FATE'S JOURNEY

SCOURGE SURVIVOR SERIES – BOOK FIVE

JL MADORE

PROLOGUE

FATE'S JOURNEY

*B*lue bolts of magic cracked overhead. The cluster of supporters at the ancient ruin site broke into chaos. Samuel launched from the assemblage with his wand pointed. Another blue beam of energy exploded across the evening sky, and I followed the trajectory of his attack. The stream of blue magic collided with an invisible force, lighting up an iridescent shield.

Abaddon.

The plague of the realm held Lia captive within a magical field. His hulking frame loomed forward, pressing her against the wide trunk of an ancient tree.

The ground shook. Knocked to my knees by an explosion, I twisted and watched my sisters vanish. I should dematerialize too, but the moment held me captive.

Lia was my friend. And Jade. And Lexi.

What would happen to them?

Talon warriors burst into war-cry as a wave of deformed Scourge Raiders invaded. Like putrid ants to a picnic, the incoming forces reeked of death and rot, their soulless lives dedicated to an evil master.

With the issue of Lia's mating rights forgotten, the hearing transformed into a battle of life and death. Debris flew. Bodies scrambled. Blood spilled. Was this their reality? The promise of violence awaiting the members of the Realm of the Fair?

A tattooed warrior gripped my elbow and yanked me toward the trees. His wrenching hold suggested he was unaffected by my station as a Fae Fate. Or perhaps the man-handling indicated exactly what he thought of me as a Fae Fate.

Another explosion detonated.

The forest spun, and we were knocked off our feet. In a tangle of silk and leather, we collided, first in the air and then in the scant brush. The impact of the forest floor brought to focus the fragility of ribs. I cried out at the snap, breathless beneath the weight of the warrior.

I gasped, jolting from memory, my hand gripping my side. The pain of the injury had subsided weeks ago, the fracture reknitting the moment I materialized back Behind the Veil.

Still, the trauma stayed with me. No matter how I tried to put it behind me, those haunting images returned in vivid replay whenever my mind had a moment to wander.

"Zophia, are you listening?" Zana stood, hands on hips, before my loom. The four of us had been tending to our daily duties in the Hall of Destiny while she droned on about realm dwellers not deserving the right of free will.

I adjusted the silk sleeve of my gown and gathered my braid over the crook of my arm. "Honestly, no. However, I've heard it enough, I could retell it to you verbatim."

Zana scowled. "Watch yourself, sister. Holding yourself above your peers only gives you farther to fall when someone knocks your pedestal. You hold *them* in higher esteem than you do your own family."

Zinnia glanced up from reading her destiny bowl, her frown more grave than usual. "Why *do* you dote on them so, Zophia? They're ants —plankton, really. If you want a pet, speak to your mother and choose anything the universe offers."

I regarded the three of them, their dark hair, iridescent skin, and midnight blue eyes a mirror to mine, yet there ended any similarity. "They aren't pets, and they aren't plankton. They're people. And several of those people are our family. Extending a polite greeting to Jade, Galan, Lia, and now Samuel would go a long way in showing the members of the realm that we're not heartless, manipulative bitches."

I finished updating the tapestry hanging framed in my station and sent it back to join the others in a gentle breeze. With a change of direction to the flow of wind, I called for the tapestry of the Talon soldier who risked himself to shield me from the Scourge.

Jade said his Talon *nom de guerre* was Savage.

The man sparked a mysterious curiosity. Mute. Violent. He covered his flesh with black ink and sneered his disdain for the world, but something in his ebony stare told me there was far more to the man than an antisocial Talon Enforcer.

And who could refute the charms of a good sneer?

Zora ranted on. "Those immortal nuisances are *not* family. Realm-bound are bugs. Do I care what the gnats in the garden think of us? They are beneath your interests. A collection of nothings who almost got you killed."

I laughed. Puzzled when no tapestry came forth, I upped the demand on the wind and re-sent the call. "No one dies from broken ribs. Stop fussing. I'm perfectly well."

"Wrong," Zinnia said, swiping her fingers through the image of her seeing bowl. "People do die from broken ribs—punctured lungs, torn aorta, et cetera."

I gave up on Savage's tapestry, determined to resume my search when I could concentrate. "And yet, not one person who succumbed to those injuries were an immortal Fate of the Fae Pantheon."

Zora swiped through the surface of the image in her bowl and offered a sympathetic glance. "Being Keeper of Lives, Zophia's connection to those of the realm is deeper than our own. Let's be thankful she wasn't killed, and put that whole nasty Scourge business behind us."

I smiled, grateful that at least one of my sisters had an ounce of understanding. Zora didn't speak up much, but when she did, her input was well-thought-out.

"Right you are," Zana said, strutting to the butler's cart and pouring herself a glass of sparkling punch. "Why waste breath on the weak, irrational, and unworthy. They are savages, the lot of them."

I chuckled. "Ironically, it was a warrior named *Savage* who risked his life to keep me safe. We mustn't judge the realm by the actions of a few malicious people. Remember, the person spearheading the violence of the realm is one of us, not them. Abaddon is Rheagan's right hand. In a way, our Pantheon is at fault, not the members of the Realm of the Fair."

Zana frowned, something dark flitting across the perfection of her face. "Be mindful not to entangle yourself too tightly with them, sister. A hair's breadth separates interacting and interfering. Then where would you be?"

～

With Zana's words of caution still nagging me, I left my sisters to their gossip and sought the company of the only person who wanted nothing but my unguarded love.

～

"Mother? Are you here?" I eased open the moss-laden door and peeked inside her woodland cottage. The place smelled of lavender, comfrey, and a dozen other herbs and essential oils. No light or candles lit the space, save for the few enterprising rays that outsmarted the ivy taking over the stone of the house.

I picked up a sprig of lemongrass and headed down the limestone walk toward the garden. "Dandy, where is she?"

The peach cockatoo perched on the gate rail raised his salmon crest and bobbed his head. "Mistress is and yet she ain't. Mistress can and yet she cain't."

"Uh, huh. You need a new line, Dandy."

"Dandy is a dandy," he squawked, and ruffled his feathers.

"Yes, you are at that." I stroked the parrot's head and left him to his bobble-heading.

The meandering path to the riverbank ebbed with life. Lush foliage on both sides of the walkway grew more dense and wild until barely enough space remained to walk two abreast. My mother wandered these grounds endlessly and was out here somewhere. Castian warded this entire wildlife sanctuary to keep her, and her animal creatures, safely contained.

"Mother? Helloooo, where are you?"

A sing-songy *whoooop* sounded in the tree behind me, and I braced for impact. Leaves rustled, and Hoola thudded onto my back, wrapping her long hands under my chin. I rubbed the leathery pads of her fingers and tilted my head to greet her. "Hello, Hoola girl, where's Mom?"

Reaching around, I removed the hoolock gibbon from the back of my neck and shifted her to my hip. Rubbing a hand down her cinnamon and ivory fur, I gave her a gentle butt scratch and glanced around. My mother's ape companion was never far from her side.

"So, what are the two of you up to today? Is it otters sliding at the riverbank or meerkats digging in the desert sands?"

Hoola squirmed, and I set on her back legs and took her hand in mine. She toddled along beside me, waving her free arm in the air as gibbons do. The moss and limestone paths throughout my mother's sanctuary made travel easy enough but the sheer volume of the biosphere settings and natural habitats made the possibilities of her location pretty much endless.

My stomach growled. "Time for treats and tea, Hoola. Point the way."

Hoola stared up at me and smiled a goofy smile, showing me her discolored teeth. Sadly, I hadn't inherited my mother's ability to speak with wildlife.

"Zozo?"

I turned toward the rainforest and stopped cold. "Mother, what are those?"

My mother held a basket writhing with tiny, sunshine yellow snakes while a much larger one coiled around her arm and across her shoulders. "*Bothriechis schegelii*," she said, placing a hand on her hat as the breeze blew her hair into her face. "Look, babies. A healthy brood. Twenty."

"Congratulations," I said, now understanding why Hoola waited on her own. "Are you ready to say goodnight to your viper friends? I'll walk you back and make you some warm milk and brownies if you like."

Her face lit up, and she ducked back into the trees. When she returned, her empty basket swung carelessly at her side. With the snakes settled back in the forest, Hoola abandoned me like a hot rock and leaped into my mother's arms.

"You look tired, Zozo. Did you miss your nap?"

I hooked my arm through hers and leaned my head on her shoulder. "I'll catch up on my sleep tonight but tell me, what adventures did you and Hoola have today?"

We strolled together, retracing our steps to her stone cottage until an immense bumblebee buzzed up the path. The bee hovered and hummed by my mother's face, and we stopped so they could chat.

"Yes, of course, dear." My mother nodded and pointed off to the left. "I revived a lovely patch of purple Bougainvillea this morning. Come back at dawn, and they'll be in full bloom."

She stared after her friend and waved goodbye, then looked at me. Her eyes widened. "Zozo, you're here. What a lovely surprise. Did I know you were coming?"

I gathered her elbow in mine once more and headed back to the cottage. "I came to bake with you before bed."

"Can we make brownies and warm milk? That's my favorite. Hoola's too. Dandy prefers rice cakes."

"Rice cakes over brownies, that's ridiculous."

Mother shrugged. "He is a strange one, that Dandy."

I leaned my head against her shoulder once again and absorbed the warmth she had always offered. "That's all right. Everyone has their own way of looking at the world."

I rose the next morning, thankful my sisters preferred beauty rest and waited until the world readied to receive them in all their self-important glory. I laughed.

No world would ever be ready for them.

"Good morning, Zo." Castian stood on the expansive back lawn of the Fae palace surrounded by his beloved deer. The herd nuzzled and shuffled to gain an advantage but Castian never left them wanting. Before he left to begin his day, they would each have their fill and then some. "What have you there, sweetheart?"

I held up the bouquet of purple bougainvillea, and the breeze picked up the succulence of their scent. "I spent the evening with my mother last night and picked these for Abbey. Is it all right if I go in and give them to her?"

Castian smiled the soft, private smile he reserved for a precious few. "She will love both the visit and the flowers, I'm sure. Thank you. And how is Shalana? I really must take some time to spend with her."

"Good. Her animals are thriving and keep her busy. Her focus slipped a few times last night, but she seems content."

Blessed to be among the inner circle of Castian's affections, I never took for granted the lengths he'd gone to protect my mother's reputation and her happiness.

He extended his palm to a submissive doe who had been pushed aside by the others. "Few things soothe a soul like those you love living well and thriving around you. Give her my love when you see her next, would you?"

"Of course."

His ruminative tone gave me pause. "Uncle? Risking the possibility of upsetting you, may I ask how you think Abbey is doing? Lia told me of the giant hawk which led her through the forest to find Jade last month. Do you think that was a coincidence?"

Castian rubbed his empty hands together and shook his head. "Abbey is coming back to us. She feels safe in her animal form but as Jade spends more time with her, and with the birth of the twins grows closer, she's fighting her way back from wherever her mind took refuge. I'm certain of it."

The pain in Castian's words made my chest ache for him as well. I prayed he was right. I left him with a quick wave and closed the distance to the palace.

Castian's wing took up the east end of the palace. The marble steps, the grape vines, and porch all lay bathed in the warmth and glow of morning sunlight. I pushed back the glass wall of his private sitting room to welcome the day into his suite. Abbey remained peacefully still, washed by the warm velvet breeze.

"Good morning, Abbey. I brought you flowers from Mother's sanctuary." I rounded the dais, where she had lain in stasis for the better part of two decades, and fetched the vase from the hutch. "I was speaking with Castian about Jade and the twins just now. Did he tell you that your grandbabies are doing better? Since binding Jade's powers, the pregnancy has settled, and the three of them are doing very well."

Disposing of yesterday's rose medley, I dumped the water in the ensuite sink and replaced it with fresh. "Did you hear Galan's sister, Lia, mated Samuel. Love is a crazy thing, isn't it? Galan is trying to be supportive, but it's clear he's losing his mind. It's all tense and awkward between the four of them right now but I'm sure with a bit of time, and likely a few drag-out fistfights, everything will smooth out there too."

I placed the vase back where I found it and dried my hands on my dress before picking up Abbey's hand. "Can you smell the bouquet? It reminded me of the summer you were pregnant with

Jade, and you snuck me down to the realm to go to the beach. Remember?"

I searched her face for any sign that Castian was right and she was making her way back to us. Part of me would always believe, but another part of me hated to see Castian build up his hopes. As God of gods, he had few vulnerabilities. The depth of his love for Abbey was his biggest. His guilt over what the Scourge did to her nearly destroyed him.

They deserved better.

I squeezed her hand. "Come on, Aunt Abbey, you want to be here when Jade gives birth, right? Castian needs you. He puts up a good front but misses you every minute of every day. Find your way home to us. I promise you're strong enough to survive this."

After folding her hands over her stomach, I left her to herself and returned to the Hall of Destiny. My sisters' stations, the three seeing bowls of past, present, and future lay unattended. I slid into Zinnia's seat and stroked a finger through the waters of the present.

Show me my Haven family, I thought.

The physical manifestation of my powers fluttered my hair in its breeze as the image on the water's surface formed.

I checked on Jade and Galan at home in her manse, Lia and Samuel recuperating at the Silver Citadel, Bruin and his human mate Mika at the Dens, and then expanded to the other members of Jade's extended family. Lexi, crazy in love with her Fae doctor, Rowan, and thrilled with their budding new family with Elani and Coal. The four of them thrived in Attalos, which was healing after the damage Rheagan had caused. Then there was Julian, their genius brother, the man in charge of Haven security. He seemed anything but content.

But they were safe and well for the moment.

I dipped my finger. With a gentle ripple, I tugged the images this way and then back, until I found Savage. He sparred with another dark-haired, Talon soldier with eyeliner and piercings. With long, black staffs, they fought one on one, while six young men, wearing Academy uniforms, watched on.

Where Savage was built with brute strength and covered in

tattoos, the other male was athletic and trim, his brow, lip, and ears adorned with nickel piercings. As their sparring shifted from offense to defense, the muscles on their backs and chests tightened and released, glistening beneath the glow of the sun's rays. The one with the piercings was beautiful to watch in action. Confident. A little cocky.

"Spying, little girl?"

I jumped. "Simply ensuring all is well with a few friends."

"Realm friends? Really?"

Where Castian's brown hair hung in long, soft waves to his shoulders, my father's military short shear made his features look severe. The two were visually identifiable as brothers, but my father's handsome rang sharply where Castian's was more of a "sweep you off your feet" suave.

I dried my hand against my dress for the second time and strode to my station. My sisters determined the outcome of lives. I recorded the events. Busying myself, I sorted through the first half-dozen realm births and called the tapestries forward. "What brings you to my doorstep, Dane?"

"Do I need a reason to visit my daughter?"

"History would dictate, yes." I set the first tapestry in the frame of the loom and verified the details of the birth. After selecting the correct colors for the weft threads, I stepped on the pedal and shot the shuttle through the shed to the end. Gripping the beater, I tightened the thread into place and adjusted it to detail the unexpected struggles of the mother. I stepped on the next pedal and shot the shuttle back.

"Why won't you call me Dad or Father, like your sisters?"

After releasing the tapestry, I sent it back to its place with more force than I meant. Calling the next one into place, I repeated the process. "A father is someone who does more than sleep with women and impregnate them. It's an earned title in my mind. So, what can I do for you?"

"You've been to see your mother, haven't you?" He strode to the side of my loom and leaned, so I had no choice but to look at him. "You get this way when you spend time with Shalana."

I finished recording the birth of a Centaur child, released the tapestry, and called the next into place. The breeze brushed my face, and I flipped my braid behind my shoulder. "Yes, I spent time with her. Yes, it still makes me mad. And yes, I understand there wasn't any lifetime commitment, but you discarded her. Have you ever thought you might have some responsibility in her mental state now? Actions have consequences."

"I'm no more responsible for your mother than you are."

"And the fact that you believe that is why you remain Dane, sperm donor extraordinaire."

I sent off the third tapestry and called the next. When I looked up to grab the shuttle, I had the room to myself.

The day passed with little incident. Ironic, my sisters thought that refusing to speak to me was a fitting punishment for stepping outside their box of approved behavior. To me, them doling out the silent treatment made for a great day.

To say their concern stemmed from a place of affection would be a gross overstatement. I was their half-sister and only a fraction of what they thought a sister should be. Their mother, Allysa, oversaw those who passed to the After and had very different views on life than my mother. Likely, the only thing they had in common was sleeping with my father.

But then, hadn't everyone?

With the major and minor events of the day recorded, I tried for a second time to call the tapestry for Savage's life. The frames, once again, remained as quiet as the Hall of Destiny.

Savage was a moniker taken on by the adult, but he remained the child born and the boy who grew up to become that man. There should be something of him recorded.

Very strange.

Unsure of what to make of it, I called Abaddon's frame. I'd studied the man's tapestry so many times over the past weeks it must be close to threadbare. What transformed man into monster? Nature? Nurture? I had expected a dark and twisted past filled with damaging events and, at first blush, dark fibers seemed to dominate. But upon closer scrutiny, light tones and the colors of innocence had woven throughout his beginnings.

Abaddon's tapestry told the tale of childhood much like any other. Son of a single mother. A twin brother to play with. The three living and growing as well as any other. At the point where his mother died, muddy browns and violet gained strength. Then, in his early twenties, a new strand emerged. Whether it represented a person or a new course chosen remained uncertain but, from that moment, black threads strangled out any sign of lightness.

More recently, the addition of silver and champagne strands spoke of innocents added into his life. Lia was one. He'd targeted her as the vessel to host Rheagan. Hours on end, I poured over the threads, searching for a way to help her reject his claim of mating. Not that I *could* help. Pantheon laws forbade anyone except the Fates of Past, Present, and Future from influencing the lives of the realms.

Why they held the reins, I never understood.

Sadly, Lia's recent escape from Abaddon's control meant only that he would target another. He would never give up on his plan to reinstate Rheagan. He would find another vessel suitable to house Fae royalty and try again.

Staring at the still empty docking station, I called forth the tapestry with a stronger force. When it too refused to come, the hair on my nape rose.

Impossible. The tapestry loom was my domain. My lot in life. Was the tapestry not responding or physically not there?

I extended my call one last time. Try as I might, nothing came to me. What was going on? I needed to figure that out. If someone was tampering with my station . . . I couldn't even begin to imagine the damage they could cause.

CHAPTER ONE

$\mathcal{I}$ materialized before the cluttered desk and empty leather chair of Julian, adopted son of Reign. Brought to the mountain as a teen, he became the last added and second oldest child in Jade's family. Everyone spoke of his gifted intellect, yet the security of Lia's hearing had been left to him, and people had been hurt.

"Fuck you, brother," a man said, rounding the corner from the corridor. "Rude. You kiss your mate with that—*Ahhh*."

Julian almost collided with me and stopped short. A tidal wave of mocha liquid splashed off the side of his oversized mug and down the front of my dress.

"*Shit*." Julian set down his coffee and grabbed paper towels. "Bruin, I gotta bounce, I just spilled hot java all over a Fate."

The coffee burned my waist and scalded my right leg.

After tossing his phone to his desk chair, he ripped a wad of white squares off a roll and handed them to me. "The door sensor notifies me when people come into my space. If you'd used the door like everyone else, you wouldn't be wearing my mid-morning fix."

I dabbed the towelettes at the caramel mark and tented the fabric away from my skin. "When I venture to Haven, I come with a purpose.

Delaying to use a door, as if I were a mortal of the realm, serves no one."

Julian shook his head, jogged out of the control room, and returned a moment later with a wet hand towel. He scrubbed at the coffee, and I noticed that the stain mirrored the same rich mocha color of his skin. By the time he drew back, the fabric was not only stained but now drenched.

"Fuck. I'm making things worse."

I let the fabric fall back into place and ignored how it suctioned to my skin, cold and wet. "Forget the dress. It's only an heirloom my mother made with her own hands, but I—"

"You're kidding, right?"

I exhaled and forced a smile. "Of course I am. It is a dress like any other. It was an attempt to lighten the mood."

He frowned. "After the clusterfuck at the hearing, no chance of that. Besides, you can poof the stain away, right?"

I glanced at the wall of monitors above his desk. Images of Haven grounds flashed up in timed circuits. "I didn't inherit Fae 'poofing' powers, but the Brownie who tends to Palace laundry is quite talented."

His frown grew more pronounced, his mint green eyes accented by his dark brow. "Sorry. I'm known to make an ass of myself when I'm focused on a problem. Can we start again?"

I set the towel and balled-up paper wad on one of the guest chairs and tossed my braid behind my shoulder. Stepping toward him, I held out my hand. "Hello, Julian. I apologize that I interrupted your morning unannounced. Do you have a moment to speak with me?"

He squeezed my fingers in greeting. "You are a welcome distraction from brooding. Though, I guess I don't have to warn you, I'm not fit company at the moment." He gestured to a small seating area at the back of the room. "Let's sit."

I propped myself on the edge of a wide club chair, and he sat deep in the leather sofa set perpendicular to it. My knees almost brushed his slacks, so I eased back a few inches. "This morning, I noticed something in the tapestries of my station. I wondered if you might be able to help me sort it out."

"What did you find?"

"I cannot say, precisely. Instead, I would like to ask you a few questions without you asking any yourself."

He wetted his lips and chuckled. "I'm more of a quid pro quo kinda guy."

"This is not a point of negotiation. I seek answers and am unable to provide private insights to members of the realm."

He laughed again, but his tone held no amusement. "Doesn't that get old?"

"What?"

He sat forward, elbows on knees, and laced his fingers. "I watched the footage of the attack a hundred times and you Fates knew exactly what was about to happen. Does it ever get old watching us mere mortals twisting in the wind while you four laugh from your perches on high?"

I shifted, sitting fully on the chair. "I assure you, I did not know of Abaddon's plans."

"Bullshit. The split-second things went south, your sisters up and vanished. No look of surprise. No moment to gather their thoughts before scurrying away. Just poof. Gone."

"Yet I remained. Surely, *I* wore a look of surprise."

"Honestly, no. You seemed fascinated."

"And you stand as judge to how I should have responded to the situation? Tell me, how did I look after my ribs were crushed beneath Savage as explosions detonated all around us?"

Julian pursed his lips into a hard line.

"Believe it or not, I worry about my family here in the Realm of the Fair. I care what happens to them. If I didn't, I wouldn't have asked for your help."

Julian sat back and rubbed a hand over his mouth. "Fine. Ask your question."

"The warrior, Savage, what do you know of him?"

He locked gazes, his eyes focused and piercing. "I'm sure there's nothing I could tell you that you don't already know from reading people's minds and accessing his life details through your position as a Fate."

"I called his tapestry forth, yet nothing came to me. That has never happened. I am at a loss. I thought you might help."

He laughed and got to his feet. "You thought wrong."

The edge in his tone surprised me. This was more than him having a bad day after the infiltration of Haven. "Have I done something to offend you?"

"How would I know? You Fates rummage through the details of people's lives, pulling your strings and playing your games. Should I feel bad when your ability to spy on one of us doesn't work? If Savage's life remains private, I won't be the one to air his personal history."

I clasped my fingers together in my lap. "As Jade's brother, I expected more from you. Are we two so different, Julian? You and I both oversee the lives of those in our care. We both hold secrets to a great many dangers which our charges need never know about. Where I hear thoughts, you use listening devices. Where I read tapestries, you research backgrounds and watch with cameras."

I gestured behind him to the wall of monitors.

His gaze narrowed. "But when *I* see a disaster about to unfold, I act to stop it. You sit safely Behind the Veil with your meddlesome sisters, passing the popcorn and recording the damage done. Doesn't that bother you?"

Deeply. Being weighed and measured on the same scale as my sisters was something I'd grown weary of centuries ago. I rose to take my leave. "I apologize for wasting your time, Julian. I shall leave you to your brooding."

"Why come to me at all?" Julian strode forward, his aftershave subtle but notably musky. "Jade would have been your first choice to get information; Lexi, your second. Yet you skipped over them and came to me."

I shrugged. "I imagined a professional kinship between us which does not exist. That was my mistake."

He canted his head, his mouth curving up into a sly smile. "You want Savage's military, not his personal info, why?"

His insight was sharp. "I was reminded last night that a fine line separates interaction and interference. For Jade and her family, I seem to test that boundary. Forget that I came. I wish you all well with what comes."

"Wait. What's coming? Did you see something?"

And with that, I dematerialized out of the Gatehouse.

Over the next days, I busied myself Behind the Veil. I tended to my station, focused on my mother, and worked on convincing myself that my sisters were right. As bizarre as that concept sounded maybe, on this point alone, their view held merit. There was a tangible divide between them and us. I confused things by blurring that line.

I paused to turn the page of the novel I was reading aloud. "Setting my glass down, I dried my palms along my thighs. Nate was the only man I'd ever slept with. What if I froze or didn't remember how—"

"Hey there," Jade said from a few feet away. "Sorry to interrupt you two."

I glanced over Abbey's platform to where Jade stood. The tassel of the bookmark tickled my hand as I closed the novel and rose. "That's all right. I'm sure she'd much rather hear about your day than listen to me read. I'll let you visit."

Jade's long burgundy curls brushed her rounded cheeks as she strode into the sitting room. Her belly, swollen with the growing twins, consumed the space before her as she walked. It marveled me how two children could be entwined inside a pocketed section of her body and her still be able to walk around and function.

"You're staring," Jade said. "Am I as massive as I feel? Galan says I'm resplendent as ever, but I think that's Elven code for *You now rival the size of the manse, Blossom*."

I chuckled. "Galan's right. The two of you are blessed."

Jade ran a hand over her belly. "I know—and I agree—but I admit,

I'll be glad when I'm solo in my body again. Sharing my personal space with kids who think nothing of kicking my bladder and grabbing hold of my insides sucks. My organs are not toys."

She raked her fingers through her hair and caught the silver matrimonial braid she shared with Galan. After tucking the loose strands behind her ear, she gestured to the chairs. "Let's catch up. I haven't seen you since you visited Samuel and Lia at the clinic after the attack."

"No, you two visit. I should get back—"

"You're not dodging me, are you?" She settled into a comfortable position, adjusted her blouse, and pointed to the chair opposite her. "Sit. Tell me what's doing."

I sighed and reclaimed the chair I'd been sitting in. "It's easier for me to remember my place Behind the Veil if I don't get tangled up personally with realm lives. Here, my duties are clear. There, I feel torn between wanting to help and being hated for things I can't change."

Jade wet her lips. "Julian mentioned he's been practicing his apology since you left him feeling like an ass last week. He said, if you're ever interested in hearing anything from him again, he's waiting to fall on his sword."

"He wasn't altogether wrong."

Jade frowned. "He didn't tell me what was said but knowing his mood after the attack, I bet an apology is the least he owes you. He thought he had locked things down for Lia's hearing, and then Abaddon's raiders not only infiltrated but destroyed the place. He doesn't handle failure well."

"No. He seems to set himself above such things. In truth, he seems to set himself above a great many things."

Jade stretched her neck. "He dug himself in deep, eh? Well, he'll have to dig himself out. Let's talk about something else, 'kay? How are you?"

Good question. "Polite answer or truth?"

Jade laughed. "I don't give two shits about polite. Truth with me. Always."

I picked up my glass from the side table and sipped at the berry nectar I'd been drinking. Where to begin? "My station ties my hands, and that ties me in knots. I have no friends. Those I hoped might be friends despise my birthright as a Fate. My father is an untrustworthy cad who lies as smoothly as he speaks the truth. My sisters want nothing more than to be rid of me. My mother declines more every day. And I'm beginning to think I'll die an angry, untrusting shrew."

Jade sat back and blinked. "Well, I guess I asked for it, didn't I? First off, I am more than your friend, as are Galan and Lia. We might be a new family, but we are family. After how you helped him and Lia, Samuel is another person squarely in your corner. Then there is Lexi, Reign, and a host of other people who care about you."

She grunted as she hoisted herself to the edge of the chair. "Second, I'm an asshat. After all the time and love you've spent devoted to *my* mother, I'm horrified I never once asked you about yours. I think people hear 'Fae goddess' and assume your life is champagne and sunshine. That's bullshit, and I should have known better. I'm sorry."

"I shouldn't have said anything."

Jade shook her head. "You said what needed to be said. I can't help with your job, your dad, or your sisters, but tell me about your mom. You said she's declining. Maybe I can help. What does she suffer from?"

The thought of outing the great Shalana turned my stomach. She was one of the most loved and praised of the Fae gods and had earned every bit of respect bestowed upon her. In her glory, she ruled the natural world like no other could, a formidable goddess, revered and even feared.

I glanced at Abbey, lying in stasis beside us, and wondered how long it would be before oblivion claimed my mother. "You have enough to worry about. Visit with your mom, and we'll catch up soon. Over lunch?"

Out of my chair, I sailed through the open patio doors and headed to the marble steps, down to the grounds. The deer, scattered across the emerald back lawn, lifted their heads from grazing and trotted my way.

"Okay," Jade said behind me. "Chasing people down was easier when I wasn't a two-hundred-pound, waddling duck."

I sighed and hurried back to her. "Why are you chasing me at all? Visit Abbey. I'm fine, truly."

Jade laughed. "It seems you missed your father's gift for lying in the gene splitting. You suck at it, Zo. And if you're angry and alone in the world, I'm not letting you go it alone. You're worried about your mom. Maybe I can give you some insight. I've treated all kinds of disorders and ailments. Nothing sends me screaming. I'm good at what I do, and I'm discreet."

I knew that. I did. But my mother was, well, my mother.

"Trust me, Zo. It would be good for you to share the burden. We, the worried daughters, need to stick together, right?"

Despite the choking fear that none of this would end well, I hoped Jade's healer perspective might highlight something Castian, and I, might have missed. "Swear to me that her condition goes no further than the two of us."

"Shalana," Jade repeated for the sixth time. "*The* Shalana."

I gestured for her to watch her footing on the stone path winding down to my mother's cottage. "Yes. Shalana, Goddess of the Woodlands, Keeper of the Wild, Mother of Nature is also my mother."

"Aust is going to—" She shook her head. "Sorry. Right. I won't say a word. But wow, Shalana. That's big."

I chuckled. Jade's father was the God of gods, the biggest of the big. That she was awestruck to learn my mother's identity warmed me. "That is how I want her to be remembered by the members of the realm. You understand, don't you?"

Jade nodded, screening her eyes from the sun as we approached the gate and Dandy standing watch. "I do. I just can't imagine how I never knew she was your mother."

"Have you met my father?"

"Once," Jade said, stopping at the gate. "A few months ago, I visited

Castian and walked into the middle of something. I'm not sure what they were talking about, but by the looks on their faces and the energy in the air, they didn't agree."

"They rarely do."

"Dandy is a dandy," my mother's doorman said.

I stroked the peach crest of the cockatoo and nodded. "You are indeed, Dandy. Where's Mother?"

"Gone," the bird replied, his neck swaying as if to a musical rhythm only he heard. "More gone than gone."

"Be nice, Dandy."

The gate creaked as I let myself into the yard. The door to the cottage hung open, the scene inside the same as always. Back at the gate, I pulled a treat from the pouch tied to the perch and offered him one. "Where's your Mistress, Dandy? Is she in the forest?"

"Mistress is gone," he said, taking the biscuit in his clawed foot and reaching down with his beak.

I patted the bird and eyed the entrance to the biomes down the path. "She can't be far," I said to Jade. "Are you good to walk, or do you want to wait here while I go find her?"

"Mistress is gone," Dandy repeated. "Gone. Gone."

The sudden rush of blood brought on a wave of dizziness. "You mean physically gone?"

Dandy consumed with his snack, and I realized I was trying to have a conversation with a bird. I jogged down the path, my heart racing. "Hoola? Hoola, where are you, sweet girl?"

A mournful *whoooop* came from the forest and I picked up my pace. At the mouth of the path leading into the forest, I met my mother's companion. Hoola jumped up into my arms and wrapped herself around my chest.

"What is it, Hoola? Where's Mom?"

Hoola's eyes glistened back at me like onyx marbles. Try as I might, I had never been able to speak the language of the creatures my mother loved so deeply.

I gazed into the dappled shadows of the forest canopy. Birds squawked. Jungle cats growled. Monkeys chattered. Despite not having the ability to communicate with them, the unrest of the animals was apparent.

"She really is gone."

Jade's face glistened with a sheen of sweat as she joined us. "Any idea where she might go?"

I shook my head, my breathing coming fast and shallow. "She's been withdrawn for decades. Mentally, she's all but lost, a child in the vacant vessel of a once powerful Fae godde—"

I blinked up at Jade as the forest spun.

Jade shifted me to lean against the broad trunk of an elm.

My vision blotched with white spots, my mind's eye focused on the champagne strands of innocence in Abaddon's tapestry. "The vessel of a Fae Goddess *for* a Fae Goddess."

"What? What are you saying, Zo?"

"It's Abaddon. He's taken my mother."

CHAPTER TWO

*I*n the thirty-six minutes it took Jade to go to Haven and return with Aust, I raced through the forest, desert, and grasslands biomes and headed along the cobbled pathway toward the moors and marshes. With no sign of my mother, my anxiety expanded well beyond my control. A constant gust of wind swirled around me, tugging at my skirt and hair.

"Zo," Jade said, flanked by Galan and their Highborne brother, Aust. The two men stood, tall and lean, from their Elven boots to the tips of their pointed ears. And their expressions looked as grave as I felt. "Any sign of her?"

I shook my head. Hoola, a secured fixture upon my chest, clung to the braid against my back and pressed her face deeper against the curve of my neck. "It's all right, sweet girl, these are my friends. They're here to help us find Mom."

Hoola clung tighter.

"Merry meet, *sweeting*." Aust bent to the small ape. He removed his mirrored sunglasses, and for the first time, I saw the ice-blue tiger's eyes I had only heard about in conversation. "Tell me, beautiful girl, where is your *naneth*?"

Aust's power of communication tingled along my skin the same way my mother's did. As he and Hoola engaged in an unspoken meeting of the minds, the energy in the air calmed. Birds flew from the forest and landed on the fences dividing the biomes. The frantic chatter of the monkeys quieted. A tiger padded out of the rainforest, its broad, striped head canted to one side.

Aust straightened and held open his arms. Hoola released me without hesitation and transferred to snuggle with him instead. With a tender caress, he ran his hand down her back and lifted her leathery hand to his kiss.

"Fash not, *sweeting*. We shall find her. Come now, we shall speak with the others."

In all my years of watching my mother communicate with her animal children, I had envied her gift. Her connection with wildlife inspired me. Intimate. Isolating. She was theirs as much as they were hers. It marked a part of her I could never truly understand. Never share.

At times, it hurt. Other times, I grew jealous. Only the knowledge that her gift was singularly unique lessened that covetous ache. Until now.

Aust shared her gift. As if he had been born of her womb and inherited it from mother to son, he possessed her ability, her manner with wildlife, her very essence of being one with the creatures of the natural world.

"Don't cry, Zo," Jade said, squeezing my shoulder. "We'll find her and bring her home. I promise."

Stupid. I brushed the diamond tears from my cheeks and shook myself. My mother was missing, and I stood there crying because the best chance to find her came from Aust being able to speak with animals? *Stupid.*

Grief rarely makes sense, Galan said directly into my mind. *When left helpless, emotions often drag a person's thoughts through pointless eddies of despair. In truth, I have watched Aust's way with animals and felt the same.*

Aust stepped back from Dandy's perch and raked his fingers through his flaxen hair. "Fash not, Zophia," he said, patting the head of the tigress as she rubbed her face against his hip. "Your mother is safe and not with Abaddon."

"Are you sure?"

He nodded. "Castian came to call. He escorted her—"

"Zozo?" My mother's smile put the warmth of sunlight to shame as she and Castian materialized onto the path outside the stone cottage. "Is it brownie night already?"

Castian released my mother's arm and kissed Jade's cheek. "Why do you all look so serious. What's happened?"

"Nothing. Everything is fine." Tears tumbled off my cheeks and clinked onto the stone walkway below, this time spurred on by sheer relief. I hugged my mother as Jade whispered to Castian, filling him in on the past hour.

"Mother," I said when my voice felt steady once again, "I want to introduce you to my friends. This is Aust, Castian's daughter, Jade, and her husband, Galan."

Though I gestured to the three, in turn, only one held interest for her. "My dear boy," she said, gliding to stand before Aust. "I'm so very pleased you've finally come. You don't know how I've struggled to wait for you."

Aust dropped to one knee and bowed his head. "The honor is mine own, Lady Shalana."

My mother cupped his jaw and raised his gaze to meet hers. "Look at those beautiful eyes. You found my idol." Her smile grew wide and proud. "You are remarkable, my son."

Aust reached into the suede pouch hanging at his hip and retrieved a small ebony statue. "We found it at Dragon's Peak when we recovered Rheagan's spell book last June. Would you like it back?"

She laughed and closed his hand over the small carved piece. "All is as it should be. Come, we have much to discuss and little time to waste."

Arm in arm, my mother led Aust down the path and into her biome sanctuary without a word to us or a backward glance. Castian removed his cloak and slung it over his arm as he led us into the cottage and out of the heat of the day. With a tight grip on my elbow, he pulled me to the side.

I apologize for your scare, sweetheart, Castian said into my mind, *but what were you thinking, bringing members of the realm here?*

"Dandy said a man took my mother. I was scared to death."

He hung his cloak on a hook inside the door and frowned. *You told them what you saw in Abaddon's tapestry. That he was choosing a new vessel. That violates the oath of your station.* The disappointment in Castian's eyes warred with worry.

I turned to the sink to fill the kettle. *I saw the thread of an innocent life woven into his tapestry and then found Mother missing. The animals were the only witnesses. Jade suggested that Aust could tell us what happened.*

I arranged four teacups onto saucers and uncovered a plate of sweets from the icebox. Jade and Galan had settled at my mother's table and were engaged in a conversation of their own. I set the plate before them and returned to the counter to steep the tea. *You know I honor my oath, but when I thought Mother was in danger, I acted as a daughter, not a Fate. I panicked with the need to find her.*

Castian scrubbed at the back of his neck, a habit he had when truly upset. *You should have called Abaddon's tapestry and sought the truth without involving the others.*

Abaddon's tapestry won't come to me. It's either missing or not responding to me.

Castian frowned. *What do you mean?*

I glanced at Jade and Galan. They were paying no attention to our conversation. *Either my station is compromised, or Abaddon's tapestry is gone. When I call it, nothing comes.*

How is that possible? The Veil is warded against Abaddon and his ilk. How could he affect your station?

I set the teapot on the table and took my seat. Savage lived in Jade's home and was a friend. The glitch with his frame not responding might be on my end, not his. Until I knew more, I wouldn't speculate about the man.

I'm not sure what's going on, or why.

Castian sensed my evasion but didn't question me further. Biding time and choosing words made up a lot of our lives. He picked up the teapot and poured for the group. *Tell me if it continues or if I should be worried*, he said.

"I think we should all be worried," I said aloud. "It's no secret that Rheagan plans to take possession of a vessel and needs that vessel to hold power and influence. She possessed Lexi's mother, the Queen of the Faery, then tried Lia to reclaim the realm throne. It makes sense that she would try to take someone like Mother, a Fae goddess with formidable power."

Castian rubbed his thumb along the delicate edge of his teacup. "I cannot ward Shalana against possession as I did with Lia. Your mother's gifts are different than mine but comparable in strength. Even with a weakened mental state, her powers surge as strong as ever."

Jade dipped her cookie. "If Rheagan possesses another of the Fae Pantheon, do you have the juice to shut her down?"

Castian smiled. "Of course, *Mir*. Your father is the God of gods, after all. I can handle my sister."

~

Despite Castian's assurance, I had doubts. As we enjoyed a companionable snack, there was a great deal of speculation over what Abaddon might try next to bring Castian's sister back to the living realm.

My mother screamed.

The four of us leaped from the table and bolted out the door. She stood at the gate, pointing at her source of upset. Animals rushed from the forest to protect their Mistress. Aust stood between her and the group, dagger drawn.

"Stand down, Aust," I said, racing to my mother's side. I put my arm around her shoulders and turned her away. "What the hell are you doing here?"

My father shrugged his broad shoulders, his coy expression uncharacteristically blank. My sisters, however, smiled with a delight that tightened my stomach into knots.

"We're not here to upset Shalana," Dane said. "We're here because it's where you are."

Me? "What do you want with me that couldn't wait until I returned to the Palace?"

"Your removal as Fate."

Dane's words floated inside my head but didn't register. "I'm sorry, what?"

Dane unrolled a scrolled parchment and read aloud. "As Enforcer of the Fae Pantheon, I must inform you that both your status as Keeper of the Lives in Progress and your right to reside Behind the Veil has been revoked. As of this moment, Zophia Ezalbet Larethan, you are a Fate no longer and will vacate the Veil immediately."

"On what grounds." Castian snatched the parchment from his brother's grasp.

Dane cast a derisive glance at my friends. "Breaking the tenet of non-disclosure with common members of the realm."

"We are hardly common members of the realm," Jade said. I'm Castian's daughter, a demi-goddess, and Queen of the Flesh. Galan is of Rheagan's bloodline, and Sentinel of Souls.

"And your freak-eyed friend?" Zinnia said. "Who's he?"

"Aust is a Fae Beastmaster," Shalana snapped. "And my apprentice, and Zophia's betrothed."

Aust blinked, looking as surprised as the rest of us.

Still, no time to dwell.

"You see," Castian said, without missing a beat. "There is no breach of duty. Each of these three has Fae stations of their own. Now leave before I fabricate charges of misappropriation of power myself—"

"Sorry, brother," Dane said, though he didn't look at all sorry. "Even if today's slip of protocol is explained, there are other recorded instances. Zophia Flashed your niece, Lia, within the Hall of Destiny one night, a week or so ago, and revealed the events of her capture."

"That was *her* tapestry," I snapped. "What laws of secrecy did that break?"

"She held no memory of the events. You interfered in the natural order of the mating hearing."

"Bullshit," Castian said.

"*And* several months ago, she shared key images with one Alexannia Grace. She divulged the identities of the assailants who slaughtered her Elf-friend, Thamior."

"Because of that," Zana said, her eyes glittering with life. "four Strati soldiers of the Faery Realm of Attalos were killed. She affected the outcome in the lives of men."

"Like you do every day," I said, my heart pounding out of my chest. "Rheagan had Tham killed to prove a point. That's Pantheon interference and our responsibility."

Zana scowled. "You didn't know that at the time."

I stared at the three of them, standing there, enjoying the destruction of my life. "How do you live with yourselves?"

"Your sisters aren't the accused," Dane said, pointing to the scroll in Castian's hand. "Shall I continue? The incidents seem slight, but add up to an undeniable breach of oath. Do you intend to argue them all away?"

Wind swirled in a vortex around us, pulling at hair and clothing, stirring up grass. I threw up my hands. As much as I wanted to knock them back a hundred feet and leave them on their asses, what good would it serve?

"No. I'm done with you. I'll stand before the Council and have my say. After that, if they don't see this for the vindictive manipulation it is, consider me gone. A Fallen Fate. A failure at all you believe a Fate should be. And thank the gods for that. I'd rather be shunned and shamed a thousand times than be like you pathetic, petty, malicious . . ." My mind spun, searching for the word.

"Fucktards," Jade said.

"That works." I unclenched my fists, my cheeks flaming hot. "I'll step down from my post for now, but won't be kept from my mother, Abbey, or Castian. I'm not going anywhere."

"You are," Dane said. "You can't be trusted. To give you access to the Palace and life Behind the Veil gives you access to sensitive details of Fae and realm activities. The Pantheon Council agreed and cast their votes."

"The Council?" Castian snapped. "I wasn't privy to any of this. Zophia hasn't even been heard."

"You are too close to this to see logic, brother. Your vote wouldn't change anything, regardless. It was unanimous."

My mother launched from my arm and screamed something unintelligible. She lashed a hand through the air and Dane, and my sisters, vanished. Hopefully, she threw them hurtling into space somewhere. Aust gathered her to his side and turned her to go into the cottage.

"Unanimous?" I said, my voice barely a whisper. My strength all but drained out of me. "Not one person on the Council thought me worth speaking to before they revoked my life? How is that possible?"

"I'm sick about this, sweetheart," Castian said, crushing the scroll in his clenched fist. "I had no idea."

I blinked back the betrayal stinging my eyes and offered what I hoped was a reassuring smile. For the first time in years, I hoped my mother had checked out mentally and had no idea what was happening in the world around her.

I wished *I* didn't know.

"Let me get Mother settled. Then I'll go. Will you explain to Abbey what happened?"

Castian nodded. "I will make this right, Zo. I swear it."

"Zozo? *Zozo?*"

I woke to the panic of my mother's voice. She stood at the center of her bed, eyes as big as saucers, her arms wrapped across her chest.

I shook myself and rubbed my eyes. "What's wrong?"

"He was here. I smell him."

I'd seen my mother like this before. Even centuries after he'd left us like litter in the street, Dane's presence still got to her. I don't know what she remembered of the past or why she hated him specifically, just that she did.

"He's gone now. Just you, me, and Hoola make three."

My mother stomped on the mattress, staring at the bedroom floor as if it held some unspeakable horrors. "Where is she?"

I searched the room. "Hoola? Where are you, Hoola girl?"

When no sound or call came back, my mother threw herself onto the mattress in a fit of clawed fingers and tears.

"It's all right. I'll find her, but you need to calm down." I tried to catch her flailing arm, to reach her. The gemstone in her ring caught my face and blood welled hot on my lip. I hissed and recoiled. "Mom. *Mom*, it's me, Zozo. I'm right here with you. Please calm down."

But she didn't. Or couldn't. Maybe she couldn't even hear me. When she got like this, she didn't seem to recognize who I was. I wiped at the moisture on my cheeks. "Mom, please. You're going to hurt yourself."

When the door creaked open, I spun to block the scene from view. Aust stepped inside, Hoola snuggling in his arms. He took one look at my face, and my mother on the bed, and jogged to my side. His usual shy reserve transformed to purpose. He handed me Hoola and hopped onto the bed.

In the next beat of my pounding heart, he'd captured both of my mother's flailing wrists and pulled her into his arms. "Good morning, milady," he said, restraining her while brushing her hair off her face with a gentle touch of his other hand. "All is well, Shalana. I promise you, all is well. Zophia is here. Hoola is here. And I am here to spend the day with you. I thought we might explore for a few hours and visit your animal family."

Shalana stilled. She blinked up at him with wide, hopeful eyes. "Would you like to meet them?"

"Yes, I would. That is, if you are agreeable to me inviting myself into your company."

"You'll stay?"

"If you shall have me, yes. How about a nice bath, something hot to eat, and then we shall go on an adventure?"

When she nodded, Aust helped her to the floor and tucked her under his arm. After leading her into the bathroom, the water came on in a rush. I staunched the bleeding of my lip with a tissue and gathered myself to help.

I stopped half way to the door and listened.

Aust's voice rose in an Elven ballad. The hard surfaces of the bathroom amplified the sound, his pitch clear, the words foreign, yet I felt their meaning as if I understood. I'd heard Jade sing before, but Aust's voice was even more amazing.

Bree was one truly lucky woman.

With the confrontation over and my mother once again sedate, my legs threatened to fail me. I sat on the edge of the bed, closed my eyes, and listened.

When he stepped out, I waved to my mother settled in a cloud of bubbles. "I shall await you just outside the door. If you have need of me, call. Then we begin a grand adventure."

"With our animal family. Right, son?"

He eased the door almost shut. "Yes, when you are ready."

Aust's attention shifted from the bathroom to me, and in the next moment, I launched off the bed and hugged him. He smelled of the wildness of nature, a scent that reminded me so much of my mother it hurt. He also smelled of suede and healthy man. That scent was all his own, and I found it remarkably soothing.

"Thank you," I said. "You're so good with her."

He pulled back and lifted my chin to inspect my face. "Oh, *sweeting*, let me aid you."

He picked up Hoola and slid into the bathroom. A moment later, he returned with a damp facecloth and shut Hoola in with my mother. "She would never hurt you."

I brushed away the last of my tears. "I don't know what to do for her when she gets like that. It's like my mother is gone. I can't reach her."

Aust backed me onto the bed and dabbed at my lip. The cloth, warm and soft, came away stained with blood. "She is never gone, merely lost. For her, it is like being trapped in a labyrinth at night. She hears our voices but cannot see to find her way to us. So, we must find our way to her."

I pulled back to look at him. "How can you possibly know that? You only met her yesterday."

He shrugged, looking sheepish. "It is our ability. I hear her the same way I hear the animals. Not words, but thoughts and impressions. It is difficult to explain."

His handsome face blurred behind another round of tears. "How can you possibly be real? And what did I do to deserve your help?"

The bed creaked as he shifted beside me. He hugged me to his side and brushed my hair from my eyes. "*Sweeting*, it is I who is blessed beyond measure to include you and your mother into *my* life."

"You're amazing. Thank you."

"I am a friend. And as such, at the risk of overstepping, I offer my company to watch over your mother while you sort things out with the Pantheon Council and the others. Castian refused to wake you last night because he wanted you to have time with Shalana, but I fear you must needs go."

I drew an unsteady breath. "I know. I want to bring her with me, but it hurts and confuses her to be away from the animals."

Aust squeezed my shoulder. "Fash not, I shall treat her as my own *naneth* and ensure her every need is fulfilled."

CHAPTER THREE

The next hours and days passed in a blur of disbelief and grief. My chest ached. My lungs failed to inflate. My entire world seemed alien. How was I supposed to connect with the people and places of the realm around me? I didn't know how.

Someone knocked on my door, and I swiped the blanket across my face. After clicking on the bedside lamp, I rolled over to see who it was. "Come in."

The door swung open a foot, and a shaft of light from the hall bathed a long slice of gold across the hardwood. Jade and Lexi let themselves inside. The two of them made quite a pair, both dressed in rock slogan t-shirts and ripped jeans. Both wore black eyeliner and royal blue lipstick. Jade stood round with her unborn young. Lexi remained petite, with her ebony spiked hair and velvety wings.

"Hey there," Jade said, coming over to the bed. "We're taking you out of the house for a bit. It's time to show you what Haven life is like after dark."

I studied their outfits more closely and still couldn't make sense of what they were up to. "Does it involve pledging my fealty to Vampires?"

Jade laughed. "No. There's a guest band at the Hearthstone tonight. The locals often dress up for fun."

"It's kind of you to ask, but you don't have to entertain me. Allowing me a place in your home, for the time being, is more than enough."

Jade shook her head. "We didn't ask you to join the fun out of obligation. We're meeting Bree, Nyssa, and some of the guys for a night out. It'll be fun."

"I'm certain you'll have more fun if I'm not there. Nothing brings down the joy of a room like a Fate." I sat upright and brushed my hair out of my face. "What's the saying? Hated by all, loved by few."

Lexi snorted. "Who gives two shits what people think? You've been exiled onto the island of misfit toys, Zo. Same as the rest of us. Embrace it, babe. There are worse things."

"It's only temporary," I said. "And although I appreciate the notion, pity isn't something I enjoy."

Lexi screwed up her face. "I don't do pity. I'm more of an in your face reality girl. You've been dumped. It sucks, yeah, but you've got a whole immortal life ahead of you to figure things out. Why dwell on it?"

I sat up straighter and brushed the sheets, diamond tears launching off the bed and falling like soundless rain to the plush area rug beneath the bed. "I'm not dwelling. I'm banned from my mother and believe Abaddon has targeted her as Rheagan's vessel. I'm panicked and angry."

Jade squeezed my arm, her emerald green eyes the same jewel tone as her father's. "Castian will get you home. He's meeting with the Fae Council as we speak and will let us know what happens as soon as he has things worked out. Until then, Aust, Castian, and I will watch over her."

"Feel better?" Lexi said. "'Cuz we gotta go if we're gonna get a good booth."

"I should still pass. I haven't eaten since yesterday, and I'm not sure whether I'm starving or about to throw up."

"Both viable options," Lexi said, pulling me from the covers and shoving me toward the ensuite. "The Hearthstone has food, and before the night is through, more than one person will fertilize the bushes. I'll hold your hair if you're one of them."

I pictured them holding my four-foot long braid as I bent over the bushes, my gown flowing in the night breeze. "I don't enjoy crowds, Lexi. People look at my skin and clothing and see nothing but a Fate."

"That's an easy fix," Jade said.

"Yep." Lexi nodded as she flicked on the bathroom light. "Jade has plenty of pre-preggo clothes you can borrow, and I am the Queen of Sephora."

"You're not going to take no for an answer, are you?"

Lexi beamed and patted my arm. "Glad you recognize that. Now, stop the negative chit-chat and let's go have fun."

Fun? The thought struck a hollow chord in the center of my chest. Had I ever had *fun*? Growing up with my mom, was fun. Shalana viewed the natural world as one giant adventure.

Since being named a Fate, I had, at the very most, took pleasure in isolated moments, experienced things, endured life. Then why did it hurt so much to have that life taken away?

"Lexi, give me one of your knives."

She slid me a sideways glance but freed the blade sheathed to her thigh. "It's sharp, Zo. Be careful."

I tested the weight of the weapon as I turned it in my palm. The grip was textured, fitted to the palm of a woman's hand. "I'm sick to death of being careful."

Grabbing my braid, I sawed the woven chestnut strands. "Always careful what I say. Careful who I trust. Careful with my sisters. For what? So an entire Council can unanimously vote me unworthy? It's exhausting being what everyone expects. Why should I play the part one more minute?"

With a final yank, the blade soared free and sliced through my hair completely. I handed her both the knife and the twined rope of my braid. "You offered to hold my hair, didn't you? Well, here you go."

"All righty then," Lexi said, a priceless look dancing in her amethyst eyes. "Did *not* see that coming but go with it."

Jade chuckled and handed me a brush. "Let's get you ready. One well-deserved reckless night, coming up."

The Hearthstone stood at the heart of the Haven social scene. Locals gathered here for the sense of community. Travelers gathered for information. And the downtrodden gathered here for the ambiance of whiskey-soaked tables, loud music, and cardiac arrest-causing foods served in baskets.

"Great, isn't it?" Lexi asked as she hopped up into a booth. Situated just off the dance floor, we were opposite the small stage and had a clear view of the entire place.

I reached to gather my dress before sitting and found only black, denim-clad legs. This would take getting used to.

I caught my look in the mirrored beer sign. Lexi had fixed my hair by cutting it shaggy at the back and along my bangs. I'd never had bangs before and was amazed at how different I looked. We'd covered my opal skin with a layer of foundation, given me the same black eyeliner and blue lipstick they wore and voila, the Fate was a Fate no longer.

"I can't get over how light I feel." I shook my head, amazed at the weight I'd been carrying for centuries.

Jade waved toward the door. The band struck a few test cords as Bree and Nyssa slid into the booth and joined us. Both ladies stared for a beat and then broke into genuine smiles.

"Holy shit," Bree said, pointing at my exposed midriff, her smile wide and brilliantly white. "You look amazing. I almost didn't recognize you."

"I'm in disguise." I accepted a pink drink from Jade and sipped from the glass. I licked the sugared rim, and the mixture of sweet and tart exploded in my mouth.

Lexi placed her fingers between her tongue and let off an ear-breaking whistle toward the growing crowd. She plunked down on the bench and grabbed her drink. "We convinced Zophia to take the night off from being herself. Tonight, she's anyone she wants to be."

"Perfect," said Bree, holding two fingers up to the bar. One of her foster brothers nodded and turned to the beer fridge behind him. "And who are you being?"

"I have no idea. I never considered anything beyond who and what I was born. If I'm not a Fate, who am I?"

"Whoa," Lexi said, snorting. "Enough of that introspective bullshit. Tonight, we drink. Get contemplative tomorrow."

The music came up, and Bree reached to grab two bottles from her brother's tray. "A toast to Zophia. After a lifetime of doing what is expected, tonight she's open to the unexpected. May you find every happiness."

The live band took the stage at ten p.m., and then the roadhouse went from busy to bursting. The five of us danced with reckless abandon for the first set but eventually, Jade had to sit, and I had to use the washroom. I'd lost count of how many pink drinks passed my lips, but my bladder hadn't.

It was many. Many many.

I exited the ladies room and nearly crashed into a group of men coming up the back hall.

"Hey there," Julian said, catching my arms before we crashed. "Sounds busy tonight. You having a good time?"

He, Cowboy, and the pierced warrior I'd seen sparring with Savage had arrived through the rear exit. The scent of exotic tobacco clung to their clothes, the same way their t-shirts clung to the sculpted musculature of their chests and arms.

I straightened and nodded. Not even Julian could dampen my spirits tonight. "Very good. Excuse me."

I practically skipped up the hall and hopped back into our booth. The three men followed.

"Hey Blaze," Cowboy said, his southern drawl slow and sexy. "How you feelin', sweetheart?"

Jade smiled and scootched over to make space. "Like there are two disgruntled aliens battling for space inside me." As if to prove her point, her belly shifted and rolled with the movement of her unborn twins.

"Man, that's just wrong," the pierced one said, a look of disgust blanketing his face. Strobing lights from the dance floor caught the nickel piercings through his brow and lip. The man wore as much black eyeliner as we did. I wondered if that was his flair for fashion or something else.

"So, Jade, introduce us to your friend." Julian gestured to me across the table. Cowboy gave him a puzzled look, but before he could say anything, Jade laughed and spoke up.

"Oh, sure, this is my friend, Destiny. She's had a falling out with her family and is at Haven for a bit. This is my brother Julian, and then, Cowboy, and Kobi."

I looked at Jade, wondering what I missed. Cowboy rubbed a hand over his mouth and coughed to hide his laughter.

"Ah, yes," I said, catching on. "It's nice to meet you."

Julian smiled and held up my empty glass until one of the Lion-Weres nodded. "Well, I'm glad you found Haven, Destiny. We'll take good care of you until things get sorted out on the homefront."

"I gotta get a drink," Kobi said, laughing. "And you're an idiot, Julian. Just so ye know."

"Why? What did I do?" Kobi and Cowboy melted into the crowd and Julian slid up into the booth opposite Jade and I. "Ignore them. So, back to you. How are you enjoying Haven?"

The evening continued in much the same manner. Drinking. Dancing. And me keeping up the pretense of being Jade's friend, Destiny. Kobi and Cowboy let Lexi, Nyssa, and Bree in on Jade's joke and everyone played along when they returned from the dance floor. Fascinating how sweet and funny the man was with no clue I was a Fate.

When the conversation hit future occupations, I set down my drink and lit up. "I have an idea about that."

Cowboy pushed a plastic basket of chicken wings my way. "Let's hear it. What are you thinking?"

I moved two of the slathered pieces of chicken onto my side plate and sucked my fingers clean. "In the washroom, I met a woman counting a big stack of money. I asked her what she did to earn it, and she said she is a hooker. Well, I'm a weaver. I think my skills could easily translate to hooking if there's a demand here—"

The table broke out in laughter.

"What's so funny?"

Jade shot the men a stern look and fought not to smile herself. "You misunderstood, hon. Hooker is a Modern Realm term for a prostitute. The woman in the washroom made that money being paid for sex, not by crafting textiles."

Another wave of laughter took the table, and my eyes stung. I brushed at my hot cheeks, diamonds clinking off the ceramic plate beneath my chin. "You must think me ridiculous. I feel foolish."

"Nonsense," Kobi said, pushing diamonds around on my plate. "Forget about the woman in the bathroom. Look at these. You're a money-making machine, sweetheart. These purple diamonds must be worth a fortune."

"Besides," Lexi said, "that's just the Cosmos and lack of food talking. If anyone came out looking like a fool tonight, it was Julian, not you."

Julian stared at the purple tear gemstones on my plate and then studied my face. "Oh, shit, Zophia? I . . . uh." He finished the last swig of his beer and shook his head.

The table burst into another round of roaring laughter, and he raised his palms to the group.

"All right, I deserved that. Yuck it up, everyone. Get it out of your systems."

CHAPTER FOUR

I woke to the sensation of someone licking my ankle. Blinking against the fog and blotches blocking my vision, I tried to focus. There was a little girl at the foot of the bed, and she was, indeed, licking me. That is, until she bit.

"Ouch." I pulled my leg back and sat up.

"*Sorry*," Bruin said, rushing into the room and scooping my attacker up in his arms. "This one got away on me. Kiara's a biter. You okay?"

I rubbed at my ankle, disoriented by my surroundings. Gold bed linens had been replaced by navy blue. The space where I was accustomed to a kitchenette was filled with weightlifting workout equipment. The weapon's vest and men's clothing tossed around the room sealed the deal.

"Uh . . . Bruin, where am I?"

"You're in my home. The Dens. You don't remember?"

I shook my head, tugging the sheet to cover my bare legs. Okay, t-shirt and underwear. At least I wasn't naked. "And whose room is this?"

"That would be mine," Kobi said, strutting into the room from a connecting door opposite the bed. He held a black towel across his

41

hips, the rest of him bare and freshly washed. "Don't tell me you don't remember last night. I'm crushed. I consider myself unforgettable."

When the towel dropped to the floor, my gaze dropped as well. Before I was caught staring, I snapped my attention back to the man's face. The warrior grinned and stepped into a pair of black jeans without underwear. Disjointed images from the night before flashed through my mind, but nothing—

"He's fucking with you, Zo," Bruin said, dangling the little girl by one ankle and swinging her around. "Don't be a dick, Demon. Look at her face."

"Dick is my default setting." Kobi pulled on a black t-shirt and then collected his weapons vest from where it hung slung over the back of a desk chair. After shrugging it on, he poked the dangling child in the belly. "And what have I told you about coming into my room without permission, little lion?"

"You eat me," the girl said, twisting as Bruin tossed her up in the air.

"That's right. I'll slather you with barbeque sauce and roast you extra crispy." With that, he flicked his thumb against his forefinger and flame leaped from his flesh.

Kiara squealed, and Bruin set her on her feet. "Say sorry to Miss Zophia for biting her, and to Kobi for trespassing."

"I's sorry," she giggled, her gaze locked on the flame in Kobi's hand. "No eat me, Koki."

"You're lucky I already had breakfast, little monster." Kobi extinguished his thumb and tugged a lock of her hair. "Now go beat up your brothers."

Bruin pinched her bottom and the two left, Kiara screeching in laughter all the way down the corridor.

Kobi closed the door behind them and turned back to me, an evil grin firmly in place. He scratched the back of his neck, and my eyes followed the flex of muscles across his arms and chest. "Now, back to last night."

I wasn't sure I wanted to hear what happened. The warrior was tall, dark, and notoriously promiscuous. Though I was far from being a prude, if Kobi and I had gotten naked while drunk and I couldn't even remember it . . . my life truly was spiraling out of control.

"You really don't remember?"

I shook my head. "Did Bree and I sing to the moon?"

Kobi laughed, grabbed a wooden chair from beside the dresser, and spun it around. Straddling the seat, he rested his arms on the back. "Not sure about that. Jade tired out around midnight, and Nyssa and Lexi walked her home. You and Bree rocked on with us at the Hearthstone for a while, then came back here for an afterparty."

"How did I end up in your bed?"

"Around 3:30, you waltzed in, passed out, and here we are."

"And my pants?"

Kobi waggled his ebony brows. "Gone before you arrived. I can't help you there."

"And where did you sleep?"

He pointed to the bed and laughed again. "Listen. It was late, and you were out. I'm an Incubus Demon, not a twenty-year-old, frat boy creeper. When I hit the horizontal, my partners are fully aware, I assure you."

"And why did I come here? What did I say?"

Kobi fished a pack of cigarettes out of his vest pocket. "We didn't get that far. You lifted your shirt and danced around a bit, asking if I liked your lacy underthings. I said I did. Then you crawled onto my bed and face-planted into my duvet."

I closed my eyes, my cheeks burning hot. "I don't remember any of that."

"You were pasted."

The next round of questions skidded to an abrupt halt as my alcohol overindulgence swirled in my gut. Kobi seemed to recognize the impending outcome because he gripped under my elbows and ushered me to the bathroom.

The tile floor chilled my shins, and I shivered as I retched. A warm, damp cloth draped across the nape of my neck. "This is getting downright domestic, lacy girl. You're tarnishing my image as a selfish asshole."

I heaved again, gagging as my eyes and nose watered.

"The view makes up for it. Damn, you've got a great ass. If you were feeling better, I would *sooo* drop down and ride you from behind."

I spat bitter bile from my mouth and waved for him to get out. "Don't worry. I think your image is safe."

～

After the vomiting spell in Kobi's bathroom ended, I found he'd left for his Talon shift. I took the opportunity to shower and get freshened up before searching his drawers for a pair of pants. Everything he owned was so . . . male. The thought of coming out of his room wearing his clothes was too much to face. I decided to dematerialize back to Jade's guest room.

I got nowhere and tried again.

The queasy unease rose once again as my form remained as solid and corporeal as ever. Either my power to dematerialize had been stripped with my station and my right to visit my mother, or Bruin had upped his security since I'd visited Lia a few weeks ago.

"Knock knock," a woman said, on the other side of the door. "It's Mika, may I come in?"

An indigenous woman peeked inside the room. I had yet to meet Bruin's human mate but recognized her from my sisters replaying her Were bonding almost nine months ago. Gods, how they laughed at the chaos they had caused by joining an authoritative, overprotective Were with an independent human journalist. It was a nightmare for everyone while they sorted things out as mates. It almost ruined Bruin and Lexi.

"Please, come in," I said, "though I apologize for standing here with no pants."

"Thus, the reason for my intrusion." Mika stepped further into the room with a stack of folded clothes between her palms. "I wasn't sure about your style but was pretty sure the back-combed rocker hair and painted on ripped jeans was only for the Hearthstone band night. I brought you a selection. Borrow whatever you like."

I accepted the clothes with my thanks. "Did we meet last night? I'm embarrassed to say I don't remember anything after the bar."

"Nah, don't worry about it. I've woken Blackout-Betty a couple of times myself. Nothing to be embarrassed about. You were with friends, and it was just good fun."

I looked at the tousled sheets of Kobi's bed and blushed. "Kobi assures me nothing happened, and—"

Mika waved away my concern. "Kobi paints a macabre picture of himself but anyone who truly knows him—and that's likely no more than two or three people—knows that he's far more than he shows the world. The first time I met him, he and Bruin saved me from being raped by three angry bikers. If he were the type of man to take advantage of a woman who couldn't give proper consent, he'd never live in my home."

Kobi had said as much, but hearing Mika vouch for his character went a long way to ease my mind. I slid on a pair of navy slacks and held up a copper peasant blouse.

"Aust said you've been dealt a lot. He's worried about you and your mom."

"He's sweet to worry."

"That's the way he's wired. Too sweet for his own good. He didn't come home last night, and when I spoke to him this morning, he seemed upset. Any idea what that was about?"

I leaned toward the mirror and fingered my damp hair. My reflection seemed so unfamiliar: the short hair, the clothes, the leftover makeup from last night. "He stayed with me and my mother last night. I'm not sure what upset him . . . well, beyond the obvious."

Mika brought her braid forward and played with the end. "No offense, but I don't want Aust drawn into someone else's drama. He's been hurt enough. He deserves better."

I turned in time to see Mika close the door behind her, leaving me feeling like I'd just been told off. I wasn't taking advantage of Aust's loyalty to my mother, was I?

～

The moment I stepped onto the outer plateau of the Dens, the zing of my powers tingled in my cells. *Blessed be.* So, the block on dematerializing *was* an increased security measure. I exhaled, surprised at both how vulnerable mortals must feel unable to exit a situation at will, and how vulnerable I felt thinking that Dane had somehow taken that from me too.

The thought of my temporary exile burned hot in my blood. I threw my molecules to the wind and made my way across the mountain to a door I swore I would never pass through.

Walking up the beige hall and into the surveillance room of the Gatehouse, I waited until Julian gazed up from his monitors. "I opened the door, and a chime announced my arrival just as you asked. Will you speak civilly with me today, or is the man from the bar only sweet to drunk strangers?"

Julian gestured to the chair opposite his desk. "I deserve that. I made you feel unwelcome, and you bore the brunt of a very bad mood on a very bad day. It won't happen again."

I didn't think it would. "When I came before, I was bound by my station not to reveal things I knew. I'm now suspended from my position and, for the moment, don't feel the same obligation of duty."

"I'm sorry, I didn't know. Jade only mentioned trouble with your family. For what it's worth, you're the only Fate anyone respects. It truly is their loss that you're no longer one of them."

I took the chair offered and ran damp palms down the crease of my slacks. "For now, at least. And while I'm not bound to silence, I want to revisit our conversation. This time, hopefully, with a more successful end."

"The one about Savage."

"Among other things, yes."

"I still don't understand why you're fishing for info on Savage."

Never had I brazenly stepped beyond the tenet of my duty. To discuss what I must to get answers was an outright betrayal of my station. But it was no longer my station.

I gathered my hands in my lap and exhaled. "His life history is one of the two tapestries I found inaccessible in the Hall of Destiny. At first, I thought the frames were blocking me, and simply refused to heed my call. Upon further thought and investigation, I am now convinced they were removed."

"Removed? Does that happen?"

"Never."

"Could someone take them?

"I don't see how?"

"Why would someone want them?"

"Information gained. Information to be kept from others? I honestly don't know."

"So, who has access to take them?"

I sat back and folded my hands in my lap. "Only someone who can enter the Veil, who possesses the divine ability to call a tapestry forward."

"Someone couldn't just go back and grab it?"

I frowned. "It's not like selecting a blanket from a linen closet, Julian. There are more than a hundred thousand members of the Realm of the Fair. Each tapestry is enchanted to respond to a summons."

"And I take it they aren't labeled."

"No."

"And every member of this realm has a tapestry?"

"Yes."

"So, if someone did steal them, they'd first have to call the tapestries forward and then get themselves out of the building and away from the Palace without raising suspicion." Julian tapped on his keyboard, and notes appeared on one of the large screens on the wall. "Is this Hall of Destiny in a private section of the Fae Palace or on the grounds somewhere?"

"It's a separate building, but within the restricted grounds of the royal family."

"Who wouldn't seem out of place . . . who also has access to the Hall and possesses the power to call forth a tapestry?"

"That is the crux of it. The only ones who fall into each of the categories you mentioned are the original three, my sisters, and me."

Julian stopped typing, his pale green gaze meeting mine. "That's a very short list."

"I know."

"And an alarming list as well."

"You share my concern."

Julian reached into a drawer of his desk and pulled a long red strand of candy out of a plastic package. "Licorice helps me think. Or at least I say it does."

He handed me a piece and stepped away from his desk to pace the room. "Okay, so let's work our way backward. We know you didn't take it. Next, your sisters."

"I can't see any of them interested enough in realm life to care. Especially in Savage. To them, he is simply a termite crawling on the mound."

"I didn't get a warm and fuzzy when they were here for Lia's hearing."

"They would never jeopardize Castian's anger for what . . . curiosity? Mischief? What would be their gain? They enjoy the fallout of meddling. It makes them feel powerful. Superior. What would the theft of two tapestries give them?"

"Two that you are aware of," Julian said. "You can't be sure there aren't others. As you said, there are over a hundred thousand members of the realm."

"I hadn't considered that, but you're right."

"Okay, well, Savage shielded you from the attack. Maybe your sisters wanted to fuck with you?"

"I don't think so. I only mentioned him after I found the tapestry missing. Their attention span doesn't support a plan that takes days or weeks to come to fruition. It might have been months until I called that particular frame."

"Okay, so, they either have a different motive, or we're looking at the original three. Man, I don't want to go there. That's scary shit."

"I know. Honestly, Castian has no reason to take it secretly. He has full access to everything. Besides, when I mentioned my troubles with the loom, he seemed genuinely concerned."

Julian reached over his desk and grabbed a handful of licorice and started chewing on a second. "Rheagan is a frightening thought. That she could get her hands on the lives in progress of all the members of the realm. That's a shit-ton of access to information."

I bit the end of the red strand and chewed. What a bizarre, artificial flavor. The sweet, textured bits in my mouth slid across my tongue, both smooth and chunky.

Rather disgusting.

"I don't think it's Rheagan. Castian warded the Veil against her, and though no one is certain what her powers are after all these years, in her non-corporeal form, I doubt she could access my station and make away with the tapestries."

"You're assuming she's still an evil fog floating around somewhere. Maybe her lapdog found her a body."

I shook my head. "I don't believe so. I studied Abaddon's tapestry up until Lia's hearing. He hadn't moved on any other innocent."

"What about after the hearing?"

I set the remainder of my strand of candy on the desk. "That's the most alarming point. Abaddon's record of life is the other tapestry missing. Without it, there's no way to know what he's doing or has done."

He stared at me, shaking his head as he started chewing on his third strand of licorice. "Oh, I am hating this. Okay, on to the last name on your list."

"Dane."

Julian frowned. "Do you think Dane would work behind the scenes against his own brother?"

"He's never liked living in Castian's shadow. He also petitioned the Fae Council to have me removed from my station behind Castian's back. I hadn't told anyone except Castian about the missing tapestries. Maybe he thought if he got rid of me, no one would figure it out."

"Have you ever seen him lurking around near the Hall of Destiny? Maybe scoping things out? Maybe figuring out how to gain access?"

I shook my head. "He wouldn't need to. He knows the stations of the Fates as well as we do and drops in unannounced all the time."

"Why, what business does he have there?"

I stepped to the water cooler by the door. After filling a tiny cone cup with water, I washed away the foul taste in my mouth. "He's our father."

Julian stopped chewing, his pale gaze bright against the warm mocha of his skin. "You're the daughter of one of the original three?"

"All four of us are, yes. Though, I have a different mother and was raised apart from them."

"Thank the gods for that. Or goddess, I guess. So, who is your mother?"

Though members of the Pantheon didn't offer the twists of the royal family tree, Aust and Jade knew who my parents were. It wasn't a secret exactly, just private. "My mother is Shalana."

Julian choked on his candy. "That's one powerful parental pairing, Zo. I had no idea. So, you must be like, super juiced with Fae mojo."

I crushed the little paper cup and tossed it in the recycle bin. "Julian, focus. I think my father took Abaddon's and Savage's tapestries. Why? What's the connection?"

"Between those two? I don't see one. Savage is one scary mother, but he's tight, and he's one of the good guys. I'd guess there are more tapestries missing and it's just a coincidence you discovered those two."

"And there's no chance he's fooled all of you?"

Julian frowned. "There's always a chance."

Good. At least he admitted there *could* be something there. "Take Savage out of the situation for a moment and focus on my father and Abaddon teaming up. What's to be gained?"

"A power play for control of the realm?"

I nodded. "What if Dane wants Rheagan back. She's his full-blooded sister, and Castian is their older half-brother. I can tell you from experience that an extra half matters. Maybe Dane wants to reinstate his sister as ruler of the realms, so they can work together to make him God of gods."

"And unseat Castian? Shit, Zo, that's one hell of an accusation to hurl against your father."

"Not really. Castian is more of a father to me than Dane ever was. Dane beds women endlessly in the hopes of siring a male heir, but fate is a funny thing. All he got was four girls."

"But do you truly think he's got the cojones to go against Castian? To actively help Abaddon reinstate his sister?"

I pointed to the plaque on the wall. It was a poem. The prophecy given to Galan and Jade last summer by the Oracles.

> Journey of Fate, two realms to purge
> Weapons drawn against the Scourge
> Blaze of passion,
> Trust unearthed,
> Cleansing of past,
> Spirit rebirthed,
> Fate or free will, which to choose?
> With love to gain and life to lose.
> Darkness hides in familiar form
> A brother's betrayal, a sister's storm
> Empower lost souls or evil shall reign
> Noble the child of argenteous mane.

"I've been staring at this in Jade's front foyer for days. Think about it. This all started with the release of the Highborne Exiles, and seems to be chronological. The first couple lines about Journey of Fate and facing the Scourge, that's Galan, Tham, and Aust beginning their *Ambar Lenn,* and the rise of Scourge violence."

"Yeah, we figured that. Then the next four lines are Jade, Mika, Lexi, and Lia all finding their power and their place with the men they love."

"Right. Then, Fate or free will, which to choose? With love to gain and life to lose. That's me. I chose free will and am no longer a Fate. I lost the life I knew because I couldn't stand aside and do nothing."

"Darkness hides in familiar form/A brother's betrayal, a sister's storm," Julian read off. The muscle in his jaw flexed as he clenched his teeth. "Do you truly think Dane would help Abaddon reinstate his sister over Castian?"

"I do."

He went back to reading the prophecy. "Empower lost souls or evil shall reign . . . Lia has Tham working on that. They're gathering angry souls displaced by the Scourge to fight back."

I nodded and read on. "Noble the child of argenteus mane. That could be Galan or Lia? They both have silver hair."

"The Highbornes are the Noble Children of Castian."

"It makes sense. Dane is part of this. I feel it."

Julian cursed and took out his phone. He pushed a button and then held it up to his ear. "Yeah, we need to talk. Shit's hitting, and we're in the splash zone. Yeah. Twenty minutes."

CHAPTER FIVE

*T*wenty minutes later, Julian and I stood in Jade's front foyer amongst the assembly of those the prophesy involved, their mates, Reign, and a few Talon. We'd gone over our suspicions and our interpretation of the prophecy line by line. The group agreed that my theory held water.

"Sav should be here," Kobi said.

I shook my head. "He's involved in this somehow."

"Bullshit," Cowboy said, his southern drawl thick.

Reign frowned. "In all fairness, Zophia, you don't know that, and you don't know him. We do."

"Do you really?" I looked to his friends and fellow warriors. "Do any of you know his personal details? His family? Where he came from?"

Blank faces stared back at me. "In over three-hundred years of recording the lives in progress, two tapestries defied me. Savage and Abaddon. Whether you believe me or not, there is a connection."

Fuck you, Fate. The words speared my mind, ringing in a fury that almost buckled my knees. Savage descended from the top of the stairs, his boots cracking out a thunderous beat. *You show up and in mere days try to turn my world on its ass? Fuck you. You want an enemy, fine. Done deal.*

"None of this is what I want," I said, the crowd parting to give the warrior the floor. "Facts speak for themselves."

What facts? he said, his hands moving as his words bombarded my thoughts. *The fact that you can't control a throw rug and are so pathetic that you'd rather ruin my reputation than admit you're a joke? My only connection to Abaddon is my obsession with putting the fucker down. When I sharpen my blades, I imagine how they'll rip through his flesh. When I close my eyes. I dream about slitting his throat. If that makes me a bad guy, fine. I'll live with that.*

"And your connection to Dane?"

Savage's body threw off a violent surge. My breath came out in a white cloud as the temperature in the entrance hall dropped at an alarming rate. No normal human could do that.

Curses erupted from the crowd.

Savage dropped his hands, the next words for me alone. *Stay out of my life, Fate. If you see me, be smart—turn and run.*

"Why do you hate my father so much?"

Who the fuck is your father, and why would—

"Dane. Dane is my father, and you hate him. Why?"

A gleam of realization lit his dark gaze.

"What does it mean to you?"

Sweet dick all. Like I said, stay out of my life and out of my way. When the opportunity comes to take Abaddon down, no one gets between me and the kill. Savage spoke the truth. Reeked of hatred. Of determination. Of betrayal.

How did Abaddon wrong you? I asked, straight into Savage's mind. He locked his thoughts. I forced my way inside his mind. *Who is he to you?*

The silver gleam of a knife flashed as voices rang out. Savage lunged like a grizzly bear launching to take down a weaker prey. My hands flew up, and I thrust him across the foyer with the force of a gale wind. I pinned him to the thick, paneled doors across the polished marble space.

The others retreated as I stalked forward.

Savage fought my powers with more strength than he should ever have possessed. I doubled my efforts and my skin burned. "I am a *fucking* Fate, remember? Daughter of an original. Not some pathetic girl for you to bully into submission. I will find out what Abaddon and my father are up to. I will protect my mother from them. And if that upsets you, I will go through you without a second thought."

"Enough." Reign set a heavy hand on my shoulder. "Despite his ill-temper, Savage has proven himself a dedicated, honorable warrior. Release him. Focus on the true enemy."

I flexed my aching fingers and let Savage fall to the floor.

He crouched, and his warrior mates tensed. We all seemed to question if he would retaliate. He sneered but didn't move.

Let him sneer. "Fine, but Savage is not involved. Until I figure out the connection, I don't want him in the discussions of what next steps to take."

Reign narrowed his gaze at me. "You don't get to give me orders about my men or my tactics. Fate or not, you'd do well to remember that. I'll agree to your terms for now. Savage, continue to work on the assignment I gave you yesterday until we sort this out."

After the drama with Savage in the foyer, Reign escorted me, Kobi, Cowboy, and Julian to the war room in Jade's home. He sat at the head of the table, tall, broad and intimidating. At least, *I* found him intimidating. Which, considering I'd been brought up by aggressive, powerful men, said a lot about the man.

He tented his fingers together and sighed. "And you think Abaddon will take your mother as Rheagan's vessel?"

I rubbed my temples. The pressure in my head threatened to explode out my eyes any minute. "The last thing I saw in Abaddon's tapestry was the beginning of an innocent's thread. He needs a vessel that can contain and support the power of a Fae goddess; a body

Rheagan can thrive in. I've checked the bloodlines, young and old. My mother is his best chance."

"I'm sorry, Zo," Kobi said. He set two tablets and a glass of water in front of me. "That sucks all around."

I dropped my forehead to the polished wood table and closed my eyes. My nerves were frayed, my heart aching, my mind full of action, yet nothing was being done.

"Kobi could guard her," Julian said.

I shook my head. "For how long? All day, every day? Forget that he has a life and a duty here, he's a stranger to her. She accepted Aust because she senses his gift. His energy resonates with her. Kobi will make her nervous. No offense."

"None taken." Kobi leaned back in his chair, scratching the scruff on his jaw. "I've never been a favorite on the parental scene. Even with my own."

"What about bringing Shalana here?" Cowboy suggested. "We could watch over her and ensure Abaddon, and your father, can't access her. Aust feels most comfortable hanging with the Weres at the Dens. If her gift is the same, it might work."

I shook my head. "Abaddon got to Lia here on Haven grounds. *Twice.* Rheagan almost got her at the cemetery too."

The argument halted as a golden mist materialized in the room. I rose from my seat and met Castian with a hug. He squeezed me tight. He smelled like home and everything I missed. "I told them not to involve you. You have enough to worry about without my theories."

Castian kissed my temple and pulled back to study me. He stroked my shaggy haircut where it lay against my shoulder and smiled. "Nonsense. Theories are merely facts waiting to be proven. I consider everything that comes to mind when dealing with Abaddon and Rheagan."

"But Dane is your brother."

"And that makes him immune from ill intent?" He walked me back to my seat and pushed my chair in as I sat. "I am brutally aware of who Dane is and what he's capable of. It's a basic truth that if you have something of value, there is always someone who wants to take it from you."

Reign poured a dram of whiskey and slid it down the table to where Castian took a seat. "That's awfully glib considering we're discussing your brother plotting to overthrow and betray you. That's treason."

"He's done worse, Maximus."

Worse? I didn't know what he referred to, but the look on Castian's face warned me not to ask.

"We could confront him," I said. "Take me home, and we'll see what's really going on. We could inventory the tapestries and see if there are other frames tampered with."

Castian emptied his glass. "Your father has usurped the Fae Council. I don't know if he threatened them, bribed them, or simply convinced them you lack any regard for our laws, but they won't discuss your reinstatement, or you returning home."

I notched my chin up. "I need never darken their doors again, but they can't stop me from visiting my mother and Abbey forever."

Julian refilled his glass and pushed the bottle back to his father. "Maybe if we eliminate Shalana as a viable vessel, Dane will lose interest in blocking you from your life."

"Not likely." I pulled the bottle to my palm with a focused breeze. I poured myself a glass and welcomed the sweet burn down my throat. "I've never fit with him or my sisters. My mother's status as a pawn has nothing to do with that."

Castian stood and eyed everyone at the table. "To that point, let me be clear. Zophia is under my protection and therefore under yours. Guard her with your lives for I shall end them if even a scratch mars her perfect skin."

"Uncle, please, that's not necessary."

Castian's chestnut waves brushed the collar of his cloak as he shook his head. "No argument. Stay out of harm's way until I can fix this and get you home."

"You're leaving? So soon?"

He winked. As bergamot and lavender wafted in the air, his form dissolved into mist. *Gotta go, Zozo. The brownies are ready, and your mom likes them warm.*

I stared at the space as he disappeared and ached to follow him home. I couldn't stand being so far from her and having no way to watch over her. "Okay, so, if I can't return home, I'll agree to bring my mother here? How soon can we arrange it?"

"Tomorrow," Julian said. "I can have this place wired—"

I shook my head, cutting off his suggestion. "Not under the same roof as Savage. If Bruin's willing to have us, I think Cowboy's suggestion of staying with the Weres suits us best."

Reign nodded. "Done deal. I'll arrange it."

Alone in the meditation garden planted by Grandfather Hawk, my mother and I watched the tangerine rays of the sinking sun. They reflected off the copper roof of Jade's mansion in the distance. Had I made the right decision? Was Bruin's home, carved into the side of the mountain, safer than Jade's home, where the Talon soldiers resided? Was I wrong about Savage and the threat he might pose to my mother?

In my centuries living as a Fate, I knew the answers. I searched the seeing bowls and read the tapestries—the truth at my fingertips. Life in this realm festered with turmoil, pain, and uncertainty. How could they stand it?

"May I join you?" Grandfather Hawk shuffled along the rail and gestured to Hoola clinging to my neck. "And who is this?"

I welcomed him to sit on the bench beside me and tucked her face into my neck. "Hoola has never ventured beyond Mother's sanctuary before. It's overwhelming for her to be here. For both of them."

As if to make me a liar, the little ape jumped from my hold and ran on her back legs toward Aust rounding the path to join us. With her gangly arms waving in the air, she met him and jumped into his embrace.

"Hello, *sweeting*," he said, accepting her kiss, wet on his lips. "Are you and your *naneth* settled?"

She gave him a whoop, and he shifted her to sit on his hip.

Aust came around the back of the bench and knelt beside my mother. "And how do you fare this evening, milady? The view is resplendent, is it not?"

Shalana, who had been quiet since her arrival several hours earlier, stared out at the setting sun. Aust whistled and Faolan, his wolf, trotted over and laid her head in my mother's lap. "At nightfall, I thought we might enjoy a tour of the Haven forest. You can ride Jade's jaguar mount, Naith. I would like to introduce you to the wolves and the woodland creatures here on the mountain. My wildlife friends are eager to meet you."

"New friends?" Mother asked.

"Many new friends. Would you like to meet some now?" He pointed to a pair of raptors gliding in lazy circles just above the plateau. Aust locked his gaze on them. The air around him grew still and silent. A moment later, the birds let off a shrill squawk. Tilting their wings, they soared over to land on the rail.

Mother smiled, and I had never been so relieved in my life.

"Grandfather," I said, "would you sit with my mother for a moment while I speak to Aust?"

"It would be my greatest honor."

Aust bowed to my mother briefly and then joined me near the three totem poles. I wrapped my arms around him and fought back tears. "You are amazing. I know she has taken up your time lately, but I'm so grateful."

Hoola pushed at me to release my hug. Then, she laid her head on his chest and stroked his cheek.

"Jealous little thing, aren't you?"

Aust chuckled. "I have worshiped your mother for my entire life. It is a dream come to reality that I now speak with her and call her friend."

I squeezed his arm and patted Hoola's side. "You bypassed friendship by a huge margin. You're her imaginary son-in-law, after all."

He dipped his chin and smiled. "Does that then give me the right to ask my imaginary betrothed what worries her so?"

There was no sense denying it. Since the moment Shalana arrived here, I knew this would never work. "She needs to be in her own home with her animals. Having her here makes *me* feel better, but she is suffering for it."

Aust nodded. "I thought a forest run might help. You are welcome to join us if you like. Bruin, Bree, and Cowboy shall shift and join the wolves while Julian tracks our group to ensure nothing unexpected occurs. The wolves are fierce protectors, and we shall take care of her at all times, I promise you."

"I have no doubt. You go. Just don't stay out too long. She is dealing with a lot. Tomorrow morning, could you take her home and watch over her while I figure something else out?"

He bowed his head. "It would be my greatest pleasure."

CHAPTER SIX

nce Aust and Bruin helped my mother onto Jade's giant black jaguar and headed into the forest, I dematerialized and wove a path on the wind in the opposite direction. I gathered myself at the door of the Gatehouse and entered as any member of Haven would have.

"Twice in one day," Julian said, as I came around the corner. "I take it you are here to watch over the forest run?"

"If you don't mind."

"Not at all. In fact, Kobi's in the kitchen getting some snacks. We'll make an evening of it." Julian grabbed a silver remote and pointed to the wall. The four wall-mounted monitors merged into one large picture.

Julian hustled down the hall, and I watched my mother. She knelt on the forest floor, surrounded by a pack of almost two dozen wolves. The dominant members nuzzled and rubbed against her, and she spoke to each in turn, stroking their coats. Then, she called forward the submissive wolves and gave them equal affection.

"Where's the camera?" I asked

"Aust is wearing a chest cam, and I can switch to a security feed if we want to zoom out or check something specific."

"Hey beautiful, you following me?" Kobi joined us, carrying a couple of bottles of liquor, a six-pack of beer, and a container of cookies.

I laughed at their idea of snacks. "Do you believe in fate?"

Kobi arched a brow, lifting the ring piercing beneath a flip of his ebony hair. "I can't say I'm a fan. I'm more of a 'choose your destiny' kinda guy."

I declined the wine but took the glass to the water cooler and filled it up. "We wouldn't want a repeat of last night."

"Speak for yourself." Kobi handed Julian the beer and plunked on the couch. "If a night of indulgence brings you out of your shell, drink up, lacy girl."

"Did I miss something?" Julian pulled a can free of the pack and set the rest on the glass coffee table in front of the sofa.

"Drunken misadventure," Kobi said, "but one that implies a deeper desire hidden within."

"Ha! You wish." I reached for a chocolate chunk cookie, and Kobi grabbed my wrist. With his gaze locked on mine, he raised the treat to his mouth and bit a piece off.

"Damn straight I do. Any itch you've got, I'll scratch it."

Julian pushed the coffee table with his boot, and it crashed into Kobi's shin. "Can you say Castian's niece, dipshit? Sorry, Zophia. Kobi's sextathalon nature gets the better of his judgment most of the time."

I ran my thumb across Kobi's lip and gathered the chocolate there. With a coy smile, I sucked it into my mouth and licked it clean. "You say that like it's a bad thing."

Kobi laughed and took a long swig of his beer. "This surveillance watch just got a whole lot more interesting."

"So, let's watch," Julian said, looking worried.

I leaned back into the couch, took possession of the cookies, and eyed the screen.

Naith stayed on the path flanked by natural wolves, while a Were bear, coyote, and wolf ran in front and behind the pack. Aust ran beside my mother, not as a tiger but in his true, Elven form. The grace and strength in his stride as he dodged trees and leaped over branches was a thing of beauty. As graceful as the jungle cat himself.

My mother had good taste picking him as my husband.

"See something you like," Kobi asked, his mouth curved in a crooked grin.

"What? Why?"

"Cause you just sighed one of those feminine sighs that means some man is doing something very right."

Had I? I swallowed. "It's the cookies. They're delicious."

"Uh huh."

Julian reached for one and nodded. "Elora made them. Can you imagine your mother cooking stuff like this every day? It's a wonder Aust isn't three hundred pounds."

"Nah, that boy's in peak physical condition," Kobi said, casting me a sidelong smirk. "Always running, that one. Can't blame him. He's had a hard-on for Bree since the first day he got here and hasn't gotten to work off any of that energy."

"That's none of our business." I tipped back my glass and drank my water. "Bree adores him. He adores her. Whatever it is, I'm sure they'll work it out."

Julian and Kobi shared a look.

"What? You don't think so?"

Julian shrugged. "Don't get me wrong. I'm all for the two of them hooking up. They'd be saccharine sweet. But Bree's Coyote is stubborn and holding out for a stronger mate."

"Is the Were part of them that distinct that they can disagree like that?"

Julian laughed. "Growing up, living with Bruin, I could tell when his bear was restless, when it was cranky, and when it was about to lose its violence-loving mind if he didn't get laid."

Kobi finished his beer and popped the top of a second. "We're two nights from the full moon. And it's the last moon cycle before the Equinox. There's more Were mojo in them these days than human. They're all fighting the effects."

On the screen, the forest party maneuvered the path. I wondered if

Were mojo might be responsible for my libido acting up lately. Likely, that was just an excuse. I was restless, and Haven was populated with beautiful, fit, warriors.

Julian's phone went off. "Damn straight. I'll be right there." He stood and headed for the door. "Elora's made stone baked pizzas. If we want one, I gotta claim it before Sin and Savage eat them all."

"No mushrooms," Kobi called.

When the chime sounded, Kobi shifted fast. He took the cookies from my lap and set them on the table. "We've got fifteen minutes max before he gets back. No time for a sextathalon but we can take the edge off."

I sputtered on my water. "What makes you think—"

His nostrils flared as he inhaled. "Incubus superpower, baby. Your arousal peaks every nerve I've got. You've been up in your head for too long. You need this, lacy girl. Unless you say no, I say we seize the moment."

He leaned in, his mouth hovering, his breath warm on my lips. I swallowed. Nowhere had he made physical contact with me, yet I felt his touch as keenly as if we were naked. Without considering how to answer, my body responded.

I clutched the back of his neck and pulled his mouth to mine. The hair at his nape was ebony silk, and I tightened my grip. His tongue swept my mouth, a male groan caught in our kiss. He tasted of chocolate and hops, and I wanted nothing more than to consume him.

Gods, he was right. I *did* need this.

Our mouths ground together while he undid my waistband and slid beneath the lace of my panties. His fingers met the damp heat pooled between my legs and the room spun.

"Fuck, you're burning up." The leather couch creaked as he shifted me across his lap. Sure fingers delved between the heated folds of my flesh. I cried out as his thumb rubbed over the tight nerves of my sex. "Been too long, lacy girl?"

I turned my head to catch his mouth again. He was gifted, whether as a man or because of his incubus demon nature, who knew? Who cared? Sprawled across his chest, I reached back and ran my hand down the front of his pants. His cock was solid and thrust against my hand.

My scattered gaze caught the screen as Aust panned the camera toward my mother enjoying her time out. I closed my eyes and focused on Kobi.

He growled against my lips. "Rub me. Harder."

I rubbed my palm over his trapped erection. "Get in my shirt."

"Yes, ma'am." Kobi's free hand came up under my blouse and pushed my bra out of his way. He cupped my breast then found the aching tip of my nipple.

The pinch and twist set off a shockwave of sensation. His mouth captured my cry, and I arched into his hands. His fingers grew warmer. Heated against the cool air of the room. I wriggled my pants down and undid his. "More access."

"No argument."

I tore from his grip and spun. On my knees, I moved to straddle him.

He cursed. "There's no time for that."

I didn't care. The penetration of his tongue. The grinding wave of my building orgasm, I needed him inside me. I gripped his jaw. "I won't take long—"

"It's your call."

"Is this a bad time?" a man asked, not five feet away.

Kobi tossed me onto the couch and rose to block me. "Who the fuck are you?"

Blouse adjusted, I righted my pants. My legs trembled and when I stood, a rush of moisture wet my panties. "This is Dane. The better question is, what the fuck he's doing here?"

"Language, little girl," Dane said, waving his finger in the air. "Slumming it doesn't mean you drop to the level of the common. I raised you better."

"Ha! You never raised me. Why are you here?"

Dane shrugged and looked around the Gatehouse. "You've been away from home for days. Can't a father ensure his child is well?" He frowned at Kobi, watching as the demon adjusted his pants.

"Really, Zophia? Could you not aim higher than a gothic pin-cushion?"

I rolled my eyes. "You judging sexual indiscretion is not only an oxymoron—it's hypocritical and hilarious."

"Now, now. We're in mixed company."

I laughed. "Cut the world's greatest dad routine. You've seen I'm fine. Now go."

He pointed at Kobi. "Keep your dick out of my daughter. She's worth ten of you."

Kobi grinned. "And twenty of you, by what I hear. And I believe she asked you to go."

Dane dematerialized.

I flopped to the couch, flushed and shaken. "Julian is right. It *is* annoying when people just pop in unannounced."

"What was that about?"

I pointed to my mother on the monitor. "He likely realized Shalana wasn't where she should be and came snooping. I guess he found what he was looking for."

"Shit." Kobi jogged to Julian's desk and grabbed a headset. "Okay, boys and girls, that's enough fun for one night. Let's get Shalana back to the Dens."

CHAPTER SEVEN

"*Y*ou okay?" Kobi rose from lounging across the end of my bed, drink in hand.

I left the bathroom light on and eased the door almost closed. The shared ensuite connected my room to where my mother and Hoola lay sound asleep.

"On what front? My father being a duplicitous jackass, my mother, one of the most powerful women in existence, unable to defend herself because she's losing her mind, or me, a discarded throwaway in my own life?"

"Lady's choice."

I ran my fingers through my hair and forced my gaze to meet his. "I was about to mount you like a wanton whore and have unprotected sex. So much for the grace of the gods."

"Hey now," Kobi said. "Don't you dare judge yourself for empowering your id—at least when I'm the other half of that equation. And unprotected sex, while normally unadvisable, is a moot point with me. Incubus Demons don't contract or carry sexual diseases, and I took reproduction off the table a decade ago. You're safe with me."

Safe? "I don't feel safe."

He sipped from his tumbler and passed me the glass. "You are. You and your mother."

The whiskey was aged and smooth. I tipped back the glass and hoped it would warm the cold spot deep in my belly. "The buzz of a thousand cicadas fills my head. They're all screeching at once, so I can't hear myself think. My mother can't stay here, but she can't stay there alone either. If Abaddon isn't coming for her, then I'm causing her more harm than good. It's all spinning around in my head in an endless swirl."

Kobi took the empty glass from my hand. "I can fix that. Will your mother wake?"

"No. The two of them are good until morning."

"Are you okay to leave here for a couple of hours? We can materialize back here at a moment's notice."

I thought about that. Too wound for sleep, with Kobi this close and being this sweet, I was liable to throw him to the floor and burn off some of this tension. "Bruin's nanny, Ceri, is curled up on a pallet beside the bed in her Puma form. Bruin thought she could keep watch and soothe Mom by being close."

Kobi laid a heavy arm around my shoulders and turned me toward the corridor. "Then let's blow this place for a bit."

After a quick word with the lion guarding my mother's door, Kobi and I headed toward Bruin's suite. Apparently, Kobi's plan hinged on Bruin giving us the okay. Before we got to the end of the hall, we came upon him in one of the other suites. He sat cross-legged on the rug between four small beds in the quad's nursery.

Kiara, the only girl of the four orphaned Were-lions, toddled over to the end table beside the pink bed and picked up a gilded frame. With the glass pressed tight to her naked body, she wrapped her arms across her chest and carried it to where her Alpha and three brothers awaited her return.

"Thank you, kitten." Bruin kissed her on the forehead and set the frame on the rug in front of them. "We ready?"

Four cherubic blonds with wide amber eyes nodded and wove their little fingers together.

"What do you do when all is quiet?" Bruin asked.

"Live and love the way Momma wanted," they answered.

"That's right. And what do you do when danger abounds?"

"Train hard, be brave, and make Papa proud."

"And what do you do if you smell the stench of Scourge."

"Shift forms, make tracks, and don't stop running."

Bruin opened his massive arms as the four launched from their prayers into his embrace. With all four of his wards locked in his hold, he stood and headed to their beds. One of the boys cupped Bruin's cheeks. "You'd find us, right, Alpha."

"My bear and I would level the two worlds before anyone harmed you guys."

"Oh," Kiara squirmed. "Momma's pi-cher."

Bruin dropped the boys onto their beds one at a time and then waited for her to replace the photo of their parents back into place. Then he scooped her up and tucked her into bed.

"Sweet dreams, monkeys."

The kids giggled. "We're not monkeys. We're lions."

"Oh, right," Bruin said, closing the door. "Good thing you reminded me."

Bruin waited until the children shifted into four golden lion cubs and then turned off the light. As the Were King, last living Bear of the Were race, Bruin was respected as one of the fiercest males of the realm. To witness such a display of fatherly devotion was touching. To know that he was this devoted to children when they weren't even his own—it hurt.

It really did.

Bruin joined us in the corridor. "Hey guys, what's up?"

"Keys," Kobi said. "Zophia needs to clear her head, so I thought I'd introduce her to your girlfriend."

Bruin chuckled and pulled a keyring out of his jeans pocket. He twisted the metal loop and handed Kobi a key.

"And please call if anything happens with my mother," I added. "Anything at all."

Bruin nodded. "Will do. Helmets and leathers. Mika's gear should fit you, Zophia. Be good to her, Demon. I mean it. Not a scratch."

"Yes, Dad," Kobi said, waving over his head.

~

Bruin's Harley rumbled as loud as his bear did when angry. The vibration rattled in my chest as the night wind whipped my hair and chilled my cheeks. Over the past half hour of dipping and swaying to the contours of the road, my hold around Kobi eased from a crushing cling to my hands waving in the current of air pushing over us.

"This is amazing!" I said, the panic and betrayal in my heart finally loosening its grip on my heart. I pointed at the glimmer of a road-house rooftop off the road to the right. The sign read, Psycho Suzi's Roadhouse. "There. Let's go."

Kobi geared down and laughed. "You do realize that *I'm* usually the bad influence, right?"

The bike slowed, and we pulled into the private parking lot. A smattering of trucks covered the asphalt square while a long string of motorcycles lined up against the brick building. Kobi headed over to the bikes and backed us between a chrome-on-chrome Harley and a red sports bike.

The engine cut off and the echo of silence quickly filled with the sound of country music and the crack of billiards balls. The clop of hooves to pavement brought two Centaurs past, and we nodded as they headed inside.

I hopped off the back and unstrapped my helmet.

Kobi set both helmets on the seat and pocketed the keys. "You sure you wouldn't rather go to the Hearthstone? There's no telling what kind of element we'll find in here. We're off sanctuary grounds."

I unzipped the leather jacket I'd borrowed and tousled my hair. "Don't tell me you're afraid of the fringe."

Kobi laughed and held out his arms. "A demon living in a Fae realm is well beyond the fringe."

"And can the demon dance?"

He cocked a brow, the piercing through it catching the light of the moon. "Incubi are well-versed in all things that get people off. The tough guys polishing the brass rail don't know what they're missing."

"People?" I repeated, arching a brow. "Not women?"

He waggled his brow. "Life's too short to censor pleasures. Does that shock a goddess of the Veil?"

I laughed. "I'm a voyeur by birth, and an immortal. You'll have to work really hard to shock me."

His grin triggered a sexual tightening deep inside me. "Challenge accepted—but just so we're clear—it's all in fun."

I swallowed, ignoring the ache. "Agreed. Life's too *long* to buy into the whole soulmate forever scenario. We need to grab happiness when we can because it's fickle and fleeting. Does that shock you, Demon?"

He pulled me against his chest and fingered my hair behind my ear. Leaning close, he kissed my cheek and whispered in my ear. "Pleasantly, yes. I find you more intriguing by the moment, lacy girl."

I bit my lip, weighing the pros and cons of abandoning the bar idea and finding a shadowed spot close by. Then again, if I truly was exiled, I had nothing but time to entertain myself in this realm. "How's your two-step. Can you do country?"

"Cowboy is my wingman, now that Bruin and Mika are hitched. What do you think?"

I nodded. "From the moment Cowboy's parents named him, that man had no chance to be anything but a country boy."

Kobi's eyes lit up. "Get the fuck out. You know Cowboy's given name? Give it up."

I laughed. "I know it, but there's no way you'll ever get it out of me."

Kobi pressed his lips once to mine. "It could be our little secret. You know, pillow talk between lovers."

"Nice try." I turned toward the entrance. With a little extra swagger in my hips, I climbed the three wooden steps and looked over my shoulder. "We aren't lovers."

"Yet." Kobi chuckled when I caught him eyeing me. "The night is young, lacy girl."

～

Psycho Suzi's Roadhouse boasted the same pitted wood and tin signs of Hearthstone's décor minus the ambiance of community welcome. Filled with women wearing leather and men who looked like they'd just got back from the battle, Kobi fit right in. I drew attention.

As we stopped to gain our bearings, Kobi lifted his chin toward the bar. A woman wearing a bustier made of chains slid out of her booth and gestured for us to take it. We made our way through the crush, and he kissed her cheek as I settled onto the bench opposite him. "Thanks, beautiful. I owe you one."

"Hold you to it," she said before dissolving into the crowd.

"You know her?" I asked.

"I know lots of people. What are you drinking?"

Aside from him being in the service of my uncle and the derogatory comments he made about his nature, I didn't know where the bravado ended, and the man began. I doubted many people did. "Double whiskey on ice."

Kobi hopped up and headed to the bar. The music seemed oddly out of step with the clientele, but the leather and chain gang shuffled across the wooden dance floor, regardless.

Through the throng of bodies, I caught sight of a young girl with mottled blue skin. Tall and slim, with an unnaturally long neck, she stood at a highboy table on the other side of the crush. At first, I wondered if she was old enough to be out at a bar at night, but then I saw the man standing just over her shoulder.

My curiosity heightened. What was *he* doing here?

"I bought the bottle," Kobi said, sliding back onto the bench. "Save us waiting for service."

I glanced back to where I'd seen Savage and sighed. The dancers filled in, blocking my line of sight. "You ready to hit the dance floor?"

Kobi raised a brow. Ice clinked against the glass, bobbing in the amber liquid. "Are we on a timer I don't know about? What about your drink?"

I emptied the tumbler in four deep gulps. "Just anxious to get you on the dance floor."

Kobi sat back and frowned. Pressing his palms flat against the table, he tapped his fingers on the surface. "That's the first time you've lied to me, Zophia. Make it the last, or this is over before it starts."

He waited until I nodded and then nodded in return.

Sliding off the bench, he stretched his neck and offered his hand. The reach of his arm exposed the gun sheathed against his side. "Ready to hit the sawdust?"

He led us toward the crush of dancers, and I realized something so obvious I felt stupid. Kobi was a male's male, his body sculpted by practice and battle, from conflict and killing. Most of the men at Haven—Kobi, Bruin, Reign, Cowboy, and the rest—were not only the fighters they seemed, but killers. Takers of life. Violent and volatile.

As the Keeper of Lives over the past centuries, I valued life as a miraculous and precious thing. If things went badly here, I did not doubt Kobi would kill to keep me safe.

"What's going on in there?" Kobi tapped my forehead.

Nothing was on my lips but his warning from a moment ago remained fresh in my mind. "Just sorting through the realities of life in this realm."

He frowned. "Do you want to head back to the Dens?"

I stepped chest to chest with him and slid my arm around his waist. "Not a chance. You promised me a tour of the dance floor. Show me what you've got, Demon."

Kobi was, in fact, a remarkable dancer. Our bodies moved in a synchronized flow which implied far more familiarity than we possessed with one another. And while I half expected him to use the physical closeness to further his seduction, his hands and body remained in polite positions and proximity to mine.

As we moved with the crowd, the blue girl remained at her table in the back. The man she'd been speaking with moved to the bar. Where was Savage? Was it Savage? Maybe it hadn't been him. I couldn't be sure.

A slow song started, and Kobi paused. His gaze said the next move was mine. I pressed against him, the softness of my breasts meeting the hard ridges of his chest. My reward was an unguarded smile. Running a finger over the piercings in his ear and brow, I brushed my lips across his. "Despite the reality of my life right now, this was a great way to end a stressful day. Thank you."

His gaze grew heated, his scent shifting to something spiced and musky. "It could have been better without your father interrupting us in the Gatehouse—"

A tap on my shoulder had me stepping back.

"Settle a bet." A whiskey-soaked man with a paunch belly eyed me up and down. Squat and muscled, he was almost the same height as he was broad. "My buddy says you're one of those Fate bitches. I say no Fate would come to Suzi's. 'You know of any other race with skin like hers?' he says. So I come over to find out. Where you from, baby?"

I stepped in front of Kobi and pulled his hands across my front before he could reach for his weapon or start a bar-brawl. "You're right. I'm not a Fate. Tell your buddy he's buying the next round."

"So, what are you?" He stared with an unwelcome level of interest. Others noticed and stopped to stare too.

"She's a woman of worth, ass-lick," Kobi said.

I patted Kobi's fists where they clenched at my navel. "I'm just a girl out for a night with a friend. So, if you'll excuse us." I turned in Kobi's arms and reached around the back of his neck. His gaze had darkened to black, the playful seducer gone, the demon warrior at the foreground.

"Ignore him," I whispered. "Let's grab our bottle and take a road trip."

He nodded and we headed back to our booth. We hadn't gotten ten feet when a vice-grip on my wrist yanked me back.

It was the same man, looking more determined. "You know, now that I see you close up, I agree with him. You're a fucking Fate. I'd bet my life on it."

Kobi grabbed the guy by the arm, drew his gun, and pushed the barrel to the center of his forehead. The smell of burnt flesh hit my nostrils at the same moment the man hollered and released my arm. Kobi pushed him back, a red handprint welted and smoking on the man's flesh. "You *are* betting your life on it, so be sure it's worth it to you."

"Don't threaten him." A second man rushed in. He stared from his friend's arm to Kobi and back again. "What the fuck are you?"

"Nothing anyone with half a brain messes with. So, the question is, do you have half a brain?"

"Fuck you. You think you're a big man because you have a gun? You know how to shoot that thing, slim?"

Kobi grinned. "I do, so you'd be wise to drop this. Get back to your evening, and we'll be on our way."

"Like hell," someone said from behind me.

"Yeah, it's a lot like that." Kobi handed me the gun. His eyes flipped to demon red as he turned back to our admirers. "Don't say I didn't warn you."

The dance floor exploded into a flurry of fists and blood. Glass shattered, men flew. Someone grabbed me around the waist and dragged me backward. I spun to hit them with the gun when I recognized the black glare staring down at me.

Stay here, Savage said, shoving me behind the bar. He tightened my grip on the gun and pointed the muzzle toward the grungy floor. *Don't kill anyone unless you have to.*

He launched straight into the fray, fists up. Within moments, he worked his way back to Kobi.

When Kobi saw him, he lit up with a genuine smile. The two of them settled in and fought back to back. They had obviously done this before and seemed to enjoy it.

They worked through the drunken attackers in tandem. The thud of fists to flesh died down, and soon they made their way back to the bar. Savage held up two fingers. The burly gray-haired woman beside me set down her bat and uncapped a couple of bottles.

Savage kept one and handed the other to Kobi.

Instead of taking a drink, Kobi guided me past our empty booth and grabbed the bottle of whiskey from the table. "Let's get some air, shall we?"

The moon hung low and almost full, reflecting silver off the chrome and glossy paint of the motorcycles. Once we reached Bruin's bike, Kobi and Savage shucked off their jackets and tipped back their beers.

"Thanks for the assist, my man," Kobi said. "It looked like that beast in plaid got you good with the pool cue."

Savage lifted his shirt to reveal a red welt coming up purple across his side. The tattoos on his arms and neck continued across his entire upper body.

Kobi dumped the melted ice from my glass and poured me a drink. "You good?"

"Fine." I drank a fair bit and found it was truer than I realized. "That was my first bar brawl."

Kobi eyed his bloody knuckles and flexed his fingers. "Are you planning on making them a regular thing?"

"First-hand experiences—absolutely. Drunken bar fights . . not necessarily. It was over a lot faster than I imagined."

The entrance doors slammed open and paunch-belly, and drunk-buddy hobbled over to two bikes parked on the far end of the row. They never looked our way, though I had the feeling they knew exactly where we were.

Kobi finished his beer and set the bottle on the pavement. Savage did the same. With his hands empty, he signed a few signals and then headed back inside.

"What did he say?"

"Reign has him working this bar. If he finds out anything about

Abaddon or his plans, he'll report it in the morning. You're wrong about him, you know."

I finished my drink and set my glass beside the two bottles. My fingers fumbled with the strap of my helmet under my chin and Kobi reached over to help me out. "Any chance you'd let me drive the bike?"

His roaring laughter drowned out the low murmur of male voices and thumping music inside the bar. The jocularity ended fast when he met my gaze. "Sorry. I wasn't laughing at the idea of you driving. I imagined what Bruin would do to me if I let it happen." He lifted my chin with his finger and leaned closer. "Not tonight, and not with this bike, but if you want to learn, I'm happy to take you out and teach you."

I stepped back and wandered down the line of motorcycles. The artistry of the custom painted designs was one thing, but the freedom and power they represented . . . "You must think I'm ridiculous."

"Why the hell would I?"

"How could you not? For centuries, I've recorded the lives and events in this realm yet know nothing of life. I understand the dangers you all face, yet have never experienced the loss of a loved one or the threat of life and death. I've never actually done anything. I've only ever watched."

He toed the dirt with his boot and frowned. "You sell yourself short, Zo. Conquering the spin cycle and watching someone you love bleed out in front of you doesn't suddenly make you an authentic, card-carrying member of the realm. Where shit counts is in here."

His fingers splayed on his chest as he stepped forward. "You know which side of the line to stand on when push comes to shove. If you take a deep breath and your lungs fill, there's still time for all the other shit. Give yourself a break. Continue to seize your moments one experience at a time, and you'll get there."

My gaze locked on his mouth and I seized my moment. The instant our tongues met, I groaned. His lips were like warm silk, his tongue a seasoned marauder. I met him, body to body. I coiled my leg around his thigh and ran my hands up the back of his shirt.

If Dane hadn't interrupted us at the Gatehouse earlier, I wouldn't be aching with a consuming hunger that scorched my insides beyond all sense. *Dane.* Betrayal pierced me anew. My breath caught, but I wouldn't let him win. He removed my responsibilities, fine. With nothing to weigh me down, freedom to act was my new life's purpose.

An Escalade parked beneath a crooked oak tree at the back of the parking lot gave me an idea. I rubbed the straining denim of Kobi's pants, and his hips thrust into my palm. "Follow me." I threw my molecules into the night air and headed across the parking lot.

Car locks and windows kept out humans and people who couldn't dematerialize but did nothing to deter preternaturals who needed an entry point. I rematerialized on the back seat of the massive vehicle, and Kobi misted in, right behind me.

"I like the way you think," Kobi said, pulling the latch to lower the seat back to recline. He hovered over me, a silent promise dancing in his gaze.

Everything about him radiated sex. From the grace of his body to the smell of his skin to the way the simplest touch from him made me wet. "I can't wait to get back."

Kobi didn't need convincing. He had Mika's leather gear off me and tossed in the back in a matter of seconds. His boots and pants were gone a second later. Tall and lean, the man had the body of a well-conditioned athlete. My lovers before him had inherited their physique from the Fae bloodline. Members of the Pantheon. Aristocrats. Kobi earned his body by fighting and having endless, amazing sex.

"You're truly safe?" I leaned back along the leather seat and let my knees fall open.

He knelt at my feet and licked his lips. The sudden hunger in his face hit me low in the belly. "One-hundred percent." His finger trailed through the moisture heating my sex, and I shuddered. "You're not shy, are you?"

I swung my legs over his shoulders and arched my hips. "Not even a bit."

His breath tingled warmly against my flesh as his head dropped. The texture of his manicured goatee prickled and brushed my flesh. My hips bucked, and he laid an arm across my pelvis. "Gods, you taste as good as you smell."

I cried out as he spread me wider and lapped hard against my core. Fingers and tongue. Lips and goatee. The sensations overwhelmed. My legs trembled as he folded and pinned me to the seat to gain the best access.

The cab of the truck filled with the heady fragrance of sex, the tinted windows providing them an insulated playground of light and shadows. Kobi's fingers delved, titillating and teasing, as my release built in a thundering rush. I dug my heels into his back and gripped his hair, urging him on.

Kobi was aggressive but not harsh. Greedy but not selfish.

His fingers gripped my hips, pulling my core against his kisses as if nothing was enough. I came hard, shattering and bucking to relentless swipes of his tongue. He eased off only while I rode out my release and then came at me again. Over and over, he repeated his ministrations, my body defenseless but to come for him again and again.

I wasn't quiet. I cried out in the glory of it. Called his name. Only after I begged for him to be inside me did he relent.

Even inside a vehicle that large, it was awkward having him come over me. His legs were long, his body humming like the sexual predator he was by nature. The interior spun as he repositioned us. Suddenly, he was on his back, reclining, and I lay on his chest.

"You wanted to ride me earlier," he said, positioning himself at my core. "I'd hate for you to miss out on one of your experiences."

The penetration was a raw pleasure. I stiffened, grabbing the seat behind him as I adjusted. I slid down his shaft like wet satin on hot steel, but he was large and incredibly hard. "My legs can barely hold me."

Kobi chuckled, the vibration shared through our joined bodies.

"You'll need to work out if you're going to keep up, lacy girl. You've spent too much time sitting at your loom."

Kobi took my breast into his mouth, and I threw my head back. Firm hands gripped my hips once again and guided me up and down until I thought I might pass out.

It was so good. So incredibly good.

Damp with sweat, my body ignited again, clenching and pulling at him deep inside me. Kobi's hips flexed as he slammed me down one last time. He came with a hoarse groan. The sound echoed inside the enclosed space as the corded muscles in his neck strained.

It was a long while before we could breathe well enough to speak. We laid, still joined, the stale air of the truck cab rife with the smell of our bodies.

"Car sex," Kobi said, kissing the top of my head. "Is that a new one for your list?"

"The being in the car part *and* the sex in the car part."

"Really? You've never been in a car?"

I toyed with his nipple ring and laughed. "No, but I'd say we checked it off the list quite effectively."

Kobi chuckled beneath me, his hand squeezing the globe of my butt. "I'm glad you consider it covered. When I can walk again, maybe we should get out of this guy's truck and home to bed. I gotta work in the morning."

CHAPTER EIGHT

*A*fter Jade and Aust left to escort my mother back to her sanctuary, I wandered the abandoned living areas of the Dens and wondered what I might do to fill my day. Kobi was off on warrior duty. Bruin, Cowboy, and Julian left to ready for the Were Solstice Summit, and Mika and Bree were heading out to the ancient ruin site to tend to details for that as well.

As they paused in the foyer rotunda to slip on their jackets, I read the missive of welcome painted on the stone wall: *We believe in the right to bear arms and the right to arm BEARS.*

"Might I join you, ladies?" I asked. "I find myself searching for purpose this morning."

Mika chuckled. "Of course, come along. Have you ever seen Were males working up a sweat? It's a beautiful sight. We couldn't let you miss it."

Bree nodded and held the door open for me to pass. "It's such a hardship spending our days overseeing construction. Sharing the burden of our duties will be good. Come along."

Mika, Bree, and I made our way deep into the forest, to the outer edge of the destruction left by Abaddon's attack. The ruin site had long stood a tribute to the ancient ways of the Fae gods. The ley lines crisscrossed deep within the grounds below making it a particularly magical location.

Abaddon's bombs had detonated within the clearing of the standing stones, bringing the nomenclature of *ruin site* to an incredible new level. Trees lay uprooted, cavities of earth blasted open like gaping maws, stone pillars and plinths splintered as if constructed of kindling and not stone.

"Bad, eh?" An indigenous boy with a purple mohawk sidled up next to me. "It's a shit-ton better than last week. We thought we were in backhoe territory. Seriously, it looked like there was no coming back from the damage done."

"It's horrendous. Infuriating," I said. "I witnessed the battle, yet still find the damage hard to believe."

"It's an eyesore, for sure. I'm Nash, by the by." He held out his hand, and I accepted his greeting. The crescent moon tattoo encircling his eye crinkled with his smile. "You'll want to wear one of these while you're on site."

He stepped under the shelter of a temporary lean-to and came back with a white domed hat. "Bruin's orders. All the lovely ladies get a hardhat. I guess the men are thick-skulled enough not to bother."

He handed it to me and waited expectantly. As I placed it on my head, I realized this was another new experience. I'd never worn a hat before. Never seen one made out of . . . whatever this was. I shook my head a little, and the weight shifted. I wasn't fond of the sensation but, trying not to hurt his feelings for the thoughtfulness of wanting to keep me safe, I thanked him regardless.

"Listen," he said. "Since you're one of us now, you'll need clothes and things of your own. I'm the go-to guy for the Talon and guests of Reign and the family. Let me know if there's anything I can get for you. You know, to help you settle in."

Settle in? "As much as I appreciate your intentions, I'm sure we won't need to bother about that. Castian is working to have my exile reversed. Once he sorts things out, I'll return home and resume my station."

"Oh? I hadn't heard that. Well, that's great news. You must be excited to get back to your life."

"I am, yes." *Was I? Wasn't I?* Well, I wanted to resume at least parts of my life. I missed tending to the tapestries. The Palace was where I grew up. No, the Palace was just a building. What made it a home was my mom, Castian, and Abbey.

"Honestly, Nash, I hadn't given it much thought, but I see your point. I might not be a guest of Haven much longer, but I also can't keep wearing Mika's clothes. Thank you, yes. I suppose a few things of my own would be nice."

We talked a bit about the shops in the marketplace and how I could shop there and tell them Nash would settle things up for me at a later time, but truly I lost focus.

Who would I be if stranded in this realm for eternity?

"Nash, getcha ass over here with the chainsaw," someone yelled from across the clearing.

"That's my cue. Gotta jet. Stay safe, Zophia."

Surprised he knew my name, I watched him trot off to help with a fallen pillar buried beneath the trunk of a tree.

A buzzing whine of a machine rent the air, followed by the crack of splitting wood. I covered my ears to baffle the din and strode in the opposite direction to gain some distance.

Closer to the forest, on the opposite end of the clearing, I scanned the progress of construction. Timber frames outlined a labyrinth floorplan I couldn't decipher as bare-chested Weres lifted, sawed, drilled, and leveled. Tanned and gorgeous, every muscle honed to perfection, they glimmered with sweat under the glow of the morning sun.

"Was I right about the view?" Bree said, her coyote letting off a low growl of approval.

She handed me a bottle of soda, and I sipped at the chestnut-colored liquid. Sweaty and physically perfect, the men before us all moved with the same confident, sexual lope that Kobi possessed. Images of us in the back of that truck replayed in an exotic memory reel in my mind. I'd been trying not to think about him all morning and was failing miserably. "How long are Talon soldiers on duty in the field each day?"

Bree inhaled, and her gaze narrowed. "The demon, eh? You two are an unexpected pair."

"We're hardly a pair, I've known the man three days. But to my surprise, we have more in common than you might think."

She stared at her bottle, chasing condensation with her thumb. "Be careful, Zo. I've known Kobi for years and he's not a *we* guy, he's a *me* guy. He's a seducer by design, and you're off balance as it is. It's tough to deny the animal inside."

I swallowed another drink and screwed the cap back on. I'd seen Kodi's demon several times while tending the tapestries. His animal saved Lia from possession and came out when situations seemed most dire. I had no problem with him.

Bree's animal, however, I took great issue with. Her coyote refused to accept Aust, and I found myself offended on his behalf. "Can I ask a personal question?" When she nodded, I continued. "When you shift, are you the coyote or are the coyote and you sharing space?"

"Both . . . sort of."

Bruin sauntered beneath the shelter and kissed his mate.

Cowboy sidled up beside us, his ripped jeans hanging low, a hammer in his hand. "What's the girl talk? Anything juicy we menfolk should know?"

Bree tossed her empty bottle at Cowboy's head and laughed when he ducked. "Zo was asking about the relationship between a Were host and base animal."

"Oh"—Bruin laughed—"so, a light conversation."

Cowboy scooped the plastic bottle from the ground and tilted it in deference. "A lot of people think we're two separate entities sharing one body. It's more interwoven than that. It's like one entity with two distinct personalities. One based on logic and emotion, the other based on instinct and emotion."

"There's lots of emotion," Bruin said. "Most often stubborn and aggressive."

"And sexual," Cowboy added.

The two bumped knuckles.

"Aust, my man." Cowboy met Aust chest to chest as they greeted one another.

Aust kissed Bree and Mika on the cheek before coming over to greet me as well. "Sweeting, what is it that has you looking so alarmed. Are you well?"

"I am," I said. "I thought you were spending the day with my mother. Has something happened?"

"Fash not. Castian came to call while Shalana and Dandy were napping in the hammock. He sent me to help with the construction, as he was going to fix your mother lunch and then take her to view a new section of rock terrain he added. He brought her some new goats."

"Goats," I said, tears welling.

"Have I said something to upset you?" he asked. "Should I have stayed? Should I return?"

I shook my head and laughed at his panicked expression. "I'm fine. Exploring new biomes is something the three of us usually do together. I hate missing things with her."

"Everything all right?" Bruin asked, joining us. "Hey, what's doin', Zo?"

"She missed the unveiling of the goats," Cowboy said, slinging a tool belt around his hips.

"Goats?" Bruin looked confused.

Cowboy shrugged. "That's what she said."

"So, this section," Mika said, shoving them toward the work area, "is where the main entrance will be. Two-storey glass facing east to greet the dawn of each new day and on the west side, the same to greet the rising moon."

"The glass will be bulletproof and shatterproof, of course," Bree added.

"Twelve-gauge glass-clad polycarbonate," Cowboy called over his shoulder. "Nothing but the best."

Mika snorted. "With Bruin and Julian in charge, who would expect anything less than a fortress."

Bree smiled, waving me over to the wooden table under the shelter. "What do you like for décor, Zo? We were thinking slate floors and pine finishes, maybe in a darker stain."

"Are you asking my opinion?"

Mika nodded. "Yeah, what do you like?"

It struck me that no one had ever asked my thoughts about something so mundane before. And though the outcome didn't affect lives, I found I very much enjoyed being included in the discussion. "Who will be staying here?"

"Nine Were Primes and any mates attending the summit. We want a grandeur fitting their stations, yet textiles and finishes respectful of the setting and the Were affection for natural materials, *annnnd* it has to be built within three weeks."

I glanced back at the skeletal framework rising from the decimated grounds. "Oh, my."

"Yep," Bree said. "That pretty much covers it."

With that in mind, I set to work, sorting through what they had gathered for consideration. "This stone would be lovely for the hearth of the fireplaces. You have fireplaces planned, yes?"

After spending the better part of the morning with Bree and Mika in the clearing, they returned to the Dens with Aust, Bruin, and Cowboy to get some lunch. I decided to explore the marketplace and find something to eat there.

The Haven marketplace started at the Hearthstone and outlined a treed courtyard square with a dozen glass-fronted shops and produce carts. It became painfully apparent, as citizens of the mountain bustled and busied themselves, that each person living in this mountain refuge led lives of purpose. The contributions of the many building a better life for the collective whole.

My duties as Keeper of Lives had always left me feeling proud to serve the realm. I missed that. I missed learning about the struggles and triumphs of these amazing people and recording them. Even if I were to return to my life tomorrow, it would take me weeks to catch up with what I'd missed already.

"Zophia . . . *Zophiiiia?*" Lia tilted her head into my line of vision. Her Highborne blue eyes twinkled as her silver locks blew back from rosy cheeks, exposing the gentle points of her ears. "Merry meet, my friend, what in the realms are you doing wandering around the Haven Marketplace? Are you well?"

I blinked, surprised at how absorbed I'd been in my mental musings. "No. In truth, everything is a horrid mess."

In a rush, I recounted the past few days, my worries about my mother's safety, my loss of purpose in a world I felt disconnected with, and how I was torn between wanting to go home and the prospect of creating a life of my choosing rather than of obligatory duty.

"Well, if there is anyone else who knows more about being thrown away by a beloved community to find herself lost in the bustle of the Realm of the Fair, I would be surprised. I know exactly how your heart aches."

Lia looked me over and then chuckled, glancing down at herself. Gone were the floor-length gowns and formality the two of us had always worn. Pants and blouses reflected our new reality. Lia touched my hair where it fell in a shaggy line around my shoulders. "Striking. Did Lexi have a hand in it?"

"Only after I hacked off my braid with her knife."

She laughed. "It's a wonder she let you touch one of her knives. She's quite possessive of her weapons. She and Bree cut and styled my hair too, when I reinvented myself."

I linked my arm in hers, and we walked the cobbled sidewalk outside the shops. "Speaking of the new Lia, how was your first week as Queen of the Realm?"

Lia rolled her eyes. "Not all that different from life before. Strong-willed men tell me what I must needs do and still seem surprised when I have thoughts of my own."

"Not Samuel, surely?"

She broke into a smile far too telling. "No. Samuel is ever

supportive and feeds my heart with more love and confidence than one female deserves."

I squeezed her arm. "I'm glad. After what the two of you went through the past year, you both earned a little bliss."

"Bliss the lady says?" Samuel stepped off a shop's stoop beside us and kissed his bride on the cheek. Tall and lean, in black slacks and a crisp, white shirt, Lia's wizard husband was the picture of chic contentment. "Is that how my beautiful bride describes her life these days?"

Lia wrapped her arm around his waist and pulled him in step with us as we continued toward the Hearthstone.

"Have I gotten a few things right then, Luv?"

Lia looked up and offered him an adoring smile. "A few. Mayhap a few more than a few."

Samuel winked and shifted his attention to me. "We owe our happiness to you, Zophia. All of it. If ye hadn't convinced yer sisters to let us be, we'd be living a verra different reality. I want ye to know, if ye ever need anything—ever—all ye need do is speak the words."

Lia nodded. "I have a wonderful idea. You should come live with us. I would love having you as my confidant and advisor. Gods know I have much to learn about the realm and its members. I would value your insights. Who knows, we might even be able to beat back some of the dominant male ideals if we work together."

I shrugged. "Castian is working to get me home. I'm sure I'll be back at my loom and avoiding my sisters very soon."

"And what if yer dismissal stands? What will ye do?"

Lia scowled at Samuel. "You knew about this?"

He tapped her nose. "Only just, Luv. I ran into Julian in the shop. But aye, Lia's right, Zo. Ye should come to stay with us 'till ye get yerself sorted."

"Thank you both, but I'm sure I'll be returning to the Veil any day." I held my hands up. "I am a Fate, by blood and by destiny. Who am I, if not the Keeper of Lives?"

"A powerful woman, and with unwavering compassion and selfless loyalty to justice. Ye'll find this realm has need of such qualities. If things dinnae work out as expected, ye'll find yer place soon enough, I have no doubt."

I wished, not for the first time since this all began, that I could talk things through with my mother. Shalana was known for her strength and wisdom. Her counsel had always guided me through the toughest moments of my life. Now, the role of mother and child had reversed, and I found myself wondering what she would have me do.

"Besides," Samuel said, drawing me from my thoughts, "Lia and I know too well the sting of a father's betrayal. Dinnae let the man define ye. Though it hurts to yer depths, it's best to know who ye can count on. Focus on the ones who deserve yer love and—Hey, Julian, what is it?"

Julian slid his phone into his pants pocket, his warm mocha complexion drained. "It's Jade. Elora found her unconscious on the kitchen floor. Something's wrong."

CHAPTER NINE

*J*ade's home had always emitted an energy all its own. The air circulated, filled with the scents of Elora's cooking, leather, and expensive aftershave, giving it a homey feel. The warriors who lived there faced death each day and as a result, lived each moment to its fullest. And while the atmosphere might be a little rough around the edges, it boasted a sense of camaraderie, belonging, and oneness.

Rushing into the foyer, the utter silence of the space struck me as wrong. Everything hung still—as if the mansion itself was holding its breath.

Elora rushed from the kitchen corridor, headed toward the main staircase. Lia raced to join her, and the two went up together. Samuel took the stairs two at a time behind them, and they were gone.

The clash of billiards balls made me jump.

"Come on," Julian said. "Let's see what we can find out."

Following Julian's lead, we headed into the living room. A leather-clad warrior leaned over the farthest felt table, lining up his shot. By the tattoos on his arms, and the close, military cut of his hair, it could only be one person.

"Sav," Julian said, jogging over and bumping knuckles. "Hey, Princess, what the hell happened?"

Lexi chalked her cue, her wings fluttering idly with the flex of her muscles. "Elora found Jade collapsed in the kitchen an hour ago. It looks like she went for a snack and got zapped with an electrical shock off something. The energy surge jolted her powers from the Fate's binding spell. Castian and Rowan are doing what they can to settle things, but the shit is hitting."

Savage finished his next shot and leaned against the table. With his hip propped against the edge of the table, the sheer mass of the man made me want to retreat. He wore the same angry scowl as usual, but the open hatred he'd shown me before seemed to have subsided—at least a little.

Instead, an edge of worry creased his brow.

You could help, Savage said, projecting his thoughts. *You're no longer bound to sit on the sidelines. Make yourself useful.*

I ignored the tone, recognizing the frustration I felt every time my mother was suffering, and there was nothing I could do about it. No doubt, if he could stab someone or invade someplace to make things better, he would. "My affinity is wind. It's Zora who controls electrical fields."

Then go ask her.

"Of course, though I'll need someone to Flash me Behind the Veil. My ability to access the Pantheon—wait, did you say Castian was upstairs with Jade?"

"Yeah, Jade's his daughter. He came the second Reign called him. Why? What's the look for?"

"Did Elora see a loose wire or anything that might have caused the shock in the kitchen?"

"Not that I know of."

The shock came from a woman, not an appliance.

I spun to the entranceway. An Elven male stood tall and proud. If it weren't for him passing through the sofa as he made his way closer, I might not have realized he was a ghost. His features had been passed so closely to his son, there was no doubt in my mind who stood before us.

"How do you know?" I asked Aust's father.

I was in the kitchen waiting for Elora when Jade came in to feed her young. Your Faery friend is mistaken. There was no electrical shock. It was a magical jolt from a blue-skinned girl that caused this.

"Blue skin? Are you certain?"

She was standing as close as you are to me now. She peered into the kitchen from the window, raised a hand, and then, a moment later, Jade collapsed.

I glanced at Lexi, the blood draining from my head. "Tell Samuel it's a spell, not a shock. Maybe he can help."

"A spell? Who cast it?"

"A blue-skinned woman peering in the kitchen window."

"Fucking Shavandra," Lexi said, running toward the corridor. "Find her, Julian."

"Who's Shavandra?" I asked.

Julian pulled his phone out of his pocket and was tapping his screen. "Abaddon's sorcerous bitch."

The room started to spin.

"Abaddon drew Castian down here on purpose. He needed to get rid of him to go after my mother. Rheagan is going to try to take her, I know it. I need to get home."

Julian cursed. "We need to be damn sure before I order a Talon force to surge Behind the Veil."

I'll take you to check it out, Savage said.

"No. I don't trust you."

There's no one else here that has clearance Behind the Veil. Jade. Galan. Castian. Samuel. Everyone's a little busy right now. Are you willing to risk your mother's life based on your bias about me?

"You're hiding something. Lying about something."

Everyone is hiding something, Zophia. That doesn't mean I don't want the same thing you do.

Hearing Savage say my name surprised me. He'd never called me anything but Fate or fucking Fate.

Look, if you're right, Rheagan is getting hold of your mother as we stand here debating. Let's get gone.

I nodded. "Yes, of course. You're right. Let's go."

Flashing was a crude and jarring mode of travel compared to dematerializing, but I was in no position to complain. My ears rang, the ever-present knot in my stomach tightened, and the palace grounds spun until the effects settled. The result was the same, however, and that was all that mattered.

"Follow me." I dematerialized and headed to my mother's compound. The moment I hit the walkway outside the little, ivy-covered cottage, Savage was beside me.

Dandy squawked a panicked shrill inside and in the back of my mind, I hoped Savage's presence was a case of "the enemy of my enemy is my friend."

A dreadful foreboding told me I would soon find out.

The door swept open, and Dandy flew into my arms, tromping and flailing for a perch. Feathers flew, his wing hit me in the face, and I nearly dropped him.

Savage withdrew dual knives and stormed toward the dark hall to the bedrooms. The sight of the hulking warrior racing into my mother's private space brought dark blotches before my eyes. Despite my body's thoughts to the contrary, fainting wasn't an option.

"Mother?" I cried. "Where are you?"

My sneakers skidded on the wooden floor of the master bedroom, my scattered gaze skimming over the dark space. The canopy bed, the reading nook, the shadowed corners.

"Mother? It's me, Zozo. I'm here."

But she wasn't.

At least not anymore.

If not here, where else might she be? Savage sheathed his blades, the action softening his menacing appearance to only slightly less deadly.

"Castian may have taken her to the palace. He has several guest suites in the private quarters of his wing."

Then that's where we need to be.

Taking form on the terrace outside Castian's suite, my heart sank. The glass doors to Castian's private wing hung open, and my worst fears took hold. With the God of gods tending to Jade in the Realm of the Fair, those doors should be sealed. No way would he ever allow access to Abbey when he wasn't here.

The alarm sounded a heartbeat before the terrace doors flew open and palace staff started flooding out. Dozens of workers dressed in full livery emerged. En masse, they hemorrhaged from the grand façade, scurrying down the marble steps to the grounds below. They looked as frightened as the deer on the lawn scrambling away from the exodus.

I caught the arm of a Brownie as he reached the marble steps. "Pim, what's happened?"

"We are invaded, Mistress." His complexion faded from its usual lilac to a sickly puce. "By all manner of reeking beasts."

Scourge. Oh, gods. Somehow, they were here.

"Savage, we need to . . ." Where was Savage? A thunderous crash inside preceded the smashing of glass.

The state of Castian's private living room made little sense. Half a dozen Scourge soldiers battled the Palace Guard. The stench of rot contaminated the air and clung foul to the back of my throat.

I gagged as the guards struck the decaying Raiders. Chunks of soulless bodies landed in heavy, wet heaps across velveteen sofas and glass-topped side tables.

Maniacal male laughter twisted the knot in my stomach. By the window, Abaddon held Savage pinned by the throat. Matched evenly in size and build, Abaddon gloated with a level of sadistic pleasure I'd never seen.

Savage's mind exploded with a bombardment of violent emotion. This *was* personal. I was right about that. But I may have been wrong to question his allegiance.

I thrust my hands out and knocked Abaddon back.

Savage drew a gulping breath and despite looking winded and shaken, regained control. The two locked back together, grunting and clawing at each other as much like animals as Aust's wolves as they set upon prey.

I abandoned the chaos and ran into the corridor. If Castian had entertained my mother or brought her here before he went to help Jade, she might be in one of the guest suites.

Focused on getting to my mother, everything disappeared around me. She would be all right. She had to be. The rubber soles of my sneakers slapped against the hard, polished floor.

She would be all right.

The hit came from nowhere. Knocked sideways, I crashed into the wall and crumpled. My elbow cracked against the polished floor. A shooting pain exploded up my arm.

I lost track of what . . .

I blinked back to consciousness, trying to see beyond the spots invading my vision. A boot kicked my hip, and I rolled face first against the wall. The attack continued.

A menacing growl vibrated from across the room. My heart shuddered, panic pumping through my cells. I struggled to roll over, tried to see what would attack next.

In the next heartbeat, my attacker was gone, and Kobi's demon stood next to me, wings up, his skin smoking.

He held no weapon, but then the light caught the curve of his talons. He was the weapon.

"Thank you," I choked out. "Glad you're here."

"I've got these assholes, Zo," the demon said.

Somehow, I pulled myself to my feet. I slipped on a smear of bloody marble and used the wall to catch myself. Where was the blood from? I took a scattered inventory. A hot stream of moisture slicked the side of my face and neck.

With a bloody hand against the wall, I hobbled as quickly as I could manage. Fire radiated elbow to shoulder. Broken. Or badly dislocated. I was more concerned with the head injury. If I blacked out, I'd be of no use to my mother.

The doors to Castian's guest rooms were closed and free of the stench of Scourge. Hope flickered in my gut that maybe they hadn't discovered her whereabouts. She might be safe in one of those rooms.

The hair on my arms raised as I breathed in.

Magic. Original Three powerful, but not just the signature of Castian and Dane. Rheagan was here. I sensed her presence.

Following the surge of her energy in the air, I passed the guest chambers and headed straight into Castian's private bedroom. I must have cursed or gasped or something because my father turned the moment I crossed the threshold.

"What a surprise. Have you come to see us off, darling?"

Dane held the upper arm of two women. On his left, my mother struggled, lashing at his hold. On his right, my aunt Abbey strode beside him offering no resistance.

Abbey's burgundy locks hung to her hips, her arms wrapped around an ancient book. She cradled the tome against her chest as if it were the most precious thing in all the realms. Decades had passed since Jade's mother had held any sentience but watching her now, I couldn't comprehend . . ..

She was awake, standing, breathing, yet when she looked at me, there was no light of recognition in her eyes. She regarded me as if I were a piece of furniture in the room. I was a stranger.

No. She was.

Before I could reason how Rheagan could possess a human, Dane's power surged. He vanished, and Abbey and my mother disappeared with him.

CHAPTER TEN

"*H*ey there, lacy girl. Welcome back." Kobi hovered over me where I lay on the sofa. He wore his Talon leathers, his arms and neck covered in blood, and his hair disheveled, as if he'd run his fingers through it like a madman.

I struggled to get up, and my body screamed in agony. I fell back, and when the room settled, I searched for the source of his injury. "What's happened to you? Are you all right?"

"Not my blood, but thanks for the worried look. Can you dematerialize and heal yourself?"

Heal myself? My stomach heaved, my head throbbing beyond anything I'd ever suffered, my arm numb and aching at the same time. Time and place came back to me. "My mother . . . and Abbey. Was anyone able to follow them?"

"I'm sorry, Zo. But we'll find them, I swear."

"What about Savage? Where is he?"

"He got you settled and waited with you until I arrived. Where he is now, I have no idea."

I stared at the empty dais where my aunt had lain for almost two decades. "I need to speak to Castian."

Three cracks of lightning struck. The power of the bolts, hitting in angry succession, shook the palace. The crystals on the overhead chandeliers sent prisms of light dancing around Castian's sitting room, tinkling a little melody.

My stomach rolled along with the ominous growl of thunder. "Who told him?"

"Reign needed him to send a team up here to help. It didn't matter who told him, though. He was bound to lose his shit."

Tears brimmed my eyes and tumbled down my cheek.

Kobi knelt beside the sofa and brushed away my tears with his thumb. "Zo, you're in pain. Focus on healing yourself."

Focusing on my own condition sickened me further. My elbow, my hip, my head. I'd failed my mother and Abbey when they needed me. They were in the hands of Abaddon, Rheagan, and my father.

My father. My stupid father. It didn't matter that I thought little of the man who sired me. I'd always hoped that one day he would prove himself and earn my respect.

"It all hurts too much."

Kobi straightened and looked to the other warriors in the room. "Leave us. Give us ten."

When we had the room to ourselves, he eased himself over me and slid into the space at the back of the sofa. Gently, he rolled me to face him and pulled me into his arms. "Zo, I'm going to help you, 'kay? Deplorable thing that I am, I can leach your heartache, so you can heal yourself. It'll hurt a little at first, but I swear, if you trust me, it'll be over quickly."

I met his gaze as his eyes flashed scarlet and his incisors grew. A shiver jolted through me. Trust was tough for me.

"Sorry," he said. "This isn't really a second date kinda thing to expose you to. You can say no, and I'll understand. Even if you allow it, it'll likely kill what's been brewing between us. It's just . . . you can help your mom if you're back on your feet and that's what's important. Let me do this for you, Lacy."

I heard the doubt in his voice, saw the vulnerability in his swirling gaze. He was exposing me to something of himself, but what I saw wasn't deplorable.

"I trust you," I said, and strangely, it was true. Where had Kobi come from that I would offer myself up to him not knowing what would happen next. "Go ahead. You be you."

He fingered my blouse down to my shoulder and brushed my collarbone with his lips. "The more you relax and give me, the better this will work for you."

He sank to my collarbone, his breath warm against my skin.

I cried out as his teeth sank into flesh and muscle. The pain, sharp at first, soon dissolved into a bizarre sensation of tingling throughout my entire system. Invasive. Seductive. A Siren's call for my cells to release things better left buried.

I tensed.

The sensation increased. Images flashed.

The pain inside me welled. Like toxic bubbles in a glass of acid champagne, pain rose and gathered. It followed Kobi's call. I wanted him to take it, but at the same time, didn't. I was afraid, and it hurt. The judgment. The rejection. The betrayal.

He growled, pulling my body against his with a strong arm. His hips ground against mine, his erection unmistakable. Sweet mercy, how could he possibly be so turned on? The world was crumbling around us; warriors might be back at any moment; we were both broken and bloody and . . .

His groan of pleasure awoke my own hunger. I pressed my hand against the straining fly of his leather pants and a sadistic steel rod pulsed against my palm. This was Kobi's nature. Primal and raw. Consuming my pain fed the demon inside him.

"Take it," I breathed, giving myself over to him. My nipples hardened, ached to be noticed, teased, sucked on. "Take it all."

Kobi swallowed, sucking greedily. Gods, the sound that he made, the growl vibrating out from between the teeth buried in my shoulder. His hips rocked as he consumed the acid of my life's heartbreak and left me with a euphoric lightness. A relief of a weight taken.

Too soon, he reared back, fangs extended. Eyes aglow, the muscles in his neck strained, he was fierce and terrifying. He was the most incredible vision of passion I had ever witnessed. The vulnerability I'd heard in his voice still haunted me.

"You're safe with me too, demon," I said, recounting his words from before. "One-hundred percent."

~

With the physical and emotional agony of my mother's abduction drained, I dematerialized without issue and knitted my injuries back together upon the steps of the Hall of Destiny. Taking the ascent on a run, I pushed my hands in front of me, and the doors flew open. The thundering echo had all three of my sisters squealing and ducking for cover.

"Did you know?" I shouted, studying one to the next.

Zinnia straightened and scowled. "What are you doing here? You're banned from—"

I threw my hand up and pinned her to the wall behind her. When Zana raised her hands, I pinned her too.

"Did you know that Dane is in league with Abaddon and Rheagan? Did you conspire with him to get me out of the way, so he could kidnap my mother and Abbey?"

"Let me down," Zinnia snapped. "How dare you."

"How dare *me*? You think *I'm* the one to be threatened? You three opened the door for Dane to start a coup for control of the Pantheon. My only question is whether you were too stupid to realize his plan or if you were in on it?"

Zora looked like she might move to defend Zinnia, but I shook my head. "I am far more powerful than you three, and you know it. I can do this all day. Tell me. Are you in on it?"

"What are you talking about," Zora said, her eyes wild. "Daddy would never—"

"Get your head out of your ass."

Kobi snorted beside me. I guess the vernacular of Haven was rubbing off on me. "Dane has betrayed Castian, helped Rheagan possess Abbey, and together they kidnapped my mother. Were you part of it, or no?"

"No!" they shouted in unison.

I dropped Zinnia and Zana to the floor and stomped to the bowl of Past. Swiping across the surface, I called forth the events of Jade's life for the past few hours. "The first thing the three of you are going to do is remove the restriction on my entry to the Veil. Then you're coming with me to Haven. You will stabilize Jade's powers again and stay there to ensure the twins survive this."

Zinnia laughed. "Why in the realms would we do that?"

I pointed to the image on the undulating surface of the seeing bowl. "Because Jade's attack lured Castian away from my mother and Aunt Abbey. You paved the way for this. You three and Dane put this in motion the moment you had me removed from my life."

"We didn't know this would happen." Zora gasped.

Zinnia shook her head. "You can't honestly believe we'd go against Castian."

"Can't I?" I stepped away from the Seeing Bowls and propped my hands on my hips. "Seems to me, being daughters of the God of gods holds more prestige than nieces. In Castian's current state of mind, how hard do you think it would be to convince him you three were looking for a social upgrade?"

"You couldn't."

"You'd honestly set us up?"

"But we're *sisters*."

Now it was my turn to laugh. "Oh, please, we've never been sisters. It just took me eons to realize it. Now, get your silk-covered asses to Haven and help Jade. Say nothing to her about her mother's abduction. If anything happens to her or her babies, I *will* tell Castian my version of things, and we'll let the chips fall."

Kobi laughed beside me. "And in this scenario, you be the chips, bitches."

"Are you as aroused as I am? I want to rip your leathers off."

Kobi snorted and pulled me to the side as several Talon warriors passed us on the way into Reign's war room. Cowboy tipped the brim of his black hat, smirking as he went into the briefing. Damn, I forgot how acute Were hearing was.

"It's the leaching," Kobi said, leaning close. "I'm afraid with an incubus demon, all roads lead back to sex. It doesn't usually hit this strongly; then again, I've never leached a goddess before. I'm sorry."

I watched his lips move, just inches from mine, and fought the urge to claim his mouth. "I'm okay with an altered libido, just not at this moment. Is there any way to turn it off?"

He raised his palms to the wall on either side of me, caging me in with his body. The lift of his arms exposed a tanned band of skin between his t-shirt and the top of his leathers.

I gripped his hips. "Not helping. I want to drop to my knees and explore your belly with my mouth. Undo these stupid pants and bite your—"

"Zophia?" Aust said, jogging up the corridor. "Sweeting, I heard what happened Behind the Veil. How can I be of aid?"

Kobi stepped back as Aust joined us. Aust's nostrils flared, and he paused. "Apologies, I interrupted a private moment."

"Nah," Kobi said, shrugging off his jacket and draping it over his arm in front of himself. "Good timing, Highborne. There's work to be done. Come on. We better get inside."

I wanted to whimper as those two gorgeous, virile men ushered me into a room filled with a dozen other physically perfect males. This leaching effect had unleashed something truly wanton in me.

"Later, Lacy," Kobi whispered, as he pushed in my chair. "I'll even you out as soon as we get a chance. You've got this."

Did I? It didn't feel like it. Aust and Kobi sat on each side of me and thankfully, aside from Cowboy and Aust, everyone else seemed oblivious to my inappropriate state of arousal—except maybe Bruin.

Stupid Were senses.

"Zophia," Reign said, snapping my attention back to the meeting, "have you any idea where your father might hole up to avoid discovery?"

"No. I don't know much about the man's habits beyond womanizing. Since you're asking, I take it you don't have any news of where Abbey and my mother might be?"

"Not yet, but we'll find them."

I had no doubt they would. My big concern was when. A surge of need tore through me, and I fought not to moan. Something more than an aftereffect to Kobi's incubus nature was consuming me. My hands trembled, and I fought to hold the control I prided myself on.

"Zophia," Reign continued. "What are you thinking?"

I swallowed and tried to meet the man eye to eye. The fact that I looked at Reign and saw nothing but his chiseled jaw, honed warrior body, and long, brindle hair spoke more of the trouble I was in than anything.

"This is about my mother." I snapped at myself with more force than I meant to. All eyes of the room were on me, and my mind was a heated mess. "If Rheagan already claimed Abbey's body, what does my mother offer them?"

"Power," Reign said without hesitation.

Aust nodded. "Shalana remains one of the most powerful goddesses of the Fae Pantheon. Even Castian acknowledges that, in some ways, her power matches his own."

I pulled to draw breath past the weight pressing on my lungs. "And once Abaddon drains my mother's powers, and she's of no use to him? What will happen to her?"

Reign shook his head, his hair rustling against the broad banding of his shoulders and arms. I wondered how soft it would be if I crawled across the table and—

"Don't underestimate her," he said. "From what I've heard, Shalana hates Dane with every fiber in her magical being. I bet she'll put up one hell of a resistance to him and his playmates."

Fury ignited hot in my veins at the thought that my father would even put her into that situation. Reign was right, though. My mother was more than kindness and creation; her gift was also natural disasters, tempests and storms. She had more power than anyone understood.

I glanced at Aust, sitting to my right. In a room of hard lines and men with edges, his Highborne features were graceful and charming. And he smelled so good. He was nature and life, suave and suede. I swallowed. "Aust, can you use your gift to connect with my mother and tell us where she is?"

Aust's expression fell, and he took my hand. With a gentle squeeze, he clutched it to his heart, and the warmth in his ice-blue gaze nearly did me in. "Apologies, it does not work like that. I would do anything —please know that."

I squeezed back, and the warmth of the contact shot through my cells. "Don't blame yourself. I know if you could do anything to save her, you would. What about Savage? He was there. Maybe he saw something I didn't."

Reign sighed. "He hasn't checked in yet."

"What does that mean?"

"Just that. Either he's on to something or in trouble. Too early to tell."

Kobi leaned back in his chair and rested his arm on the back of my neck. He squeezed my shoulder, the contact easing some of the desperation building between my thighs. "What about a Hell Hound?" he said.

Reign stretched his neck side to side and sighed. "How does that fucking suggestion keep rising to the surface? I thought I made myself clear when you wanted to get one to protect Lia."

Kobi shrugged. "They crave malevolent spirits like the munchies after smoking Haze. They track with a single-minded obsession. And, they never stop until they find their quarry."

"That sounds perfect," I said. "Let's do that."

Reign scowled. "Traveling to the innards of Hell to steal a Hell Hound pup from the teat of its maniacal bitch mother? That sounds perfect? If we survived getting it, what makes you think we can control the beast once it's in this realm?"

"The Highborne can," Kobi said, tilting his head toward Aust. "Our boy here has Beastmaster mojo. Shalana said so. I bet he could have the thing eating out of his hand."

"Or biting it off," Reign snapped. "No. It's off the table."

"Shouldn't we consider every option?" I asked.

Julian shook his head from across the table. "Reign's right. There's no way we're sanctioning Castian's niece cozying up to a Hell Hound. That's a pink slip of death for all of us. We'll think of something else."

"While we toss around options," Bruin said, his voice tight, and his eyes gold with the strength of his bear ascending, "Zophia might like to freshen up after her ordeal. Kobi, why don't you escort her downstairs to the gym? Show her the showers and where to find a change of clothes. I'll catch you up on anything you miss."

Kobi looked to Reign, and when his commander nodded, he stood and helped me to my feet.

Bless you, Bruin.

In the next moment, Kobi had me by the wrist, and we were racing down two flights of carpeted stairs.

CHAPTER ELEVEN

"What's happening to me?" Sexual hunger clawed, heated and raw, my underwear damp, my nipples peaked against my silk blouse. I trembled with urgent need. An intense wave of lust had me only dimly aware of my actions.

"Not just you," Kobi said. "I'm sporting a fucking marble column for a cock. I nearly laid you out on the war table with everyone watching."

He opened a door on the left and closed us in.

No lights. No preamble. He pressed me against the back of the door and seized my mouth. His tongue speared me with the attack of the warrior he was, while his velvet lips coaxed me to insanity. "I gotta get at you."

Without visual cues, there was only sensation. His fingers made quick work of undoing things, and my pants fell to the floor in an obliging *plop*. The stitching on my blouse snapped as I yanked it open. I kicked my legs free and opened the front of his leathers. "Good enough. I'm dying."

Kobi snapped the crotch of my panties and gripped my bare buttocks. The door slammed hard against my back as I wrapped my legs around his hips. His hair felt like silk as I clenched rough fingers into it and pulled him closer.

He growled. "Gods, I don't want to hurt you, Zo . . . but I'm losing my grip here."

Cool air from the room hit my heated flesh an instant before Kobi's heat smothered it. He clenched his teeth. A snarl of the beast inside him tore from his throat. His hips thrust forward, and I arced at the penetration.

"Yes. Oh, yes. More." My cry was as much a shock as our loss of control. With other lovers, I'd never been vocal. He crushed me to the door, thrusting deep inside me. The stretch to accommodate him struck an indescribable pleasured pain.

He bit my lip and sucked on the sting. "Hold on, baby."

I gripped the two large hooks on the back of the door and groaned as hot, slick moisture greeted his assaulting rhythm. I met each pounding thrust of his hips, our bodies glistening as we grasped and clutched and rode each other's pleasure.

He lifted his head, and his incisors grew. His scarlet gaze leaped and danced with the flames of hell. "I can't control myself with you. I'm sorry."

"Don't be." I locked my heels tighter around his leathers. My release burned inside me, building, throbbing, consuming. "It's so good."

His groan of satisfaction ramped things up even higher. I throbbed around him, and he pumped harder. Wilder. "I want to bite you again. I fucking get off on drinking you in. I want to consume you."

"Do it. Anything. Everything."

The bite was instant and triggered my orgasm. I threw my head back and let Kobi take what he needed. He worked me hard against the door, my body's greed gripping him with each pulse of my release. It didn't take him long to join me. His breath escaped in throaty bursts as he stiffened and stilled.

Rearing back, my demon lover was the most fearsome thing I'd ever seen. Eyes ablaze, his face contorted with the ecstasy of losing control, his truest nature revealed itself.

He was terrifying and yet beautiful. How was it possible to want a man so desperately?

Kobi reined himself in and let me ride out my release. When my body relaxed, he laved the puncture points with his tongue and kissed each of the four small wounds.

"You're too fucking trusting, Zo." His expression confused me. He almost looked disappointed that I didn't fight him off and run screaming. I pressed my breasts against his chest as he stepped back from the wall. I thought of Hoola as I clung to him and we crossed the room.

The place was practically pitch dark. Only the glow given off by Kobi's demon gaze, and the safety strip lights over the door, punctuated the darkness. By the echo of sound, I guessed the room had to be an easy fifty-foot space. When he stopped, he withdrew from inside me. The absence of him struck me more acutely than should have been possible. What was this between us?

Kobi shifted me in his arms and set me on my knees. Bending me forward, I laid over a stack of what felt like . . . oh, workout mats. "I've wanted you bent over for me since my bathroom that first morning."

"You're a seriously disturbed man."

He kicked off his boots and rid himself of his leathers and t-shirt. When he knelt behind me, there was nothing between us but the silk blouse draped over my back.

He ran his fingers between my legs and up my thighs. "Gods, you're so deliciously wet, Lacy. I'm flattered. Truly."

He spread my knees wider and made room for himself. It occurred to me that maybe I should be embarrassed or feel awkward. I didn't. Kobi made me feel powerful and feminine.

"Now, keep your hands locked there and let me study you. We've never taken our time, and I want to know everything: where you like to be touched, if you're ticklish, what your limits are."

"I don't have limits, but maybe we should get back."

"Nah. Bruin will text me if they come up with anything. Besides, our arousal was bringing his and Cowboy's animals dangerously close to the surface."

I remembered how golden Bruin's eyes had been when he suggested we take our leave. "We did that?"

Strong but gentle, his fingers explored as his kisses covered my back, my shoulders, my neck. "Sex is a powerful call for Weres, especially since tonight is the full moon. I bet Cowboy is rock hard and contemplating joining us down here."

"The three of us?"

"Mhmm. Does that shock you?"

"Not as much as it intrigues me."

His throaty laugh had me pulsing again. "As much as I love the guy, I'd never invite an unmated Were into our mix."

"What makes you say that?"

"'Cause Were bonding is for life, and we both know where you rank on your sisters' fuck-you list at the moment. Imagine their delight in mating you to Cowboy in the midst of all this chaos."

"You're right. Still, it would be fun."

"Seriously? You're up for a Devil's Threeway?"

I laughed at the curiosity lighting him up. "I'm immortal. Sexual expression and polyamorous relationships are the norms Behind the Veil. Does that shock you?"

"Nothing shocks me." He licked a warm path up my neck and kissed my ear. "But now my depraved and dirty mind is filling with all kinds of new possibilities."

My nipples rose to greet his touch, my skin super-sensitive. The slightest sensations had me trembling. His breath on my back, his legs brushing mine, the warmth of his flesh. I twisted around to stroke him. "Come back inside me."

The smack to my bare backside brought another rush of moisture to my core. "Don't rush the Incubus, Lacy. I'm making sure you're slick enough for another round. I don't want you sore."

I waggled my butt against his thighs and chuckled as he cursed. "You overestimate yourself, Incubus. If you can give it, I can take it."

I expected him to come back with some kind of 'Challenge accepted,' but he grew silent and still. I risked another spanking and turned.

My eyes adjusted to the darkness, I could read the look on his face. "Hey, what's wrong?"

"Nothing. Just waiting."

"Waiting for what?"

He shrugged and sat back on his heels. "You haven't clued into the fact that I'm a demon. You're a fucking goddess, a member of the royal family, daughter of one of the Original Three, and I'm the spawn of all things vile. What are you doing, Zo? Is slumming it with me some kind of cosmic fuck-you for your father? What is it?"

I sat on the stack of mats with him kneeling between my legs. "What you or I were born isn't who we are now. Isn't it what life makes us that counts?"

"No. You have no idea—"

"—about your demon-self?" I stared down at him. "You have a winged, scaled beast writhing inside you. You like killing more than you should. The piercings, makeup, and sex are tools you use to keep people at a distance. You feed off pain, but it never quenches the ache inside you."

The horror and sadness in his gaze pierced me. "You say the words but don't know. Not really."

"You feel like you don't belong, alone in the company of many. Apart. Abnormal. You sense people judging you and wait until you make a mistake that will prove them right. Even your friends look at you like they don't quite understand you. Like you are *other*."

He cursed. "If you get that, then why? You should run in the opposite direction."

I shivered. The last warmth of our heated bodies chilled, and my exposed flesh rose in goose bumps. "You're a throwaway judged by worldview. So am I. I don't believe in love or forever. I believe in right now. It is what it is between us, no more, no less, and it's working—for me anyway."

Kobi rose to his knees, his arms wrapping around me as he lowered us to the padded floor. Warmth bloomed once again, every long, chiseled inch of his body pressing against mine. My knees fell open, and he rolled into the cradle of my hips. "It's working for me too. But seriously, you should run."

~

Deciding we'd never get upstairs if we cleaned up together, I headed into the ladies' locker room, showered, and found a pair of yoga pants and a top to match in the clothes cupboard. I tried to recall how many women there were in Talon that they'd need such a large space: Jade, Lexi, the Asian wizard that Bruin used to sleep with . . . and that was all I could think of.

The Talon needed more women in the field. I'd speak to Castian about that when things settled down. I only hoped that things did settle down.

Knowing that he was out there, somewhere, scouring the planet for his wife and my mother, gave me hope. He would raze the world to find Abbey. He loved her that much.

Part of me envied that kind of devotion to another. The other part of me couldn't grasp how it was even possible.

Finished with my routine, I headed across the hall to the men's locker room.

"Hello?" I eased the door open. There was no one in the changing area and only the sound of the shower in the distance. My voyeur instincts kicked in and before I thought twice, I strode further inside and hopped onto the men's counter to watch Kobi shower.

He seemed to sense the moment I entered because he smiled and glanced over. Without a word, he ran his soapy hands over his chest and down his ribs. Mercy, he was a drool-worthy man.

He spread the lather over his chest and arms and then washed his pelvis and groin. When he turned to rinse, I noticed the tattoo of the Talon hawk inked on his shoulder blade. The ink was altered with magic because it glowed gold the same way their brands did when they made them visible to identify themselves.

"Do you know the significance of the Talon hawk?"

Kobi shut off the water and ran his hands over his head to shuck water from his hair. "They're hunters, killers, and really fucking cool birds?"

I chuckled and tossed him the towel he'd set out on the counter. "Castian's wife, Abbey, is a Carpathian Gypsy. She can leave her corporeal body and assume the form of a red-tailed hawk. That's how she first drew Castian's eye, soaring through the skies above him."

Kobi dried off and opened the men's cupboard to grab a clean pair of leathers and a black t-shirt. He went commando, and how sexy was that? He stepped into the pants and came over to me, t-shirt in hand. "With every woman in all the realms at his fingertips, she must have been one hell of a catch to snag him. I honestly don't get it, even as I see it happen around me."

"Me either, but before the attack, their love was something to behold." I pulled at his shoulder, turning him for a closer look. The detailed depiction of the bird descending, talons extended, was slightly raised and carried a signature of magic I recognized. "Castian did this?"

"You can feel that he did it? That's crazy."

"I can also feel there's a warding in his touch. When did he do this, and why?"

Kobi stepped away and pulled his t-shirt over his shoulders. It was a shame to cover all that delicious skin, but I was anxious to get upstairs and see what was happening.

Kobi seemed anxious too, though I wasn't sure why.

"Hey, you two." Cowboy pushed himself off the wall he'd been leaning on as we reached the main floor. "You get all the kinks worked out down there?"

"Yeah, sorry about that." Kobi shrugged and brushed the back of his finger over my heated cheek. "My Incubus mojo got away on us there. Not sure what happened. You good?"

Cowboy winked down at me. "Bruin and his bear booked it back to the Dens. Not sure if Mika will thank you for that or blame you for it later."

Kobi laughed. "And you?"

He took off his Stetson and ran a hand through his wavy blonde hair. "Nothing a little alone time in one of the private washrooms couldn't solve."

"Kobi thought you might join us."

Now it was Cowboy's turn to blush. "Well, if I'd known that was an option, I would've been tempted to take you up on it. Somehow, though, I think I'm better standing my ground. Not sure Castian would take kindly to the two of us tag-teaming his precious niece. Especially in his current mood. I'm still waiting to see what happens to the demon here."

Kobi rolled his eyes. "Have you assholes got a pool going? What skin have you got in the game?"

Cowboy pulled a hand-rolled cigarette from his vest pocket and lit up. "Got a C-note on you getting your nuts twisted in a vice. Sorry, man."

"I think you underestimate my uncle. Castian doesn't judge. He's supportive and wants me to be happy."

"No offense, sweetheart, but I think it's you who might be underestimating the big guy. Tell us, how have your past beaus survived to tell the tale?"

I thought about that. The handful of lovers I'd had in the past never amounted to anything serious. Just as things began to develop into something deeper, something always seemed to come up—a change of heart, a relocation, death. "Oh dear. You think that was him?"

Cowboy snorted and smacked Kobi on the shoulder. "It's been nice knowing you, my brother. Keep your head down and your guard up."

I took Kobi's hand in mine and squeezed his fingers. "I'll speak with him. You'll be fine."

"I'm not worried," Kobi said, though it was the first time I'd heard a lie in his voice. "Cowboy's just fucking with us. Why are you here anyway, shithead?"

"Oh, right. Savage is back. He spent the night at Suzie's and overheard Shavandra in a convo with some stud at the bar. When the guy wanted to hook up with her this weekend, she said she was game but come Sunday, her boss had a big project in the works, and she'd be busy."

"What kind of project?" I asked.

"Didn't say. Whatever it is, we've only got four days to figure it out."

"And you think it has to do with my mother?"

"No idea, that's all I got. We're riding the fences until something else knocks on the gate. When it does, I'll be sure to let you know." Cowboy touched the brim of his hat and left the two of us to ourselves.

"That's not good enough." I paced the hallway. I had never experienced such helplessness, even monitoring life from the Veil. "I can't do nothing while my mother is gone for days. Abbey is under the control of a madwoman. She was just starting to come back to us."

Kobi nodded. "I get that it's hard, but what can we do? If Castian can't find them with his powers and the resources at his disposal, what chance do we have?"

I thought about that and smiled. "How do you feel about breaking a few laws and pissing people off?"

Kobi laughed. "Sounds like the perfect date. I'm in."

CHAPTER TWELVE

"*S*o, this is where the magic happens, is it, Lacy?" Kobi swiped a finger through Zinnia's seeing bowl and eyed the Hall of Destiny as if he might be in danger of catching some hideous disease by simply breathing the air. "Four sisters determining the fate of the realms. An ethereal Z-quadrangle weighing and measuring the worth of free will. Then callously voiding it and watching the chaos ensue."

I rolled my eyes and settled onto my stool before my loom. "Really? Z-quadrangle? And you were here this morning."

"I was on duty then. I didn't take it all in. All the hard and shiny. All the glittering pretense. All the marble-carved breasts and penises."

I called the first tapestry, ignoring my lover stroking the polished genitalia of the statuary. "Are you helping me find my mother or not?"

"Of course. What can I do?"

"Give me the names of any realm members who might know something. I can't call Abaddon's tapestry, but maybe I can find out what's going on from someone else's viewpoint."

"Only realm members? So, we couldn't creep your duplicitous, slimeball father?"

"No. I only have access to—"

"How dare you." Zora stormed in from the antechamber, a hurricane of swirling silk. "You aren't man enough to speak his name, let alone cast judgment."

Kobi smiled wide. "Technically, I didn't speak his name. The judgment thing—yeah I totally did that."

"You have no right to be here. I command you to get out!" She pointed to the exit and stomped her slipper on the marble tile to punctuate her point.

"Relax," I said. "We're just here to—"

"You have no more right to be here than him," she sputtered, an unattractive flush blotching her cheeks. "Leave, or I'll call someone from the Council to have you removed."

Kobi burst into a churning black mist and grew in height and mass. A massive, winged demon with swirling scarlet eyes consumed the two-story temple. His leathery tail swished as his skin exhaled smoke. "Try it, bitch. I'll swallow you whole and shit out your bones."

I would have enjoyed Zora's terror if I didn't pity her so.

"Kobi, right or wrong, I'd rather you don't eat my sister. I'm sure, if we ask nicely, she'll help us find Aunt Abbey and my mother. After all, if Castian gets his wife back, he might forgive them their part in Scourge invading his home and our father betraying him."

"I'd rather eat her," Kobi said, dragging his tongue across his ebony lips. "I'd be the hero of the realm taking out one of the Fates."

"You're already a hero of the realm, and she's too bony and sour for good eating, aren't you, Zora?"

Zora swallowed, her head bobbing. "Y-yes."

"Change back, babe. It'll be easier for her to concentrate on how she can help us if you aren't looming large."

With that, Kobi's demon beast swirled into a funnel of black smoke, and the man appeared in his place. "As you wish, milady. Now, put us to work. What do you need."

Hours later, I sent the last of the frames back, no closer to finding my mother. Wherever they were hiding, Shavandra hadn't been there, and neither had anyone else Kobi could think of. Kobi poured me a glass of sparkling punch from the butler's stand and brought it to me.

"Anything else you and your twisted sisters could try?"

I shook my head and regretted it. I'd been staring at strands and reading threads so long my head might literally explode. "Nothing that I can think of. I guess we're back to Cowboy's suggestion to wait and see what happens."

I accepted the drink and the two headache tablets he offered. "What if Abaddon tries to drain my mother's powers? Or they try to excise Abbey's soul? It's killing me that we know something is looming and there's nothing we can do about it."

Kobi frowned and knelt before me. He brushed the hair from my face and frowned. "There's still the Hell Hound idea. I know Reign killed it, but I'm sure we can get it to track your mother's energy."

"If we went that route, how would we do it and when?"

"Tonight is the full moon and our best chance to slip into Hell unnoticed."

"Tonight? Like right now?"

Kobi nodded. "That's what I'm thinking."

"And *who* are you thinking?"

"Me and Aust," he said, straightening. He scrubbed his hands against his leather pants and started to pace. "I'll handle the Hell. He'll handle the Hound. At least, I'm hoping his gift translates. Hard to know with creatures of purgatory."

"What about me?"

Kobi turned, distracted by the plans calculating in his mind. "What about you?"

"I'm coming too."

"Yeah, right. I don't think so."

I stood, fists clenched at my sides. "I *do* think so. No one goes on my behalf while I wait not knowing if the two of you are being tortured or killed. If I don't go, no one does."

He stepped close and pulled me against his chest. He cupped my chin in his hands and kissed my nose. "You coming is not an option.

Hell is unlike your worst nightmare. It's not the place for you to assert your newfound independence."

"I'm immortal."

"In the Fae realms, yes. You have no idea what the venom of a Kishi bite or the curse of a Horseman could do to you."

"I accept that risk. I can take care of myself and who knows, my powers might help."

"Look, Zo, this isn't a woman thing or a warrior thing—"

I reached forward and closed my fingers around the rings in his nipples. When he moved to draw back, I gripped harder and met his gaze. "I go, or no one does. End of discussion. I'll march straight into Reign's office and have you recalled the moment you try to leave me behind."

"You can't Flash. Maybe I leave you here?"

"I'm have a direct line of communication with Castian. How do you think he'll feel when I tell him you're disobeying Reign's orders and where you've gone?"

"Nice try. You're no snitch."

"How far would you go to keep me safe?"

He scowled and stared at me a long while. "No wonder Bruin was mental when he and Mika first started up. He tried to leave her behind once too—stranded her in a mountainside cave. She nearly killed herself by scaling a rock face."

I tightened my grip and smiled. "Women. Can't live with them, can't leave them behind."

Kobi glowered at me with impressive focus. He was silent so long, I wondered if he'd scratch the whole idea rather than take me. "You'll have to follow orders. I'm serious. Anything I say, you do, no questions."

"Sir, yes sir."

The flash of scarlet in his gaze signaled the moment I'd won, and his aggression turned sexual.

I stroked the front of his leathers and gripped the bulge.

"Interesting choice of talking stick, Lacy."

His length pulsed and thickened in my grasp. "I got your attention."

"True dat." The light in his eyes glowed with sinful delight. "We need to find Aust and get this party started."

"Well, tonight's the full moon. He's supposed to go on the Were-run with Bree and the others. If he's not at the Dens, he soon will be."

Kobi and I nodded to the guards on the outer plateau of the Dens' entrance and headed to the living room to find Aust. My demon had grown quiet—not that he was mine in any way—but I didn't know if his mood was a result of the possible consequences of bedding Castian's niece, or if he was thinking about the night ahead. Maybe it was neither, and I didn't know him well enough to guess.

Bruin, Cowboy, Bree, and a dozen other Weres milled about the main rooms, drinking and readying for the full-moon run. Were energy raised the hair on my arms, a palpable prime power emanating from each of them as their base animals struggled to take control from their hosts.

Kobi joined Bruin behind the bar and poured us two whiskeys on ice. Bree swiveled her stool toward me and lowered the bottle from her lips. "I heard about your mom, Zo. Try not to lose your mind. Reign and the boys are the best. They'll find her."

I sipped at the amber liquid and watched the way Bruin and Kobi spoke together. Bruin knew him and loved him for who he was, I could tell. They had an easiness about them I hoped maybe we two could achieve in time.

Bree leaned close. "You're really hooked on him, eh?"

I shrugged. "Hooked is probably overstating things, but he's definitely an interest. He's sweet, generous, a solid guy."

Bree stared at her bottle, chasing condensation with her thumb. "We are talking about Kobi, right? The depraved, sex-obsessed, self-centered, pessimistic, smartass of Haven?"

I finished my drink and swished the ice around the bottom of the tumbler. If Bree only saw what Kobi projected, that was her loss. I saw more. Much more.

Cowboy sidled up to the bar beside me, and Bruin came over with two more beers for his buddy. Kobi poured me another half glass and winked. "Everything okay here, ladies? What's got the two of you whispering over here?"

Bree emptied her bottle of beer and took one of Cowboy's. "Feminism. World peace. Global economics."

Bruin laughed. "You can just say it's none of our business."

"How's Mika feeling?" I asked.

Cowboy tilted his drink back, laughing as he swallowed.

Bruin cleared his throat. "Ah, good. She's good. She's enjoying a bubble bath and retiring for the night. Thanks to you two, we had an unexpectedly busy afternoon. She's worn out."

Cowboy extended his beer toward his Alpha, and they clinked bottles.

"Aust," Kobi said, lifting his chin toward the entrance. "Glad you're back, my man."

Bree met him before he made it half way across the room. She kissed his cheek and handed him her beer. "Are you ready to run? It's going to be a beautiful night to tear up the grounds."

Aust pulled the leather tie from his hair and let his blond waves fall to his shoulders. "I am, and it shall be."

Kobi stepped behind me and wrapped a heavy arm around my waist. "Yeah, about that. We're here to break up the band. Abaddon's got big plans Sunday night and, Aust, we need you, buddy, if you're still game to help find Shalana."

Aust cast a glance to Bree and then back to Kobi. "To run that pick-up errand, discussed in the war room today?"

Kobi nodded. "Yeah. The window is closing fast. We're in 'now or not at all' territory."

"Hey, losers," Cowboy said, a scowl marring his handsome face. "What's with the speaking in code? Bruin and I were at the same meeting. That particular errand got shut down."

Aust strode over to Bree. "I must needs go with Kobi and Zophia tonight instead of joining the run. If there is even a chance to retrieve Shalana from her captors, I must aid them."

Bree leaned against the bar. "Will you be back for any of it? I'll wait, and we can go out later."

Aust shook his head. "Your coyote will only hold that against me. No. There is a fair bit of travel in our task. I cannot say when we might return. You join Bruin, Cowboy, and the others for your run and enjoy yourself."

"Sorry to kidnap your date for the night," Kobi said. "We promise to take good care of him."

My heart went out to Bree. She and Aust had been on the verge of this incredible relationship for months. If not for her coyote self, they might even be mated by now.

"About this errand," Bruin said, his hard gaze locked on Kobi. "The Wolf and I should come too."

Cowboy cursed. "You have any idea how much shit this will stir up?"

"The smaller the group, the better the chance to get in and out unnoticed," Kobi said. "And probably a shit ton."

"What the hell are you talking about," Bree asked. "And why am I the only one who doesn't know what's going on?"

"It doesn't matter," Bruin said. "They're not going—"

"—to admit anything." Kobi held up his hands to his friends. "Plausible deniability and all that, boys. Now unknot your silk panties and wish us well, because we are going."

Bree pulled Aust to the side, her worry and anger filling the air in equal measure. "Don't go. I want you here to run as planned. You can't come next month during the Equinox Summit, and I can't take two more months of this."

Aust brushed her cheek with his finger. "I must needs go. Shalana bestowed upon me all I have and will be. I can do no other than make every attempt to aid her when she needs me."

"You could be killed. Kobi's a demon and a warrior. Zophia's immortal. You're just . . ."

Kobi cursed as Bruin and Cowboy growled.

"Just what, Bree?" Aust paled and gripped her shoulders. "Speak your heart's truth. Is it only your coyote who thinks me weak and unworthy?"

"I've never said that."

"I have every bit the warrior's heart and honor inside me that any male of worth on this mountain possesses."

"I know that," she said, looking to the others in the room. "I *do*. Aust is amazing, gifted, and strong. I never meant to imply otherwise, or for any of you to think less of him. I love him. I'm just worried."

Bruin laid a hand on Bree's shoulder and nodded. "We know, Coyote Girl. Take your man into the hall so that you can send him off properly. We'll give you a few minutes to set things straight."

CHAPTER THIRTEEN

I studied the writhing bodies carved and suspended on the bow of the ship. Their hair twisted and twined with wild sea plants as their frozen gowns billowed in a nonexistent breeze. The wood of the rail grew warm in my grip, and I forced myself not to glance into the darkness below.

Kobi, in his demon form, flew above. Ebony scales melted into the endless night, leaving only the glow of two scarlet eyes visible. The heavy whisper of his wings drowned out by the knock and buckle of the hull colliding with the rocky surface.

I gripped the rail tighter. No water held us buoyant as we sliced our way through the cloying mist. Our waterway was composed of spirits of the damned. Desperate, hollow eyes glowed eerily green against the darkness of the abyss below, while mouths stretched in silent torturous screams.

Aust tapped a stone against the rail. "Fash not. It shall all be over soon."

That was my greatest fear.

I shivered and stared off to the menacing shoreline. Hell's Gates loomed large against the desolate backdrop, reaching pointed spires toward swirling scarlet eddies in the sky. "I'm sorry, Aust."

"Whyever for?"

"Aside from disrupting things with Bree, I'm putting you at risk. If she were aware, my mother would be furious. I think maybe this is a mistake and we should turn back."

For the first time since I'd known him, Aust scowled at me. "Nothing Bree said was because of you. If you think it is, you give yourself more power than you possess."

"All right. Then I'm sorry you're hurting. May I say that?"

Aust swung his arm, throwing the stone well beyond our visibility in the mists. "As for turning back, what would Shalana endure to ensure safety for you or one of her wildlife children?"

"Nothing would stop her."

"Does she not deserve the same devotion?"

I set my hand over his balled fist on the rail. "I wish you'd known her before her decline. She awed people. She was an amazing woman."

"I stand in awe of her every moment we spend together. Verily, that is why I came. Regardless of what anyone thinks, I am uniquely suited to aid in this quest and shall not fail her."

The boat bumped the shore and jolted to a halt.

Aust steadied us both and then helped me to land. The heavy, humid heat of the waterway passage gave way to the dry singeing heat of Hell itself.

My skin tightened, growing pink. I called forth a breeze to encircle Aust and me, and the burning stopped. The air wouldn't be considered refreshing by any stretch of the imagination, but it kept our flesh from scalding.

Kobi landed a few yards closer to the gates and took human form. By his instruction, the three of us wore suede breeches cut to our thighs, and I had the added fashion touch of a suede bandeau strip to cover my breasts.

He claimed fabrics other than hide would melt and burn our skin. Likely true but, by the heat in his gaze, I was pretty sure he just got off playing Robinson Crusoe.

He gestured to the satchel, and Aust swung it off his shoulder and handed it to Kobi. After drinking from the canteen, he passed the water to me. "Hell Hounds guard the entry points of Hell, so we shouldn't have to venture too far inside." Kobi drew the dagger from his thigh sheath. "This is a reaper's gate. The full moon draws most demons, especially reapers, to the human realm so, with them gone, this should be easy peasy."

I didn't need powers to hear the lie in his voice.

"The trick," he continued, "will be to find a litter of pups in May. Spring has sprung, and pups are good eating. They get picked off quickly, and that makes mommy hounds more than a little protective. If there's a litter intact, that mommy will be a tough one."

Perfect. Something scurried in front of my foot, and I jumped to clear it. "Aust, do you sense anything?"

"I am catching an awareness, but cannot form a bond or conversation to determine what creature it might be. Mayhap with closer proximity."

"And what if Aust's gift doesn't work the same way on Hells creatures and she attacks?"

"Oh, she'll attack, all right," Kobi said, stretching his neck from side to side. "I'm hoping Aust's affinity keeps the bloodshed to a minimum." He waggled his brow, his piercings catching the strange red glow of the light above.

"That's not comforting."

Kobi shrugged. "Keepin' it real, baby. If you're having second thoughts, you can wait here with the boatman."

I turned to the eerily handsome wraith who captained our passage from the entrance of the Downworld to Hell's Gates. I doubted his appearance bore any similarity to the true likeness of the boatman of the damned. Though Kobi hadn't said, I was certain this minion of lost souls could alter his appearance in the same way he could.

With my attention on him, our captain made a clucking sound and drew his black tongue along his upper lip. "She's welcome to stay, Incubus. It would be my pleasure to amuse her while you're gone."

My stomach turned. Kobi's smirk inspired me to throat punch him. "You're an ass."

Kobi's chest bounced as he took my hand and gestured for Aust to follow us over the rocky terrain.

CHAPTER FOURTEEN

*T*he Gates of Hell weren't so much gates, but an ominous ornamental opening to the land beyond. Rising to tower above us from the smoldering rock ground, the boundary walls of Hell spanned as far as I could see, both left and right. Elaborate symbols covered the outer face of the archway and wall with demonic warnings depicted in sculpted relief.

The missive spalled in places and bits of the detailing had worn and fallen to the ground below. I picked up a piece and threw it back down. "Fingers?"

"Not only fingers," Kobi said. "Some of the darker wards use tongues and testicles."

I cast another glance at the wall. The size. The sheer scope of the artwork. How many hundreds of thousands of body parts had it taken to create this? The surface of the wall wasn't rough stone as I had thought; in places, you could still make out body hair and moles. "Is that flesh?"

Kobi gripped my wrist, licked my palm, and sucked each of my fingers. "Are you saying demons can't decoupage?"

"That's disgusting, and why are you licking me?"

He paused. "Would you rather the dark wards of Hell seep into your skin?"

"Nope. Go ahead. Lick once more to be sure." When Kobi finished, I dried my hand on my suede cut-offs. "So, are we not touching anything, or just the gate?"

"Especially not the gate but touch as little as possible. Contact with things here makes it hard to fight off the dread."

I sighed. "Why are we just hearing about this now?"

Kobi shrugged. "So much to tell. So little time. It's oppressive anxiety you'll feel while here. It should dissipate as soon as you get back to Haven. S'all good."

"Right. Perfect. Aust, are you good?"

Aust nodded, staring off into the distance beyond the gates. "We should begin our search that way."

"Then away we go." Kobi took my hand and pulled me close behind him. Aust came up close behind me. "Inside voices, kids. Don't draw any unwanted attention."

We walked through the entrance of Hell, and I felt the impact of dread press on my lungs. It tightened in my belly and weighed on my chest. Other than that, and the sweat building and dripping into every crevice of my body, we could have been taking a stroll in a public park.

I thought there'd be more to this, I said, directly into Kobi's mind.

It's easy getting into Hell, he thought. *The trick will be getting out . . . with a hound pup . . . before sunrise.*

Once inside the gates of Hell, Kobi's demeanor changed. Gone was the insouciant cynic and in his place stood a warrior at work. He walked with stealth and kept us to a path not in the darkest shadows but within cover. Aust and I soon learned his hand signals, crouched when he crouched, and grew as still as the rocks around us when he tensed.

The tortured wails of things unseen echoed from everywhere and yet nowhere, on the ground and from the air above. I tried to breathe through my mouth because even with my powers circulating the stale air around us, the stench of sulfur burned my sinuses.

Aust squeezed my hand, and I paused. Kobi nodded at him pointing to a jagged mound to the left and changed our course deeper into the darkness. Kobi's demon blood and Aust's Elven night vision allowed them sight. Even with my Fae powers, I was definitely at a disadvantage. I didn't know how well they could see, but I could barely make out enough to maneuver.

Aust stepped past us and took the lead. "There are a few pups close by," he whispered.

"And the mother?" Kobi asked.

Aust shrugged and shook his head.

Find the litter, Aust, I said into both their minds. *Let's get one and get out before the mother comes back.*

Whether it was his skill as an Elven tracker or being able to connect with the hound pups, Aust led us through a low opening and into a cave we could never have found without him. *You're amazing, Aust.*

"Nice one, Highborne," Kobi said, unable to stand to his full height. "Now, go make a friend and let's get gone."

Aust shuffled further into the cave. When I lost him in the void of darkness, I forced my feet not to follow. I'm not sure how Kobi knew, but he laced our fingers and squeezed. *He's fine, Zo. We're all good*

I leaned over and kissed him. *I hate it here. How did you ever live in this place?*

This area is upscale. It's unpopulated, so no one's trying to kill you at every opportunity.

The pups let off a series of yips. I held my breath.

Aust reappeared a moment later with a little ball of black tucked under his arm like a furry football. "All is well."

Kobi turned, and we retraced our steps. My heart beat a rhythm far faster than our pace warranted. I wanted out of this place. The heat. The stench. Fear and doom invaded my body and mind, more pervasive by the moment. I couldn't imagine growing up in this place. Kobi must have—

The hit came fast and hard from the left.

Kobi flew off his feet and disappeared into the shadows. My hands were up before the demonic canine turned to charge. Head down, she locked me in her red, glowing sights.

I pushed her back with a gust of wind.

The pup in Aust's arm barked. The mother snarled, snapping her fangs in the air. The sound of her fury tore at my insides, angry and primal.

"I'm sorry," I said, widening my stance. "We need him. Aust, can you explain that to her somehow?"

Aust stood beside me, dagger drawn. "I cannot sense her at all. I am trying."

"Kobi? You alive?"

A hoarse cough and weak curse were my answer.

Mommy dearest howled, long and loud, pushing against the barrier. My command of wind held strong but wouldn't get us out of this. The thing was the size of a small horse and built like a grizzly bear.

"Aust, can you tell the pup to stay put and help me?"

"Consider it done." Aust set the puppy in the shelter of a rock overhang behind us and then disappeared off to my right.

The mother seemed confused by the unseen force keeping her from her young. She stomped clawed feet, shook her ragged mane, and howled again. The mournful cry rolled through the darkness like thunder.

So much for not drawing attention.

Kobi staggered out from behind a rock. He tried to stand but his legs buckled, and he dropped to the ground.

The guttural snarl of a white tiger had my heart thundering. Another of the pups dangled by the scruff of its neck from the jaws of the majestic beast. It narrowed its ice-blue gaze at the Hell Hound mother, and I almost fainted.

"Aust? Is that you? What are you doing?"

The tiger swung his head, and the young pup let out a yelp. The mother growled, her full attention now on the greater and immediate threat.

Kobi lurched to his feet. With one hand braced against a rock, his head hung as if it weighed too much for his neck. I wanted to go to him, but feared angering the monstrous hound.

Aust waved the pup again and turned to run.

"No—" He was gone before I could get the words out.

I looked back at the pup we'd taken. Still curled in a ball, it sat right where Aust had placed it. Kobi staggered toward me, then stumbled and landed hard on his side.

"How bad are you broken?" I said, helping him up.

"I'm pretty fucking dented but not broken," he wheezed. "S'all good."

"Liar."

Kobi chuckled, and that at least made me feel a bit better. "Let's get the pup and find—"

The crashing flap of wings had Kobi tensing in my arms. "Fuck. Stay here." He burst into a black mist and shifted to his demon form mid-air.

Kobi's dragon tackled the creature descending to attack, and the two tumbled through the air. End over end, wings beat and talons scored. The beast screeched and surged upward, taking Kobi with it.

I surveyed my surroundings, me standing alone in the open while screams and growls filled the distant air. "Come on baby," I whispered, picking up the pup. "Let's find cover."

With Aust and Kobi off in different directions, I couldn't go far. If separated, we were supposed to head back to the ship. There was still time. Nothing to worry about. No. Not worried.

Come on, boys. Where are you?

A shrill cry rent the air above. A fluttering and flapping of wings. The whistle of something heavy falling to the ground grew in volume.

I cradled the warm bundle of black fur and ran.

Something hit the ground like a meteor twenty feet behind me. Kobi's dragon screamed. It surged on impact and then transformed, the man lying broken in a massive crater.

I slid down the bank of the impression and knelt beside him. Ash gave way beneath my knees, hot either from the friction of impact or from being in Hell's unearthed underbelly.

I brushed the hair from his eyes.

How could he survive a fall like that? Even if his demon dragon took the brunt of the damage, they were one. Damage done to one was done to both.

"Kobi? Can you hear me?"

The growl behind me sent a chill down my spine. The pup squirmed in my arms, whining to gain freedom. I turned my head, ever so slowly, and gazed over my shoulder. The demon dog dropped her head over the ridge and eyed her young struggling against my hold.

If she was here, where was Aust? Her lips raised on her snout and sharp canines caught the scarlet hue of the sky above.

"I swear," I said to the mother. "We mean no harm to your baby." Hell's dread weighed heavy. My hope was a dwindling thread, sheering more every moment. If ever there were a time for Shalana's genes to shine, this was it. Oh, how the thought of letting my mother down cut me to the depth of my soul.

"You see, my mother's in danger. Your young can protect her. In return, I will protect him."

Kobi moaned. She canted her head and snarled. The bristled hackles of her wiry coat stuck up in spears.

I blocked her view of Kobi and tried again. "If I had anything to offer you, I would freely give it. All I have is my vow that we mean neither you nor your litter any harm."

A glint of emotion flashed in the beasts glowing red eyes. Was it understanding or instinct? Reason or resolve?

"Please. Allow this one to lead a different life. A good life in the Realm of the Fair. Do you know where that is? Do you understand me at all?"

A pup barked in the distance and she lifted her head. After a torturous moment, she turned. I watched the vacant edge, waiting for her to return, for her to jump down into this ditch and rip us both to shreds.

She didn't come.

~

Wind is a powerful force. It can spread seeds for creation. It can level lands in destruction. And it can lift fallen warriors out of pits and carry them to safety. With Kobi elevated and hovering in my care, I had two choices: take cover in the cave or try to make it to the ship.

Leaving Aust without knowing his fate wasn't an option. Kobi needed to heal urgently, and every instinct I possessed told me the Hell Hound mother wouldn't take her cubs back to the place they'd been discovered. It seemed, at least for the moment, I was right.

I settled Kobi at the low opening at the mouth of the cave. He looked whole. If I hadn't seen him plummet from Hell's ceiling, I would have thought he simply slept. I ducked inside to set the pup down. When I returned, Aust stood over Kobi, catching his breath.

"Are you all right?" I hugged him, then ran my hands down his arms and turned him so I could check his back. Gloriously filthy and other than a dozen scrapes, surface cuts, and bruises coming to the surface, he remained unharmed.

I punched him. "You took a century off my life luring that beast away as bait. What were you thinking?"

He picked up the satchel from where I'd dropped it and crouched. "Chastise me once Kobi is well."

I lifted Kobi with my powers, and Aust crouched through the opening and directed him to the back of the cave. He laid out the groundsheet from the pack and then balled the satchel up to act as support under Kobi's neck.

I knelt and cupped his face in my hands. "Now the fun part, warrior." I kissed his split lip, wiped the grit from my mouth, and kissed him again. No pressure met mine. No sexual energy. No awareness. "Come on, Kobi, wake up. Ignite that insatiable hunger of yours."

The rough ground poked my knees, and I shifted onto my hip. I tugged his nipple ring. Nothing. I nipped at the hoop piercing his lip and fumbled with the lacings of his shorts. The ties were knotted, and I fought to loosen them.

Aust laid a hand on mine as he knelt on Kobi's other side. "Allow me."

Kobi's mind fluttered. It brushed my thoughts with the faintest touch of a feather. My lips met his with firm determination. I swept my tongue into his mouth, challenged him to duel.

Aust tugged Kobi's cut-offs down the carved muscles of his thighs, and I caressed the skin exposed. Down his navel. Between his legs.

"Aust is undressing you. Can you feel that? Come on, big man. There must be a million lude come-ons kicking around in that head of yours. Come play with us."

I ran my hands up his chest and kissed him again. "It's sexy, the three of us in this tiny cave, covered in sweat. We missed our exit before sunrise. How will we ever pass the time until nightfall? I bet you have some creative ideas."

Aust set Kobi's shorts to the side, looking puzzled.

"Sex triggers an Incubus Demon's healing. He needs us to arouse him enough to have sex."

"Intercourse is forbidden for Highbornes, unless mated. You are aware of that, yes?"

It struck me then, something I'd seen while studying Lia's tapestry before her hearing. "Kobi was injured at the cemetery a few weeks ago, and Lia healed him. Either she specifically, or something in the Highborne nature, triggered his healing stronger than other realm races. They didn't have sex. Her touch and kisses were enough."

Aust's eyes widened, and he froze.

"It's unfair to expect you to pleasure Kobi," I said, trying to breathe past the lump in my throat. "I regret putting you in this situation, but he's dying. Highbornes view sexual freedoms and acceptance in much the same way as the Fae Pantheon. Please. Will you try?"

Aust swallowed. He looked nervous. Sad. "Verily, I have no issue with the idea of sexual play. I would be happy to oblige."

"But?"

"I am a newling in all but the most casual affections. I fear I fail to possess the skill to aid him."

I let out a breath and smiled. "If that's all you're worried about, don't be. Do what feels natural. A kiss. A touch. I'll help and take it from there. I promise."

He slid his arm under Kobi's neck and gathered him against his side. With gentle urging, he kissed him, tentative at first, but gradually growing in confidence.

"He likes it when you nip the hoop in his lip."

Aust complied. He shifted, rolling over Kobi's bare chest.

"Aust has you now, Kobi. His hair is brushing your jaw, his body draped over yours, skin on skin. Can you feel it?"

Nothing happened. Hell's dread weighed me down heavier still. Kobi dead meant we all died. Dawn brought the reapers back. The boatman would leave. Aust and I had no provisions or skills to escape Hell on our own.

"Please, Kobi," I whispered. "We need you. You have to try to come back to us."

I lifted Kobi's hand and hugged it against my chest. The blood and the bruising on him was unlike anything I had ever seen, his body more black than flesh-toned.

Highborne.

I held my breath. Kobi's thought whispered weakly in my head. I didn't want to get ahead of myself. His injuries were extensive on the outside. I couldn't imagine the internal damage. I brushed his scraped knuckles against my lips and felt the tingle of his healing beneath my kiss. Studying him closely, I watched, waiting for some sign that—

"Aust, it's *working.*"

I caressed the muscled lines of first Kobi's shoulder and then Aust's. The difference in their skin was amazing. Kobi was dark, his warrior's skin tough and peppered with dark hair. Aust had skin as smooth and soft as the finest silk. Hairless. Unmarred by battles and a life of physical assault. He was a beautifully made male.

The gentle rocking of Aust's hips against Kobi's thigh drew my body into the mix. Instead of cold panic, my belly tightened with a much warmer and more welcome sensation. Once again, I stroked down Kobi's navel and caressed between his thighs. His shaft kicked against the ridges of his abdomen, and I gathered him in my grip.

My next words, I sent privately to Kobi.

Aust grinding on you makes me wet.

I laid beside them and bit Kobi's shoulder. He stiffened in my palm. With a surge of relief, I went with what was working. I stroked him base to tip, soaking in the sight of the two men. The chiseled warrior and the lean nurturer together.

You two are hot. Seriously hot.

Kobi's arm lifted, his hand seeking, finding, gripping into the back of Aust's hair. His stubbled chin lifted, and he returned the liplock in earnest. Aust responded as any healthy male would, arching, rocking his hips to increase his pleasure.

I'm getting naked. Amuse yourselves.

As sexual energy crackled in the small space, I shimmied off my shorts and untied the bandeau covering my breasts. Kobi threw a heavy leg over Aust and rolled for a dominant position. When he moaned and thrust his hips, I knew he was on the mend. *Welcome back, Demon. Glad you joined us.*

Now, my biggest challenge would be to get Aust out of this cave and back to Bree with his virginity intact.

CHAPTER FIFTEEN

"There's no way Bree's coyote can turn you down now," I said, as Kobi, Aust, and I materialized on the outer plateau of the Dens. I released Aust's hand from Flashing and stroked the pup's velvet ears. "When we tell her how you tracked down this little guy, lured away his Hell mommy in your tiger form, and healed Kobi, she'll see that you're every bit as heroic as any arrogant alpha male, Were or otherwise."

Aust's ears flushed red, right to their pointed tips. "Mayhap we should keep the healing private for now."

"Whatever you want, Highborne," Kobi said, his voice tight. "What happened is nobody's business. I hope you don't think you did anything wrong."

"You don't, do you?" I said. "You didn't even do anything sexual enough to break your Highborne vows. You saved Kobi's life, and likely my mother's, by extension."

Aust shrugged. "And Kobi saved mine right back by flying us over the reapers, to the boatman and escape."

"We're an amazing threesome," Kobi said, waggling his brow. "Let that soak in."

Aust smiled down at the pup in his arms. "Moments in my life have often been twisted by public opinion. I should like the hours shared in that cave to remain our own. Untainted. We three know what affections were shared and why. Let it be our own truth."

I laced my arm through his elbow and kissed his dirt-stained cheek. "Agreed. The only problem is that we smell like sex. There's no way a room full of Weres will miss it."

Kobi clapped Aust on the bare shoulder. "Bree understands the biology of my healing. I think she'd be cool either way, but if you want, I'll spin it, so you're left out of the carnal pleasures. Zo healed me. Tight quarters. I'll be convincing. But if you ever want to explore the benefits of a true Devil's Threeway, let us know. Boundaries or no, you're more than welcome."

I rolled my eyes.

Aust handed me the pup as his ears flushed even brighter. "The honor was mine."

I brushed my lips over the soft fur of the pup's muzzle and kissed his nose. "Let's go show everyone we're not dead and introduce them to Paladin."

The three of us entered the Dens and made our way toward the living room. In ripped shorts, covered in scrapes, blood, and filth, we were a sight. Despite our appearance, however, with the danger of our Hell quest over, a celebration was in order.

"Drinks on the house," Kobi said, bursting into the room in true Kobi fashion.

Bruin, Cowboy, and Bree had gathered by the bar. Aust rounded the leather couches, jogging straight for Bree. His beloved sat on a barstool, facing the back wall.

She didn't turn to greet us.

Kobi bounded over to Bruin. "The Hellraiser Three have returned. Did you miss us?"

"More than we care to admit," Bruin said, clapping Kobi on the back. "Thank the gods you're safe. We were worried when you didn't get back last night."

Kobi lined up two glasses and grabbed a bottle of whiskey from the back wall. "Nah, easy peasy, right, guys?"

Aust squeezed Bree's shoulders and spun her stool around. Her face was blotched, her eyes rimmed red. He hugged her to his chest and set his cheek on her head. "Bree, fash not, *sweeting*. All is well. Everything worked out. We are home."

She pinched her eyes shut and sobbed against his bare chest. It was a gasping hitch of breath and anguish. Her nose and tears ran, her shoulders rounded.

A hum erupted in my head. "What is it? Is it my mother? Has something happened?"

Bruin stepped out from behind the bar. His somber expression had my nerves on end. "Don't panic, Zophia. We don't know anything more on that front than when you left. This is not that."

That was good.

"If it's not Shalana, then what the fuck is it?" Kobi snapped. He drained the tumbler in his hand and tipped the bottle to refill. "Where's Mika?"

"Lying down," Cowboy said.

"Is it the pregnancy?" Aust asked. "Are the cubs—"

"It's not that either." Cowboy finished his beer, looking like he'd rather be anywhere other than standing in that room. "Mika's upset, Aust. I need to tell you about it, my man."

"Very well. Tell me." Aust settled onto the stool next to Bree and accepted the beer Kobi handed him.

Cowboy rubbed his palms down his thighs and exhaled. "Last night was the full moon run. Our animals have been especially anxious with the coming of the Equinox. We've been struggling to contain our primal sides—"

"My brother, I know this," Aust said, his hand up between them. "Why is Bree crying and why is Mika upset?"

Bree reached for another tissue and Cowboy nodded.

"So, during the run, our animals took over. It was a relief to let them loose, to go primal, to let our consciousness recede. But then something unexpected happened."

Cowboy held out his hand for Aust to see. Emblazoned into the flesh of his palm laid the stylized symbol and Sanskrit of a Were brand.

"You bonded with your mate!" Aust launched to his feet and met Cowboy chest to chest. After clapping him on the back in a rough hug, he grabbed his broad shoulders and stepped back. "This is remarkable. Congratulations. Who is she? Why do you not celebrate?"

"Because of who I mated," he said. "You see, it was my wolf, not me. I wasn't in human form, or it would never have happened. But with the moon . . . and the run . . . and my wolf being in control . . . I'm just so fucking sorry."

The abject misery in Cowboy's face raised the hair on my neck. Aust turned back to Bree and took her hand. Slowly, he flipped her palm up to reveal the matching tattoo.

She blinked tear-filled eyes at him. "I'm s-s-so . . . sor-ry." Her words cut off as her breathing hitched.

Aust straightened, devastation written in every line of his body. My gaze jumped to Kobi and Bruin, Cowboy and Bree, and then back to Aust. The same tortured looks reflected around the room. The wolf and the coyote had mated.

"This is my sisters at work," I breathed. "They did this. Aust. Bree. I can't begin to tell you how sorry—"

"No," Aust said, his voice a hoarse whisper. He straightened and retreated a step. "A Were-bonding is extraordinary. A pairing of souls to rejoice. You both deserve nothing less than a union blessed by the gods."

"You don't mean that." Cowboy cursed and moved directly in front of his best friend. "Hit me. Curse me. Pound me into pulp. I deserve it. But don't you dare take the high road here, Aust. You can't be okay with this."

"I never said I was." Aust's tone held a barely-restrained scream tethered beneath the surface. "Verily, I wish things different, but my wish changes nothing. Instead, I leave you to your new life. Mayhap, one day I might even be happy for you."

Aust bowed his head and backed away. Cowboy grabbed his arm, but the hold was shrugged off with a violent twist. Aust froze, his fists up, his shoulders rigid. After a moment, though, he dropped his gaze and backed away.

The pain wafting off Aust's body fouled the air as he passed me. "Aust, I . . ." *What?* What could I say to make this any better? I hugged Paladin and kissed his head.

Cowboy dropped to his knees, tipped back his head, and howled. The mournful cry tore at my gut and broke my heart.

"He's not answering." I hung up Kobi's cellphone and tossed it back to him. My nails bit into the flesh of my palms as I paced. Luckily, the floor was stone, or I would soon owe Bruin a new rug from wearing a path. I brushed past him to access the pile of necessities Nash left in my suite.

Fresh from the shower, my hair dampened the sweatshirt I wore. I managed to wash off Hell's filth, yet still my skin crawled as if covered by a legion of ants. "If Sunday night *is* the night for Abaddon to make his move, we need to get Paladin trained on my mother's scent or energy or whatever is going to lead him to her."

The pup chuffed, sound asleep on the padded chair in the corner. His little feet twitched as he dreamed, soft whines and yips coming off him as he chased some imaginary foe.

"Aust knows what's at stake here, Zo. He lost his best friend and his love in one horrible moment. As soon as he has a moment to process that, he'll be here. Don't panic."

"I have a horrible feeling eating at my gut." I slid my feet into a pair of tennis shoes and knelt to tie the laces. "We should go out looking for him. Remind him we care about him, but we're on a clock. Maybe keeping busy will help."

Kobi caught my wrist in one of my passes and pulled me into his lap. He smoothed a hand against my thigh. "Give the guy a moment to grieve. Right now, he needs privacy to let his guard down."

The warmth of Kobi's body did nothing to soothe me. I checked the clock again and yep, another minute had passed. "I know you're right, but if I ache this bad for him, I can't imagine the pain he suffers. I can't breathe."

"You're still suffering the influence of Hell's dread. It's compounding your anxiety." He brushed my hair back and tugged the collar of the shirt down my shoulder. A gentle finger touched the mark from his bite two nights ago. "I can help you with that. Set you right again?"

I slapped his hand away and stood. "Stop trying to seduce me. My mother is in danger, and Aust's life is in shambles."

Kobi sat back and scowled. "We've covered that ground. What's really up your ass, Zo? You've been throwing me stink the eye since we left the cave. What did I do?"

I snorted. "Your ego knows no bounds, I swear. Did your multitude of lady friends lead you to believe the world revolves around you? Well, it doesn't."

"Granted, but this *is* about me." He stood, his hands locked on his hips. "I get that you're worried about your mom and Aust, but if this more than the dread, I want to hear it. Is the novelty of slumming with me over? Did seeing Aust get his heart broken convince you to cut your losses?"

I flexed my clenched fists and forced a smile. "You're imagining things."

His nostrils flared, and he held up a finger. "I warned you about lying to me. Don't do it again."

"Fine, you want the truth? You almost died. I hated it."

"It was no fun-fest for me either. What's your point?"

"Don't be an ass. I don't want or need to be focused on someone else when my own life is such a mess."

"Life *is* messy. Getting your hands dirty is part—"

"Save the speech on realm life and how I haven't got a clue. Enjoying each other is one thing. Investing in someone else when I don't even know who I am is another. Don't you get that? All of who I am and have always been is gone. Haven isn't my home. It's a fallback position after being smacked in the face with the realization that I'm not welcome in my own life. I'm biding time here. This"—I gestured between us—"what's happening here, it's nothing more than a distraction."

"Lie," Kobi snapped again, stepping closer. "Your family hollowed you out, and you're throwing up walls. I fucking wrote the book on self-preservation, baby. And while I may have started out as a distraction, I'm more than that now, and that scares you more than you have the balls to admit."

"There's that ego again." I shook my head, the thrumming beat of my heart pounding in my ears. "We're displaced souls caught in a battle against evil, that's it. Adults get to have sex—even great sex—without it meaning more."

Kobi's gaze narrowed and he stalked closer. "You're losing traction, Lacy. What happened in Hell spooked you. You've never seen death before. You told me that."

I headed to the dresser and pulled a brush through my hair. "I've witnessed every horrible moment of this realm."

"From the safety of your station, you view the gore of battle through a distant lens. Today was up close and personal. You got to smell the tang of my blood and watch the life drain out of my eyes. I bet it cut deeper knowing it was your fault, didn't it? Your responsibility. Your quest to save your mother."

I threw the brush at his head. "Get out!"

He ducked and caught my arm, spinning me, so my back collided with his chest. Pinning my arms against my stomach, he struck, piercing the meaty flesh between shoulder and neck.

It's dread, Zo, Kobi said into my mind. *Let me help you.*

The physical pain eased after a racing heartbeat or two. The strange sensation of Kobi leaching my suffering tingled down my shoulder. Icy-heat trickled into my chest and rolled like an ebbing tide through my body.

The familiarity of his presence maddened me. What I'd perceived to be an invasive sensation the first time, was Kobi's demon energy dispersing within me. I recognized him now.

Seductive. Greedy. Hungry.

Despite my urge to gain distance, the oppressive dread consuming me followed Kobi's call. Other pains, old and new, rose to the surface. Judgment. Rejection. My ache for Aust. The panic of watching Kobi die. The fear of being trapped in Hell—of leaving my mother vulnerable.

His gentle pull released the heavy press on my chest. After another moment, he eased off his hold on my arms. The deep-throated murmur of his pleasure made me curse. He knew his effect on me—likely on all women.

Stupid. Arrogant. Demon.

How dare he think he knew me. *I* didn't even know me. The shiver came out of nowhere. For millennia, I believed we Fates were blessed to live amongst the gods and goddesses of the Fae Pantheon. What value did a realm of mortals offer?

What indeed.

The withdrawal of his incisors ignited both relief and regret. Kobi licked the puncture marks and sealed them closed. He looked down at me, his satiation obvious in his heavy-lidded gaze. "Better?"

I pursed my lips, shaken at how deep the roots of my affections had grown. Too deep.

Paladin barked, and my awareness jolted back to the room.

Forgive me, Cameron said, stepping around Kobi to see me. *You must needs come. It's Aust. I fear he might harm himself.*

Blood rushed to my head, and I steadied myself. "Aust's in trouble."

"And you know this, how?"

I grabbed the navy peacoat from the hook at the door and headed out the hall. "Cameron's here. He watches over Aust and Elora."

Kobi caught up to me in the hall. "What? Why is this the first I'm hearing about Aust's father haunting him?"

"He's not haunting him. And don't say anything. He wants them to move on."

"Keeping a secret this big from a friend is a shitty way to return loyalty. Aust risked his life for you and your mother."

We rounded the corner from the sleeping quarters to the living areas of the dens. All seemed quiet. Likely everyone retreated to their corners after Cowboy, and his little coyote mate, blew up Aust's life.

"It's Cameron's right to decide what his family knows. He understands them best."

Kobi grabbed his leather jacket from the closet near the main entrance and stomped his feet in his boots. Grabbing the doorknob, he swung it open and waited for me to exit. "You don't get to play Fate almighty down here, Zophia. In this realm, you're either one of us, or you're not."

Well, I guess that summed up my life, didn't it?

On the outer plateau, I turned to Cameron. "Where is he?"

At the ruin site.

CHAPTER SIXTEEN

*I*n the center of devastation, among the culverted tracks of heaving earth and pits where explosions had carved holes in the landscape, sat Aust. Knees up and head down, he perched on the upended stone slab from the decimated stone circle. And he looked bad, like a hollow, broken clone of the Elf he was just hours ago.

Unaware of our approach, he scrubbed his eyes with his forearm, as his shoulders racked. A sob ripped up his windpipe.

I materialized before him as moonlight caught the bleeding edge of the dagger. He gripped the hilt with both hands, pressing the point of the blade to his chest.

In the blink of a moment, Kobi grabbed Aust's wrist, and the two rolled from the force of the tackle. Arms and legs flailed and the two twisted in a struggle for control of the weapon. Aust cursed and fought back. He landed a violent uppercut. Kobi's head whipped back, his teeth clacking as his jaw got slammed into his skull.

Kobi bared his teeth, his eyes glowing scarlet. "Hit me like that again, and I'm hitting you back, Highborne."

Aust focused on the point of the dagger, his arm trembling with the effort to pull it closer.

Kobi shook his head. "There's no fucking way you're offing yourself over a woman. Last warning, my man. Stand down, or we're doing this."

"Kobi, stop." I shifted closer, unsure how to step into the fray. "He's hurting. Don't threaten him."

Aust hauled off and elbowed Kobi in the groin.

"Mother*fucker*," Kobi spat, his voice thready as his knees came up. "Oh, it's *on*, blondie."

The two of them went at it hard, blood spouting from noses and mouths, grunts and curses filling the air.

"It's the dread," I yelled. "He can't think."

I had no idea if either of them heard me. I thought about getting Julian to help, but Aust's agony was nobody's business. Haven was a small community. He'd have to face everyone knowing his heartache soon enough. Kobi flipped Aust onto his back and threw himself across his chest.

"We're here to help him, not kill him."

Kobi wrestled the knife away and flung it into the trees.

Aust muttered in Elvish, and the pummeling took on a violent second wave. Watching the two, it became clear that not only was Kobi in better fighting form and remained in control, but he seemed to draw perverse pleasure from the fight.

Legs and arms entwined, the two rolled as one. Whether because of friction, frustration, or sheer desperation, something shifted. Aust's fists transformed into rough fingers. His punches became grabs. He gripped the front of Kobi's pants, and his hips thrust forward.

Kobi gritted his teeth and pinned Aust's arms on the grass above his head. "Not what I'm here for, Highborne."

Aust wrapped his feet around the backs of Kobi's thighs. "You want me."

"Not like this."

Aust barked a dark laugh. "I repulse even the man who fucks the entire population of the realm."

"Flattery won't get you laid. And don't kid yourself. If not for me trying to respect your Elven beliefs, I'd flip you over and mount you here and now."

"Then do it."

"Pass. You'd regret it." Kobi dropped his head to the muscled flesh between Aust's shoulder and neck. "This is the dread talking. Let the humiliation and anger go, and trust me to heal you." Kobi's eyes glowed bright red a split-second before his fangs descended. He dropped his head and bit.

Aust stiffened. He struggled beneath him at first but then began to settle.

Get off him, Demon. Cameron surged forward.

"It's all right." I fell to my knees beside them and spoke to both father and son. "Kobi's draining the pain. The despair from Bree and Cowboy's mating magnified the effects of two days in Hell. Relax into it, Aust. Let Kobi take the burden."

And the demon can ease that? And Aust will be well?

Aust's arms got sloppy, and his fury drained. I rubbed a hand down his bare arm and drew a deep breath. The cuts and bruises that marred too much of his body, the blood and filth that smeared the grimy cut-offs he'd worn for days, these were the metaphorical tip of the iceberg wound that crushed him.

"As well as can be expected."

Staring at Kobi and Aust, entwined in a strangled embrace, seemed invasive. I'd long been the voyeur to people's lives, but Kobi was right, watching from the point of security Behind the Veil was very different.

Here, I was part of the moment. *In* their lives. Higher stakes. More overwhelming emotions. Kobi was right about that too. I didn't like it. I preferred anonymity.

The damp from the grass seeped through my pantlegs and wet my shins. The cool chill contrasted the hot stone of the cave from earlier that day. Was that only hours ago?

I took Aust's hand and squeezed my support. After what seemed ages, Kobi rolled off, and they laid side by side, chests heaving, soaked in sweat and covered in dirt.

"How do you feel now?" I asked.

He coughed a little and shook his head, as if clearing a fog.

Kobi patted the pockets of his leather jacket and pulled out a pack of cigarettes. In a series of practiced moves, he selected, lit, and drew on the white stick, his whole body relaxing as he exhaled. "Well, tonight has been a barrel of laughs."

Aust propped himself up to sit and rubbed his bloody lip with the back of his wrist. Those cut-offs did nothing to hide that he remained fully aroused. But fighting could do that to men, I'd heard. "I thought smoking came after sex, not before."

Kobi wiped his mouth with the back of his hand in the same fashion and spat blood to the grass. "Your pony still on that track, Highborne, because leaching makes me horny as fuck. I warn you, if you're serious . . . I'll take you up on it."

"No, you *won't*." The heat in my words surprised me, but I didn't dwell on that. "Aust is suffering emotional heartache. Encouraging him to betray his beliefs on mating won't help."

"You sure about that?" Kobi rolled onto his side and then made an awkward attempt to get to his feet. On the second try, he stood and steadied himself. "Seems to me, Highborne laws offer him nothing beyond guilt and suffering. What happened to 'adults get to have sex without it meaning anything more'?"

Kobi exhaled and probed the swelling gaining strength on his cheek. "Aust's Highborne nature eases the acid burning through my veins. I'll ease his pain and loneliness. I want him. He wants me. End of. You said we aren't anything beyond the casual, so it's none of your biz."

"Highbornes mate for *life*," I reminded them both. "Neither of you want that."

Kobi laughed. "Are you qualified to speak for the two of us? I would've claimed him today if you hadn't pulled me off and force-fed me bullshit about his planned future with Bree. Well, that's no longer an obstacle."

Aust flinched at the mention of his lost love, but stood and brushed his fingers over my cheek. "Join us, *sweeting*. We three are an amazing team, as you said."

"I . . . I'm sorry, but this isn't what you need. When you've given time for your emotions to clear, maybe the answer will be different, but not now. You can't decide on forever with your world flipped upside down."

Kobi sighed. "No, *you* can't. Stop projecting and stop with the cock-blocking. Either join us, sit back and watch, or get gone. I told you, life is messy. You can't hide behind the Veil and look down on people anymore. You gotta get in the game."

Kobi's dismissal slapped me as if he'd raised his hand to my face. He knew it too because his eyes rolled closed and he turned his face into the hollow of Aust's neck.

"I *am* in the game," I said, my voice too emotional for my liking. "My mother needs me. I have a Hell Hound that isn't trained, and a man I thought I could depend on who short-circuits every time sex is in the air. Grow up, Kobi."

Kobi rested an arm across Aust's shoulder and squeezed. "What our fair Fate is saying, Highborne, is that I'm not good enough for you and you're making the mistake of your life."

Truer words were never uttered, Cameron shouted.

Aust stared at me, as if trying to read the truth of Kobi's comment in my expression. "Zophia, *sweeting*, you are wrong. I am neither a child nor addled. I watched the two of you together for hours today and want that connection for myself. Mayhap we remain lovers for a lifetime, or mayhap I forsake Highborne tradition as it has forsaken me. The point is, the choice is mine to make."

"Preach," Kobi said, blowing out a cloud of smoke.

"But she is also right," Aust continued, looking to Kobi. "At this moment, Shalana and Abbey need us, and we must needs do all within our power to recover them. If you and I, or the three of us, are destined to unite, it shall happen in due course. Nothing need be decided at this moment."

I exhaled, realizing how long I'd been holding my breath.

Kobi cursed and extinguished his cigarette against the tread of his boot. "You two are maddening. You know that? So fucking logical. Fine, we table this discussion for a later date, but it's not over. Not by a long shot."

"Thank you. Both," I said. Despite the crushing pressure in my chest, our evening was far from over. "Let's get Paladin from my suite and see if we can't find my mother."

CHAPTER SEVENTEEN

My mother's little, ivy-covered cottage wasn't the same without her in it. And being there, not knowing what she was going through, stole even more strength from me than I imagined it could. It did give me a measure of comfort, though, to ensure Dandy and Hoola were fed and properly loved. And while I did that, Kobi smoked out by the gate.

He was still angry, but more than angry, he seemed hurt. I wasn't a relationship expert, but by my account, the one with more grounds to hold a grudge after what happened at the ruin site was me.

Still, I didn't like the tension between us, especially because the three of us did work well as a team and I wanted to give my mother the greatest chance of being rescued.

"Zophia, *sweeting*, did you hear me?"

I pulled my attention from staring out the window. "I'm sorry, no. What did you say?"

"I believe we are ready to return home." Aust scrubbed Paladin's ruff and handed me the pup. The moment his arms were free, Hoola jumped from beside the table, wrapped her long arms around his neck, and clung to him. Poor girl.

I kissed Paladin's velvet ear. "You think he's ready?"

Aust adjusted his suede tunic, so Hoola wasn't half stripping him with her grappling hold. "We smelled the smells, felt the signature of her powers, and I have tried to impress upon him the importance of finding Shalana sooner rather than later. I have never worked with a creature like him before, but believe he understands."

"And letting him chew one of her unwashed socks?"

"That was simply fun. He wanted it, and I thought it a small price to pay for a favorable mood and obedience."

I agreed and turned off the lights.

When we returned to Haven, the three of us went straight to Jade's house to face the wrath of Reign. There was no hiding the fact that we now possessed a Hell Hound and we needed enforcers at the ready when Aust sent Paladin into the field.

Aust took the pup to the kitchen to feed and visit his mother. Kobi went in to speak with Reign. And Hoola and I went upstairs to check on Jade. It seemed my gibbon sister refused to be left to the wilds of the sanctuary without our mom.

I couldn't blame her. I missed Mom too.

Galan sat at the top of the three stairs that led to their private suite. With elbows on his knees and his head in his hands, he may have lost himself to exhaustion. I paused and was about to turn back when he lifted his head and smiled.

"Come. Please, Zophia. Is there any news?"

"We're working on a plan to locate them. I'll let you know the minute we have anything to tell you. How are Jade and the babies?"

He rubbed his palms together and sighed. "They're resting now. Rowan is monitoring the three of them and has requested emergency equipment be brought here in case the young deliver earlier than planned. He believes that in ending the pregnancy, these struggles will also end, but no one knows the proper gestation period for a half-Fae/human/Elven pregnancy. He shall wait as long as he can before making that decision."

"Well, Rowan is a wonderful doctor and a skilled surgeon. I'm sure everything will be fine."

Galan gathered the burgundy braid signifying his mating and held it out to examine. The deep auburn of Jade's hair was startlingly striking next to his silver. "Highborne pregnancies are a mortal curse more oft than not. I had hoped Jade, and the babes, might be spared because of her genetics. I suppose it was foolish to hope."

I touched the braid and leaned shoulder to shoulder with him. He smelled like suede and the outdoors, but unlike Aust, the scent of trees and the wilds of the world was subtle on Galan. "Jade is one of the strongest women I know, in the company of her mother and mine. They will all be fine, you'll see. We have to believe that."

He kissed the side of my head and swept his hand across his eyes. "I do. I truly do."

I squeezed his hand. "Are my sisters still here?"

"They left once Samuel terminated Shavandra's spell. But they did bring two of Castian's care staff to aid Rowan. Jade, however, wants Castian himself, and knows there is something we are keeping from her."

"Well, then I should go and get back to our plan to end this nightmare. Wish us luck."

Galan kissed my knuckles and managed a faint smile. "I wish you all the luck in all the realms. Blessed be."

"Blessed be," I repeated, and headed back down the stairs.

The bass of Reign's voice boomed all the way up to the second-floor landing. I needed to get down there and take my share of the blame for our Hell excursion. In the open doorway, I hesitated, unsure of how to break into the volatile conversation without making things worse.

"I don't fucking care if we search every barn, house, and shit-shed in the two realms. We follow protocol. We don't go off task. We don't disregard orders. And we certainly don't take a civilian and Castian's *fucking* niece to Hell to get her killed. What the fuck were you thinking?"

"Zophia's immortal, and I know the Hell Realm. I knew we could—"

"You didn't *know* shit. You thought. You hoped. That, and a dollar can't buy you a fucking coffee."

"But we're good, Reign. It was a piece of cake. We got the pup, and Aust worked his magic—"

"Don't even." Reign pointed a dagger. I was thankful there was a table between them; though, the man could likely throw the weapon with deadly accuracy. "I don't want to hear it, Demon. You're done. Get out of my sight."

Kobi cursed and tore off his weapons vest. Tossing it onto the war room table, the weight of the thing carried it halfway across to his commander.

Cowboy saw me at the door and shook his head.

Ignoring the warning, I crossed the threshold and knocked.

"Not a good time," Reign said, looking up from the realm map lit up on the surface of the table. "It won't help lover boy here to give me the bleeding-heart plea of how you couldn't stand by and wait. Get gone and take him with you."

"Perhaps if I could—"

Reign stood to his full height and the other warriors in the room stilled. The power of his fury sent a rush of frigid air through the room.

I exhaled, my breath condensing in a cloud of white before me. "I respect your authority, Maximus, and apologize if I undermined it in any way by countering your decision. I, however, will not apologize for doing everything within my power to reclaim my mother. I am not one of your subjects. I do not take orders. If the Talon battles for freedom and the right of free will, it seems I am entitled to the same. I am far more than Castian's *fucking* niece, and it would do you all well to remember that."

He opened his mouth to speak, and I raised my hand. "You will calm yourself. We will wait in your library. And then, we shall come together and discuss the next stage of our plan, as a united front against the true enemy of this realm."

Reign pointed to the door, his eyes feral, his entire frame rigid. "Out. Now."

Kobi glared at his commander and then at me, but as I left the war room and headed down the hall, I was relieved to hear his boots thundering against the floor behind me. Whatever he'd been stewing over was about to boil and I, for one, was ready to face anything.

Reign's library wasn't far, but with the violent rhythm punctuating every step, it seemed like forever before we arrived and closed ourselves inside.

Kobi strode straight into the room and rebounded, finger pointed. "Don't you dare make me look bad in front of Reign and the others. Trash me personally, if it makes you feel better about yourself, but I'm respected as a warrior. I won't have you shitting on me where I work."

"You're imagining things again. I didn't—"

"And yes, that's my ego talking. And yes, when it comes to my duties as a warrior, I've earned a bit of an ego."

"Kobi, stop. You're a great warri—"

"Am I? You might have just argued me out of a job—out of my fucking *life*. Who am I if I'm not an Enforcer?"

"And who am I if I'm not a Fate? Terrifying, isn't it?"

"Why couldn't you just walk away when he told you to?"

"I wanted to be heard."

"Everyone wants to be heard, Zophia." He threw his hands into the air. "I get that you're a goddess Behind the Veil, but Reign is pretty much a god here at Haven and throughout the realm. You don't get to wrecking-ball your way through every situation, even if you are a Fate."

I swiped at my cheeks, furious that tears had the nerve to fall and make me look weak. "I'm not a Fate—not anymore."

"You still act like one."

I clenched my fists at my sides, my powers burning in my palms to let loose. "How am I supposed to act, Kobi? Please, gods, tell me because I haven't got a clue. I've lived a cloistered life with one purpose. Now, everything I understood about my life is gone—taken from me by people who should have been on my side . . . who should have loved me."

"You don't believe in love. It's a waste of energy, right? A myth. A fallacy?" The edge in his voice pierced me like a blade through my chest.

"Don't sound so cynical, you think so too."

"Do I?" He laughed, scrubbing the back of his neck. "Have you ever asked me? You tell me that you accept me for who I am, yet judge me with the same lens as everyone else."

The door swung open, and Aust stepped in, eyes wide, his expression hard. "Stop this, both of you."

Faolan trotted in at his heel, with Paladin nipping at the wolf's tail. The puppy had made a fast friend. Aust locked the door and crossed the room, hands extended. "Jade is upstairs fighting for the life of her young, and you two are in here airing your hostilities. Unacceptable."

He stormed into the mix, grabbed Kobi's wrist and dragged him over to me and grabbed mime. "The two of you, join your hands. Now. Do it!"

Stunned by Aust's autocratic tone, I obeyed. Kobi frowned, but we completed the circuit.

"Your passions are heated, I understand that, but bridge the gap between hurt and anger."

Kobi sighed. "Aust, I appreciate—"

"Not a word," he said, pointing a finger. "I care naught for your appreciation. Shut up and listen."

I almost laughed at Kobi's expression. Aust was on fire.

"I know well the hurt and betrayal of love. My village. My beloved. My best friend. When we hurt, we hurt others in turn. Mostly, we torment ourselves. If you stop to speak your heart's songs, those tender blooms you protect to the depth of your souls, the pain and confusion clear, and you are left with truth."

"Yeah," Kobi said, "and what truth is that, Highborne?"

He squeezed our arms and sighed. "You, my stubborn, oblivious friends, have fallen in love despite yourselves."

I shook my head, trying to draw breath past the pressure in my chest. "This doesn't feel like love."

"And have you been in love before, *sweeting*? Would you recognize it? Did you grow up in a home with two parents who would die for one another? *I did*. Now take away the pain of your situations and look at one another."

Kobi rolled his eyes. "You're reaching on this one, my man. Physical connection when the world is spiraling around you doesn't add up to love."

"But you do believe in love, yes?"

Kobi nodded. "I live with Bruin and Mika. I witnessed the transformation in him last August and felt the power of their love as it took them over. Yeah, it's out there."

"And you want that for yourself?"

He shrugged. "Sure. Someday."

Aust frowned. "Someday? You are a brave male of worth. Stop being a coward and pretending Zophia means less to you than she does. Admitting your truth is more terrifying than battle, is it not?"

"I'd rather be speared by a nine-inch blade. In the eye."

Aust smiled. "Then if you value *my* feelings in the wake of what I lost, mount your courage and speak your truth."

Kobi scowled, his chin jutted. When he met my gaze, licks of gold flames danced across the scarlet of his eyes. "All right, I admit it. Maybe I *do* love you. *Maybe.* I never meant for it to happen and it makes me want to puke . . . or get pissed drunk."

"That is fear talking," Aust said. "What else?"

Kobi sent Aust a look which was the ocular version of giving him the finger. "A never-ending loop is screaming in my skull. *She's a goddess, and you're a fucking incubus demon, you idiot. You're not what she wants. Or needs. If you trust in this, she'll throw it in your face.*"

"That's what you think of me?"

"I'm just sayin', if you want to run, run now. If you want to laugh at the demon who caught a case of feelings, have at it. But know that it's more than the sex—on my side anyway."

I stared at him, mouth agape. "I had no idea. I . . . uh, don't know what to say."

"Dig deeper, Zophia," Aust said, frowning. "Kobi exposed his heart. Show him the respect of doing the same."

I thought about what Kobi had said and tried to connect with what was happening in my own body and mind. "Can my soul's truth be that I honestly don't know what to say?"

Kobi withdrew his hand, and I gripped his t-shirt to keep him from retreating. "You are important to me, Kobi, yes. But love? My mind is filled with fear and anger. My mother is missing. I'm exiled from my life. I can't decide what to wear each day, let alone where my heart belongs. If your truth is that you might *maybe* love me, I'm grateful. I'm hopeful. I know that it *is* more than sex, but I need life to settle before I can say for sure what I feel."

"That is fair," Aust said, tilting his head toward me. "There is still much to do. Kiss, and let your argument come to its end."

Kobi frowned. "Not sure what wasp flew up your ass. You're awfully bossy tonight, blondie."

Aust nodded. "We are a team. Let us act like one."

Kobi took a long look at me, the hurt and anger in him visible in his dark eyes. In the end, he didn't kiss me. He shook his head and stepped back. "Give me a minute, would you?"

When he walked off toward the window, Aust pulled me into his embrace. The pain and fear of the past fifteen hours weighed heavier than my crumbling sex life, or love life, or whatever it was.

Worry sat like a stone in my gut. Aust kissed the side of my head, and I let his warm strength seep beneath my skin.

"Fash not, *sweeting*," he said. "Everything that happens has a reason. It shall all work out in the end."

I cupped Aust's jaw in my hands. "Bree is a fool. You are far too wonderful for words."

I rose to my toes and pressed my lips to his cheek. The connection was soft and chaste. He tasted like sunshine and smelled like suede and the outdoors.

Paladin barked, and Aust's hand stiffened against the small of my back.

"Look at you two," a voice crooned behind me. "My Zozo happy with her betrothed."

I spun and almost tripped on Hoola, the two of us racing to the overstuffed sofa. Hoola sprang and bounded into her lap, upsetting the huge red-tailed hawk perched on her arm. I stared as the bird settled, praying for Castian's sake it was Abbey.

"Mom, what are . . . how did you get here?"

She smiled, but her expression seemed tired. "How does the sun shine, baby girl? Power and light. No one keeps me from my Zozo. Especially not your father."

In my peripheral vision, Kobi slipped out the door. It wasn't Reign who mattered. It was Castian *I* wanted. I closed my eyes, opened a connection to my uncle, and sent an urgent call for him to come to me.

I brushed my mother's hair out of her eyes and drank in the sight of her. "Are you all right?"

Aust took the bird over to the lampstand so I could get a better look. She seemed physically intact, but something felt wrong. Whooping and chattering as Hoola was, it was hard to get a sense of anything beyond how upset she had been at our mother's disappearance.

Aust took a knee. "Milady, are you well? Is there anything I might get for you?"

"I'm very thirsty, son. Dane was never one to anticipate the needs of a woman. He locked me in a room and left me there as if I was a piece of furniture."

Aust excused himself, and I focused on the grimoire in my mother's lap. "What's this?"

"A book. I'm not sure what, but Dane coveted it, so I took it when I left. May he rot with the loss of it."

The library door creaked open, and a flood of people washed in. Aust returned with Elora, and a tray of lemonade, tea, water, and cookies. Kobi brought in Reign and Julian. Hoola clung to my mother's neck as Paladin stood on his back paws, licking her hand.

Reign stepped forward, but I raised a hand, and he paused.

I exchanged the jug of lemonade for Rheagan's spell book and then poured a glass. "Drink this and tell me all about your adventure. Where did Dane take you? Were there other people there for you to talk to?"

The air charged, and the scent of bergamot brought Castian to the group. "Shalana," he said, rushing forward. "Blessed be, dear friend. What news have you of Abbey?"

I pointed to the hawk perched by the window and Castian raced over. I stroked Hoola's back, praying that my aunt was indeed in her animal form, and not still trapped by Rheagan.

Mom bit into a cookie. "These would be better warm."

"Mom," I said. "Castian asked you about Abbey."

Shalana shrugged. "The woman with Dane looked like Abbey, but her words were wrong. She was a trickster. She talked like we were sisters, like she knew me, but she didn't. I pretended not to notice and brought the real Abbey home."

"You did great, Mom. I'm so proud of you."

"But she spoke to you?" Castian rounded the sofa and sank onto the coffee table opposite us. I don't know if he sat so much as his knees gave out, the bird on his arm rustling her wings to keep balanced. He stroked down her back and kissed her head. "My darling, I need you to focus. Can you tell me everything the woman who wasn't Abbey said to you?"

Mother smiled. "Like a memory game?"

He nodded. "Exactly."

"And if I win?"

"You name it. Anything you want."

"Zozo will make me brownies every night for forever . . . and Aust too." She craned her neck to look around me and found Aust. "Do you bake, son? We like to bake. It'll be good if you bake too."

He joined us at the sofa and squeezed my shoulder. "I assure you, Zophia and I will keep you sated in sweets, e'ermore."

"Okay, wonderful," Castian said, reclaiming my mother's attention. "Now, our memory game. What did you hear Dane and the woman who wasn't Abbey say?"

"Can I do the voices?"

Castian nodded, and my heart went out to him. "Of course. If it makes the game better, do the voices."

And she did. My mother spent the next forty-five minutes recounting word for word everything she could remember.

CHAPTER EIGHTEEN

hen Castian dematerialized from Reign's library, I followed. Wherever he was going, whatever he had planned, I wanted to be part of it. When he stormed into his private chambers, I hesitated. The thunderous boom of the door slamming behind him echoed in time with the violent skies outside. I had never seen him in such a rage. And as much as he likely needed time to himself, it was dangerous to let the God of gods boil over.

I knocked and let myself in. Blood and rubble horribly tainted the opulence of the once pristine space. Ironic really, the carnage my father left behind.

Castian stiffened as I approached but didn't turn. "You should go, Zophia. I'm not fit company."

I righted the chair in the reading nook and took a seat. "That's exactly why I'm here. I understand better than anyone the betrayal of Dane and siblings stabbing you in the gut. Yell or throw things, or sit and stew, I don't care. I'm here for you as you have always been for me."

Gripping the raised platform where Abbey had lain dormant for almost two decades, he leaned heavily into his rigid shoulders. "As much as it enrages me that my siblings cause such strife in the Realm of the Fair, what truly strikes me to the core is that it's all my fault. If I had wiped Dane from existence when he orchestrated the attack on Jade at that farmhouse, they wouldn't be suffering now. And if I had expired Rheagan when she tried to take the realm the first time, Abaddon wouldn't have culled through the realm to build his soulless army."

My mind stuttered to a halt. Was my father involved with the attack on Jade? Arranged it or been part of the violations on Abbey? Did it matter? I knew one of the offenders had yet to be punished, but —to target his brother's family?

I'd never imagined the depths of Dane's duplicity.

"Millenia of sitting back," Castian continued, his voice hard and strained, "believing our charges should find their way. To what end? It was sheer arrogance, to believe I could rule the Pantheon with honor and guidance alone. Hell, my own Fae Council turned against me."

He screamed, and the bedding platform shot across the room. The glass window-wall smashed as the dais slid out onto the balustrade and dropped to the grounds below. "Now Abbey is trapped in her hawk form; her body possessed to wage war against me. How do I destroy Rheagan now?"

"You can't."

Turmoil flashed in his emerald green eyes. "I gave Abbey immortality after her attack and Dane knew it. He also knew that with Abbey's corporal self on the line, I'd never strike against Rheagan. Why hadn't I considered that? And to hide the spell book within Abbey's platform—my arrogance truly knows no bounds."

I went to him and squeezed his hand. "You would never intentionally put Abbey in harm's way, and it's a moot point. The spellbook is back under our control, and we'll find a way to extricate Rheagan and rescue Abbey's body intact. Then, you can deal with your siblings as a husband and man, not as the leader of the Pantheon. There are no tenets to save them. You will exact justice and crush their evil uprising for good."

He nodded, staring at the rain rushing inside the smashed wall.

"No mercy shall find them. No quarter given. This ends, Zophia. And it ends now."

I hugged his rigid frame. "Where do we start?"

Lia's Advisory Council was assembled in the conference room rotunda when I arrived at the Crystal Palace with our guests. The four of us rematerialized next to the ebony table, and the heads of the major races and the Celt guardians of the Queen all turned. The looks on their faces were priceless, but I suppose not everyone had met the Gypsy Queens before.

"Sorry we're late," I said, sending a smile to Lia poised in her high-back throne at the head of the table. "May I introduce you all to the Oracles of the Modern Realm: Clare Voyant, Amanda Playwith, and Cara Zmatic."

The three gave a Queen's wave and blew kisses to the men gathered as I gestured to them each in turn.

"Queens must stick together," Cara said. She winked at Lia and flipped her fuchsia ponytail behind her broad, muscled shoulders.

"Damn, girl," Amanda said, her gaze glued on Lia too. "Look at you, rocking the red suede."

Dressed in a red suede pantsuit and halter—obviously custom crafted for her by Iadon—and sporting silver armbands which matched the color of her hair perfectly, Lia both dazzled and commanded respect.

"Sexy regal, sweetie. Oooh and we brought you the perfect coronation gift to accent the look." Clare strutted around the table and held a long, rectangular box across her wide palms. "For a beautiful and powerful leader, with our congratulations."

"Gratitude." Lia accepted the gift and set the box on the table. She untied the plush, red velvet ribbon, lifted off the lid, and tunneled through the rainbow tissue. With a puzzled look, she extracted a silver riding crop. "Uh, this is very thoughtful. I appreciate—"

"Give it a whip, honey," Cara said.

"Like you mean it," Amanda added.

Lia gripped the leather handle and cracked the crop against the conference table. The snap echoed in the massive gold gilt dome arching high above. All three of the Queens burst into a round of clapping.

"And it's versatile," Amanda said, winking. "The perfect gift for work *and* after-hours play. Are you hitched, baby?"

Lia blushed to the tips of her gently pointed ears. "Samuel and I are recently mated, yes."

The three of them eyed Samuel seated to Lia's right and hauled him to his feet. Standing an easy six-and-a-half foot tall before they slipped on their stiletto, thigh-high boots, they towered over Lia's handsome groom. Cue the congratulatory hugs and man-handling all around.

Clare kissed his cheek and left an enormous lime lipstick smack on his face. Running a wandering hand down Samuel's white dress shirt, she purred. "Good catch, girlfriend."

Cara was more interested in his kilt. "All this broody, Celtic charm, wrapped up so nice. You've always been a delicious one, Sammie."

Samuel rolled his eyes and slapped the wandering hand away from his thigh.

"Sadly," Amanda said, batting her long, gold lashes toward Lia. "we wanted to make an Oracle Sammie out of him when he visited us in Toronto, but Reign killed our fun."

Reign scrubbed a hand over his smile and leaned back in his chair. "I've missed you too, ladies. Shall we resume the strategy meeting, now that you're here?"

Cara winked. "All work and no play makes for a lot of sexual frustration, Reign. How are you doing on that front anyway, big boy?"

Reign laughed. "Yeah, right. When have I ever allowed you to open that door."

"A girl can always hope."

The snap of leather to wood brought everyone's attention to the ebony throne at the head of the table. Lia giggled and used the crop to point to three of the Celts at the table. "Please offer your seats up to our guests, gentlemales."

The members of the Queen's Council didn't look happy to give up their places at the table but did as commanded.

"Now, why has Castian gathered us here this evening? You mentioned something about a Hell Hound?"

Mid-morning burned my tired eyes by the time I returned to Haven and received Aust's message. He had my mother and Hoola with him, staying in the Were guesthouse built in the clearing. Relieved, I threw my aching body to the breeze and materialized outside the massive cabin stronghold.

Gazing up at the façade as I rematerialized into corporeal form, I paused mid-step. The building stood a marvel of nature blending with architecture. Completed to the finest detail, the landscaping and lines merged with the forest surrounding so completely, it stole my breath.

"It's something, isn't it?" Kobi stepped off the covered porch. He pulled a pack of cigarettes from the pocket of his weapons vest and placed one between his black lips.

My heartrate quickened, the familiar flutter a side-effect I now associated with proximity to the demon. Was Aust right? Was that love?

"Look at this place. I was just here, and weeks of scheduled work remained until construction could be completed. Bruin was awaiting supplies and Mika worried they'd never make it in time for the arrival of the Were Primes. How did they ever get it finished so fast?"

"How do you think?" He exhaled a cloud of sweet-smelling smoke, and I blinked, connecting the logic.

"Castian wanted a place for my mother to feel comfortable while here at Haven."

"Brains and beauty."

"Is Bruin all right with that? He doesn't mind?"

Kobi shook his head. "No, of course not. Weres revere your

mother as much as any creatures of the animal world. He's honored to host her. And what's more, with the Were Primes arriving, she'll have an army of Alpha warriors to protect her if anyone is dumb enough to threaten her again."

Castian was always thinking. It made sense and made me feel much better about things.

"So, welcome, Lacy. Now you don't need to slum around with me at the Dens. Courtesy of the God of gods, you got an upgrade. It's good to have connections."

I fought not to roll my eyes. If, after the battles with Dane and Rheagan were over, I decided to remain in the Realm of the Fair, I would earn my stay. Castian couldn't pave my way using his divine intervention. "I'll speak to Bruin and make sure he doesn't mind me staying here with my mom. With his guests coming for the solstice and the coronation, he doesn't need to be worrying about us as well."

Kobi shrugged. "That's between you and him."

I stepped closer to take Kobi's hand, and he pulled back to extinguish his cigarette on the sole of his boot. I straightened and squeezed his arm. "I'm sorry I disappointed you. I need to sort things out. Are we okay?"

He glanced at the tree line and gave me an unconvincing nod. "Sure, we're good."

I looked him over, from the hard cut of his jaw to the rigid muscles beneath his vest. "You're wearing your Talon gear. Are you back on duty? Did Reign cool off?"

He scoffed. "Like you didn't do that. Is that why you chased after Castian—to do me a solid? Thanks, but no thanks. I've made it on my own for too long to expect favors."

I crossed my arms and met his glare. "Do *me* a favor and stop thinking you've got me figured out. You get it wrong, every damn time."

"I doubt that."

"For your information, Castian and I discussed what to do now that Rheagan possesses his wife's body. We're faced with not only her powers but the combined strength of Dane, Abaddon, and his army. Funny, with my dysfunctional family threatening the freedom of the realm, it never dawned on me to bring up my asshole boyfriend's current job status."

Kobi closed his eyes. "You're right. I am an asshole."

"That's what I said. Are you trying to push me away?"

Kobi's expression changed, and the sorrow was a shock. "Thanks for the boyfriend thing, but your mom wants you with Aust and, I gotta say, I see her point. The Highborne is a saint."

"My mother has diminished cognitive reasoning and doesn't dictate my choices. Is that what this is? Are you hurt that she sees me with Aust instead of you?"

Kobi pursed his lips and stared off over my shoulder. "No."

The lie permeated the air between us. The scent was acrid and burned my sinuses. I breathed it deep into my lungs and ran a gentle finger over the row of piercings across his brow.

This was my fault.

I left him raw and rattled by not returning his declaration of *maybe* love.

"Zophia," Aust said, rushing from the house. "Thank the Fates you returned. Come. Something is wrong with Shalana."

I ran, grabbing Aust's hand as he led me into the house and to my mother.

Shalana, Goddess of the Woodlands, Keeper of the Wilds—my mother —was dying. Immortal no longer. There was no doubt in my mind and no hope in my heart as I collapsed onto the bed next to her. Her energy was off, her skin covered in burns, and her eyes held none of the magic and wonder they always had.

"What's happened? Who did this to you?"

She lifted a shaky hand, and Aust guided her to stroke my hair. "My amazing child, my greatest strength."

The welts on her arms and neck made my stomach churn. Bruises oozed across torn skin as if a magical attack bombarded her. Through a wall of tears, I turned to Aust. "What happened to her?"

"I cannot say, *sweeting*. She grew quiet soon after you left and when we arrived here, I laid her down to rest. I checked on her through the morning, but these injuries simply appeared from nowhere moments ago."

"I'm so stupid," I cried, swiping at my cheek. "Her energy was off in the library and I didn't take the time to question it. She looked fine, but shielded her injuries until she couldn't hide them any longer. Why, Mother? We could have helped you."

"No," she said, struggling to sit up. "I have lived, loved, ruled my kingdom, and earned my fame. You never once complained about having me as your mother, but you deserved better—both then and now."

"Don't say that," I gasped. "You were the best. *Are* the best. Don't leave me now. Everything is such a mess. I need you."

She shook her head. "I will be within you e'ermore, my love, I promise. And if my last act of power is to deny your father something he covets, I leave you a happy woman indeed."

My father. Hatred boiled in me, hot and consuming. "He tried to take your powers."

She nodded. "To no avail. Now, both of you come here and hold my hand for a moment."

Aust sat on the opposite side of the bed. He looked as shaken and ill as I felt. We both gathered one of her hands in our own.

"You two are my future. My creatures and my lands are now in your care. Protect them and love them as I love you both. It may seem sudden, but I've known this day would come since I set those idols in the cave at Dragon's Peak millennia ago. Be good to one another."

Tears streamed down my cheeks. I tried to speak, but my voice wouldn't come.

She looked at Aust then and said something in Elvish. He nodded, his tears brimming. "Thy will be done, milady."

My mother smiled, laid back, and squeezed our hands. Her grip tightened, her fingers digging into my flesh.

"Ouch, Mom, that hurts." A jolt of power shot up my arm, and she squeezed harder still. I shook my head. Energy flooded into me like a shockwave breaking through a levy. "Mom, don't. Please don't."

I pulled at my hand. Her grip was unbelievable, her intent clear. I sobbed. "I don't want your powers, Mom. I want *you*. Don't leave me. Stay and fight."

Head reeling, body aching, my ears buzzed under the onslaught of Fae energy. It bombarded. I absorbed the warmth of my mother's gaze one last time . . . and blacked out.

Aust held one hand while Kobi held my other. A reverent group of Haven family and friends, forest animals, and Were Primes had gathered in the ancient ruins' clearing to bear witness to Shalana, Keeper of the Wilds', return to nature. Fire. Wind. Water. Earth. Flames from the pyre. Ashes on the breeze. Tears flowing. The earth, trees, and creatures mourning the loss of their mother.

My mother.

Blessed be.

Beyond the staggering ache in my chest, an unfamiliar strength held me upright. It steeled my bones, replacing the meaty marrow with reinforced resolve. It ignited the blood in my cells. It brought my future into focus like never before. In all the centuries of my life, I had never been so self-possessed.

My mother was within me, as she promised.

Fae ley lines coursed beneath my feet, resonating with her powers. They helped build and strengthen my resolve even as my mind buckled under the weight of sadness.

Dane. Rheagan. Abaddon. They would pay for what they'd done. Pay for what they intended to do. Pay for it all.

"Be at ease, Zophia." Castian squeezed my shoulder.

I blinked. My arms, raised to the stars above, sparked with energy. I commanded a powerful vortex encircling the clearing. The angry tempest of air awaited my command, hungry to be unleashed. Those standing in the eye of my storm watched with worried gazes. Jade and Galan. Lexi and Rowan. Mika and Bruin. Lia and Samuel. Aust and Kobi. Grandfather Hawk. Reign. Aust's Highborne family.

I lowered my arms. "My apologies."

Jade rose from the chair Galan had her sitting in. When he went to support her elbow, she slapped his hand away and rolled her eyes. "We get it, Zo. And we're with you in whatever comes next."

I hugged her. "Thank you. Now, should you be out here in your condition?"

"Twenty minutes, twice a day," she said with a sigh. "That's all the doctors allow me out of bed. Never mind the fact that I happened to be a recognized healer myself."

I hugged her again. Her emerald eyes, so comforting and so much like Castian's. "Then get back and lie down before I get you into trouble. I want to meet these kids but not until they are fully cooked."

She hugged me again. "If you need anything—anything at all—you know where to find me."

Castian took my hand and wrapped it around the inside of his elbow. "She does, *Mir*. Now do as your cousin suggested and take care of my grandbabies."

Castian gathered me to his side, and the two of us stared at the smoldering pyre. Kobi joined the Weres and Aust, and his wolves plodded over to the Highbornes. I drew an unsteady breath of pine air. "Aust looks as bad as I feel."

Castian squeezed my hand under his. "Shalana meant a great deal to the man. She was a formidable woman and a beloved strength in the Pantheon. There never was, nor ever will there be, another like her."

"I can't believe she's gone."

"As an immortal, it is only by her own choice that she could have succumbed to her injuries. You realize that, yes?"

I swallowed past the lump in my throat. "It hurts to think that she chose to leave me. I'd rather blame Dane or Rheagan for taking her."

Castian kissed the side of my head. "I don't believe that is the case. At least not directly. You are destined for great things. She saw it as well as I. In a way, she set you free to discover what your future holds."

"I never wanted to be free. I loved caring for her. She was a constant in my life, and as an immortal, I assumed she'd always be with me."

"And she will. I feel her powers within you."

Faolan brushed my thigh, and I stroked her ebony ears. Paladin jumped onto his back legs and licked my hand. He'd become the wolf's little black shadow, and I had no doubt Aust had instructed Faolan to care for the pup while he mourned the loss of his mother.

Poor pup. I knew exactly how he felt.

I blinked. Now that I thought about it—I did. I knew how he felt. Images and impressions of the pup's thoughts and feelings became a tangible communication between us. I knelt down, and Faolan rubbed her muzzle against my cheek.

"Thank you, girl. Yes, she was." I blinked up at Castian through a wall of tears. "I can hear them. The animals are speaking to me."

Castian helped me straighten and kissed my forehead. "You have your mother's powers—"

The earth rumbled beneath my feet, and for the second time that month, an explosion shook the ruin site. Something heavy hit my head. Knocked off balance, I raised my hands as a second attack hit. I fell to the ground, the forest around me spinning out of focus.

CHAPTER NINETEEN

Mika

*M*ika had covered both war-torn countries and natural disasters in her previous life as a journalist. The sheer mass of the devastation had always struck her hardest. She remembered wondering, how could a place go from being a calm and scenic, natural wonder one moment to a demolished warzone in the next? She now had her answer.

Standing at the smoldering pyre with Shalana's mourners, she stood amazed, once again, how quickly the Fates could turn the world upside down.

After something exploded close by in the forest, Bruin checked that she and her grandfather were all right and then retrieved his phone. Scowling, and with his turquoise eyes flashing the gold of his ascending bear, he raised it to his mouth. "All call, my location. Hostiles on the grounds."

In the seconds that followed, two dozen men Flashed to their location and another two dozen followed Kobi as the demon raced into the fray.

Reign called out to his men, looking murderous. "Julian, get the civilians into the guesthouse and get me intel. Everyone leave Castian to settle things with Rheagan and get his wife back. Bruin, back up Kobi and find Zophia. Samuel and Savage, you're on Abaddon. Kick his ass. Cowboy, secure the Academy and the castle, and then get to Jade's. You and Lexi guard her and our family. Chiron, take the Centaurs and lock down Jade's mansion. Keep them out of this. Dane is mine. For what he did to Jade and Abbey, he's got twenty years of payback coming. The rest of you, kill Scourge and get them the fuck off our mountain."

Everyone dispersed, dematerialized, and galloped off in different directions.

Aust nodded to Nightrunner. The pack alpha cocked his wide russet head, and his ears pulled back. "The wolves can pick up Zophia's trail, but magic confuses the scents. They'll need the Weres to help."

Bruin kissed Mika and pointed to the guesthouse. "Take Lia and the others, and lockdown." He turned to the Were leaders standing along the treeline. "Shift and follow. Let your animals loose. Tonight, we track, hunt, and kill."

Lexi

Lexi caught Jade under the elbow and waited until the mountain stopped rocking before letting her go. The explosion detonated back at the ruin site and, by the sounds of things, all hell had broken loose. The 'all call' pinged on her phone a moment later. "Take care of her, Doc. Shit's hitting. I gotta bounce."

Jade frowned and raised her fist for a bump. "Kick ass for me too. Wish I was coming."

She met her sister's knuckles and nodded. "You'll be back in the game soon enough, Blaze. Now get our men home and lockdown."

Rowan and Galan closed ranks, her hubby's gaze keen and worried. "Come back to me in one piece, Trouble. I mean it."

Lexi winked and blew him a kiss. "I expect a full-body examination later."

Hustling her way back the way they'd come, she hoped there would still be some fighting left for her— "Oh shit."

There was no shortage of workout partners tonight. In fact, the size of the attacking force was incredible. She stalled out for a second as she gauged the size of the incoming army.

Hundreds—possibly thousands—of Scourge poured onto the mountainside through magical portals. Well *allllrighty* then; Rheagan was making her big play for realm supremacy.

Getting her feet moving once again, Lexi raised her blades and headed into the thick of things. "Yeah, we'll fucking see about that, bitch."

Jade

Jade watched Lexi race toward the fight and hated the sinking feeling festering in her gut. Something wicked had come to their mountain, and she knew without a doubt that Rheagan and Abaddon were behind it. An attack like this put everyone and everything she loved at risk, and there wasn't a damn thing she could do to stop it.

"Blossom, please, we must needs get you to safety." She allowed herself to be swept along by the tide of Galan and Rowan.

She tried not to think about her family and friends facing the toughest fight of their lives, about the students in the castle being vulnerable, about how many would be injured and her unable to heal them while her powers were bound.

She winced as something let loose and warm liquid rushed down the inside of her legs. "Um . . . Rowan? I think I'm in trouble here."

Lexi's handsome hubby stopped and looked at the dark patch spreading down her pants. "Are you in any pain? Is this blood or your water breaking?"

"No ide—aughh!" She gripped Galan's arm as her vision phased in and out. Her body tightened and then eased, her back burning with fiery pain. "I think these kids have waited as long as they plan to."

"What?" Galan said, glancing around the forest. "Now? You cannot bear our young in the middle of a Scourge attack."

Jade laughed until another contraction took hold and her knees buckled. "Tell that to your children."

Galan scooped her to his chest and straightened, but the strain of carrying her was plain on his panicked face.

"I'm too heavy. If we move between contractions, I can wal—" She cried out as the gallop of hooves announced the arrival of the Centaurs. "Hey, D. A little help."

Chiron frowned at them and raised his arms. "Give her to me, Galan. She'll break your back."

"You . . . implying I'm fat . . . old man?"

"I imply nothing. You're bigger than my house."

Galan shifted her into the arms of her lifelong teacher and friend. When he stepped away, Galan's arms were smeared with her blood.

Jade wasn't sure if it was the sight of the blood or the loss of it, but a wave of dizzy spun her for a loop.

Rowan cursed. "Back to the mansion. Now."

Lia

Lia settled Grandfather Hawk onto a chair in the kitchen and peered out the window wall at the clearing beyond. The darkness of night was upon them, but her Elven sight gave her perfect vision. She searched for any sign of Samuel's signature blue bolts of magic but saw nothing. If her beloved mate was taking on Abaddon, she wanted to be there. To fight at his side. To stand up for the realm she was supposed to govern.

"Stand away from the door, Lia," Julian said, gesturing for her to join the others in the sitting area. "Keeping yourselves safe is the best way to help your husbands."

Being relegated to the background while the males faced all the danger rankled her but for now, she had no idea how she might be of aid. Haven was situated on a large mountain, the school and sanctuary only a small portion of the landscape. There were miles of wild forest, miles of rocky terrain, and many settlements and villages which fell outside of the safe zone of Castian and Reign's protection.

She had no idea where Samuel might be, and no means to find him.

"Well, this sucks," Mika said beside her.

Lia found that Bruin's mate had her arms crossed and was staring out at the darkness the same way she was. "Yes. It most certainly does."

"Up you get, Fate." Someone yanked on my arm and hiked me to my feet. The forest blurred and I swallowed against the bile burning my gorge. My legs trembled as I fought to regain my wits. Where was I? What was . . .

The fog of my blackout cleared, and it came back to me in a rush. I'd been cracked in the head. I pulled back on my arm, crying out as pain brought me to my knees.

Abaddon pulled me along in his wake, his long stride putting distance between my family and us. I twisted to search the brush for Castian. Was he all right? I didn't see him. I tried to open a mental channel to his mind, but my head was one giant fog.

"Kobi! Bruin!" I screamed, as the two broke through the trees where Castian and I had been attacked. Aust joined them, looking panicked. "Aust, I'm here!"

"They can't hear you," Abaddon said, sounding bored. "Can't see you either. I dropped a veil over us."

"What do you want? Where are you taking me?"

"It's family reunion time. I'm taking you to Daddy."

Dane. Perfect. Just the asshole I wanted to see.

I glanced back at the chaos. A flood of raiders had engaged with

Kobi and his group of Talon Enforcers.

My demon lover was in his glory. He lunged, spun, and cracked off insults, taunting his enemy while wielding fatal blows. Beyond the sarcasm, piercings, and Goth makeup, Kobi was passionate, fearless, and a massive pain in the ass.

But he was my pain in the ass.

And I loved him.

Aust was right about that, but he was wrong too. Because, when I saw him at one with the wolves and raptors of the forest, orchestrating a coordinated attack on the incoming forces, my heart filled with awe and wonder. I loved him too.

They were both amazing.

And as confusing as it was to love two men at the same time, it also made perfect sense. We worked well as a team of three.

Abaddon yanked me around a rock and I had to focus on my footing. I planted my feet each step as I regained my balance. My arm hurt. I didn't remember the injury but could have banged it when I was knocked out.

"If you're truly taking me to my father, you don't need to be so rough. I'm not resisting. I *want* to see him."

Abaddon's laughter rang rich in baritone and raised the hair on my arms. Magic. It rattled my bones, the strength alarming. Abaddon stole souls for power, everyone knew that, but this was more. The man possessed a gods-given power. Charisma. The magic of persuasion strung in his very vocal cords.

"The dysfunction of this family is amazing," he said.

"You have no idea."

He laughed harder. "No. *You* have no idea."

"You're delusional."

"And you're judgmental. As qualities go, it's unattractive. You'll never land yourself a husband if you don't learn to be more accepting."

I frowned. "Like I'd take advice from the maniacal blight on the realm."

"Ouch," he said, pushing me toward a thick wall of trees. "If I had any feelings, I think that would have stung."

Following a sheer, rock wall, Abaddon led me to a make-shift war camp set beneath a massive overhang. The stench of the Scourge hit about a hundred yards out, gaining in strength to the point of gagging as we grew close.

"I'll never understand it," I said. "Why do men of the realm give you their souls when they know what they'll literally rot from the inside out."

"Is this you *not* judging?" He paused; his dark eyes struck me with a familiar light I couldn't place. "You might say that I'm persuasive. Besides, it's not one-sided. For those years they decay, they experience every moment, rapt and wild. Every impulse of power and dominance they suppressed is unleashed. Without a soul to bog them down, they are raw strength and sensation, impassioned and fearless. It's a rush."

A rush? They were mindless murderers—

We rounded the rock face and crossed the threshold into the cave-like area beneath the overhang. My father straightened from the war table he bent over and smiled. "Look at you two. Fighting like spoiled siblings."

Movement from the opposite corner of the room drew my attention and faltered. "Zinnia? What are you doing here?"

My sister strode close, a cruel smile rounding her cheeks. "Why wouldn't I be here? Do you honestly think I'd choose Castian over our own father? The man is oblivious. He believes in those realm vermin. He's weak and pathetic—"

I kicked her. She fell to the stone floor, and I fought the urge to stomp her like a brushfire. "Call him pathetic again, bitch!"

Abaddon laughed.

Dane grabbed me and pulled me back. With both my arms gripped tight, he shook me. "What's gotten into you? Since when do you use brute force to express yourself?"

"Are you *fucking* kidding me?"

"You even sound like them. Has living in the mortal realm done this? You forget that royal blood runs in your veins."

I spat in his face and called every ounce of power I had. Nothing came. I flexed my fingers and willed my command of wind to come to me. The powers my Mother had given me.

Still nothing.

Abaddon laughed harder and held up his hands. "I put a binding collar on you. Daddy dearest thought he could use his charms to tame you, but I thought it best to cover our asses."

I raised my hands to the smooth metal of the collar around my neck. Yeah, despite his incessant whoring, Dane didn't have the slightest clue about women. "You kill my mother and think I'll see you as anything beyond the disgusting waste of life you are?"

He glared at me, wiping his jaw with his handkerchief. "Stop the drama. Shalana is immortal. Even as a half-wit, that bitch is as tough as—"

I threw a punch, but Abaddon caught my wrist and stopped me from connecting. "She's *dead*, asshole," I repeated, waiting for that to sink in. "Your evil little lapdog here probably even watched her pyre celebration."

Dane's head pivoted, looking genuinely confused.

Abaddon shrugged. "Yeah, there was a pyre burning. Can't say who played the part of the yule log."

Dane stepped back and sat on the edge of the desk. "Not possible. Castian is trying to keep her from me. He thinks I'll fall for his trick." A moment later, he straightened, looking pleased with himself. "Very convincing, Zophia. I almost believed you, but if your mother were truly dead, you would be an emotional heap. You are too soft for your own good."

"I don't care what you believe. You will suffer for it just the same." Him underestimating me worked in my favor. "Why am I here?"

"To draw back your mother, of course. Where you are, she will come. I will get what I want, and you will help me, whether you like it or not."

I couldn't believe his stupid arrogance. "Yeah, well, you'll be waiting a good long while . . . because she's dead."

"We'll see," Dane said, his smile as cocky as ever. "We'll just see about that."

CHAPTER TWENTY

Aust

*A*ust jolted back to consciousness hearing Kobi's voice nearby and Faolan's whine close to his ear. As he blinked, his wolf ran her warm tongue across his face. When she shifted, her bony elbows dug into his chest and fur brushed his neck and face. "Off you get, girl." He rolled to his side and touched the burn on his chest. "Fash not."

Kobi was upon them a moment later. "Aust, my man, no time to dwell. You okay?"

"Well enough."

"Good to hear," he said, wrapping an arm around his back and hauling him to his feet. "You caught quite a blast."

He had. His head was ringing, his equilibrium off kilter. "Whose magic hit me?"

"The bitch queen herself. Rheagan and Castian are throwing it down. You should be honored."

Kobi guided them behind the trunk of an ancient sequoia and pressed his shoulders against the bark. "Catch your breath, Highborne. I need you alive, or Zo will kill me herself."

Aust shook his head, but it did little to clear the ringing. Rheagan was a powerful sorcerous. "Castian needs Paladin."

"Hell Hounds devour malevolent souls. Rheagan's in the body of Jade's mom and Castian's wife. The pup can't chow down on one of our own."

Aust was about to explain when two raiders rounded the tree. Kobi spun, his dagger eviscerating one while the second raised his ax to strike. Aust grabbed the knife sheathed to his thigh and rammed it in the attacker's throat. "I agree, but mayhap the threat of the hound destroying her physical form might be enough to have her vacate the body."

Kobi grabbed him around the shoulders, and they tumbled as one in the scrub as a bolt of orange magic whizzed overhead. "I doubt a hound will bluff one of the Original Three. Keep thinking."

Kobi rolled off his chest and pulled him to his feet for the second time in five minutes. "So, just how bonded are you to Zo, now that you share Shalana's powers?"

Aust ducked as a blue bolt of magical energy zinged past his head. "Regardless of tangled emotions, I respect your love for her. You must know that."

Kobi frowned. "No, blondie. I'm asking if you can sense her? Are you connected? Can you track our girl?"

He assessed the carnage of the forest all around them and tried to grow calm. He closed his eyes and allowed the pull of Shalana's powers to ascend. The energy fought being fractured and wanted to reunite with its other half. "I can feel her, yes."

"Perfect. Then get a lock on her and let's go find our girl."

Tham

Tham found Gemma pacing along the glass wall at the Were guesthouse. The place still smelled of freshly-cut wood and new leather, and each chrome and granite surface gleamed, polished and new. Outside, the grounds bore the brunt of a very different reality. The ancient ruin site was once again a disaster zone, the bodies of the fallen strewn amongst pyre ashes and heaving ground. "It is a true war zone out there."

Gemma turned, and he was rewarded with a glowing smile and her running over to jump into his arms. He caught her and smiled as she linked her ankles behind his hips. Her lips claimed his with an urgency that implied they had been apart for weeks instead of two days.

A moment later, breathless and far more aroused than was polite given the state of events in their world, he eased back. "Are you well, love? Are our loved ones safe?"

She kissed him again quickly and let her feet drop back to the floor. "No idea. Galan and Jade headed home before the attack, so I assume they're good. Everyone else is out there in that mess."

"Tham," Lia said, joining them. "Welcome back. Did you have any luck?"

He winked and pulled Gemma to his side, unwilling to break the connection with her just yet. "Who needs luck, sister mine. I was born with mad skills."

"Yeah, you were," Gemma said, holding up her fist for a bump. "I missed those skills too."

Lia rolled her eyes at Gemma and flipped her silver braid behind her shoulder. "Tell me what I wish to hear."

He nodded. "You have your ghost army. Cameron has them gathered at the forest's edge dispersing the weapons Samuel enchanted for them."

"Wonderful," she said, heading toward the door. "Not a moment too soon."

"Lia, honey," Julian said, jogging out of the kitchen to meet her at the side door. "Where do you think you're going?"

"Out to command my army."

"You're supposed to stay inside where it's safe."

Tham gave his little sister credit. Lia had truly grown into a confident and powerful female. She slapped her palm with the silver crop the oracles had given her and met Julian's gaze. "When last I checked, *I* was Queen of the Realm and tasked with leading the ghost army to defeat Rheagan. I cannot fulfill that destiny tucked inside a fortress, no matter who wants me to remain here."

Tham chuckled, took Gemma's hand, and jogged through the closed door. When Lia joined him outside, he gestured toward the trees. "Your army awaits, my Queen."

Lia ran a hand down her suede pantsuit and waved her crop toward the forest. "After you, brother mine."

~

Galan

Galan was losing his mind. Before they had even gotten back to the manse, Jade went limp in Chiron's arms. Rowan's face had blanked out, and as quickly as they had gotten her to the clinic, and the Fae doctor to work, Galan feared it not fast enough. Pregnancy was dangerous for Highborne females under the best circumstances. These were not those.

The medical lights were brilliant over the exam table, the illumination harsh and white. Beneath the glare, Jade's warm, copper skin seemed ghostly pale. He had done this to her.

When she went into heat last August, part of him had wanted her to conceive—even knowing the risks.

What did that say about him?

Jade's body jerked, and then his beloved screamed. More than a scream, it was a blood-curdling shriek that clawed at his eardrums.

"Get them *out!* My powers are breaking free."

Elora handed Rowan a syringe and he plunged it into her arm before exchanging it for a scalpel. "Let the meds take hold, Jade. Just give it a sec—"

"No. Now!" She pinched her eyes closed, a groan ripping from deep in her throat. She twisted on the bed. Energy crackled through the air and sparks ignited from her fingertips. "I can't control it. I'll electrocute them."

Rowan cursed. His hand came down on her stomach, and a vivid red line appeared where he pierced her skin. The stream of blood trickled down the shuddering bulge of her belly and dripped onto the floor.

Jade jerked again, and her eyes lost focus.

Galan could hear her heart thumping unevenly, and his panic rose. *Stay with me, Blossom,* he said into her mind. *You promised me forever, Jade, and I expect you to keep your word.*

"Galan, I need you!" Rowan shouted. "Like we practiced, High-borne. Into the incubator and give me an APGAR score. Elora, get ready for the next one."

Galan accepted the first of his young—his son—and carried him quickly to the incubator. He stroked his fingers over the boy's dark auburn hair and gently pointed ears. He was perfect.

"Galan, APGAR. Ogle him later."

Yes. They had practiced this. Appearance. Pulse. Grimace. Activity. Respiration. "He is not crying and is slightly blue."

"Suction him and make sure his airway is clear."

Galan worked as quickly and carefully as he could. When the child sputtered and cried out, his heart beat once again.

"Good job. Now again."

Elora placed his daughter into the second incubator, and he raced to her. Her eyes were open and alert and she sneezed as he examined her. "Bless you, *sweeting.* You have the look of your *naneth.* Yes, you do. Stunning and strong."

Rowan hissed behind him, and Galan turned. Jade had hold of his wrist, her powers out of control. "Jade, no!"

Too late.

Rowan hit the floor, his body convulsing.

~

In all the centuries I'd known Castian as a god, leader, and uncle, I'd only heard of his lethal skills as a fighter. No legends spoken had prepared me for seeing him cut his way through a sea of Scourge. Captive in my father's military camp, I watched the fight in progress. Zinnia had brought her seeing bowl. She and Dane were glued to the images like sports fans during the last minutes of the playoff game.

Castian didn't waste time or energy on Abaddon's half-dead minions. He left the raiders to Maximus and his enforcers and battled one-on-one with Rheagan.

And while he'd given Abbey immortality after her attack all those years ago, I knew it was killing him to strike out against his wife. Even if she was his evil sister at the moment.

What an unbelievable mess.

Despite my father's smug belief that he had me under his thumb and my mother would come and surrender her powers in trade, I had the upper hand. Abaddon's collar might have held enough juice to subdue a Fate, but I was more than that.

I was my mother's daughter.

The nearer Aust drew to me, the stronger the force of her powers grew. And he wouldn't be alone. Kobi was with him. I knew that as keenly as if I were the Fate of Lives Present.

"Why do you look so pleased with yourself?" Dane asked. "You're betting on the losing team, Zophia."

"Am I?" I tapped my finger to Abaddon's binding collar, and the noose around my neck popped off and fell to the rocky ground. "I disagree."

Dane's gaze narrowed. "How'd you do that?"

I raised my arms and drew the power of nature into my cells, my command of wind now extending to every rock and plant and tree around me. The wind picked up my hair and lifted me from the ground. I tipped my head back and absorbed the electrical current from every atom and every molecule.

"I told you, Dane." My voice boomed in a thunderous rush. "You killed my mother. Shalana's power is mine now. Mine to wield. Mine to protect. And mine to exact revenge."

A surge of energy signaled his call to dematerialize.

I blocked his power and laughed as his eyes grew wide with realization. "You don't get to run away this time. Not when you haven't answered for my mother's injuries. First, there was the mental assault. You took her choice away and forced her to be somewhere she didn't want to be. How do you like feeling trapped and powerless?"

He tried again to leave, his scowl deepening when he got nowhere.

"Then there was the physical assault. I will never forgive the bruises. You ceased being my father the moment I saw what you did to her." I swept my hands through the air, lifting loose rocks and wood debris from the forest floor. With a swift sweep of my hand, I commanded nature to converge on him.

He groaned as projectiles pelted his flesh, but straightened. "Is this truly the woman you've become? A vengeful brat who throws a tantrum and abuses her position when things don't go her way?"

"My position? Do you mean as a Fate? No, you had that stripped from me. As a member of Fae Royalty? As a daughter? No, you took that too. What position do you mean, Dane?"

He wiped the blood from his nose and smiled. "You don't want to play rough with me, little girl."

"Who said she's playing, asshole?" Kobi said, sauntering around the corner like he owned the place. "Hey, Lacy. What you doin' up there, sexy girl?"

I released my hold on wind and lowered my feet to the ground. When I landed, I leaned my cheek over for him to kiss. "Just waiting for my white knights to arrive. What took you guys so long?"

Aust joined us, his chest raw with the welt of a magical burn. "Apologies, sweeting. It seems Haven is under siege."

I nodded. "Right. And it's time we take one of the key players off the board."

Dane laughed. "I take it you mean me?"

"You bet your lying, whoring, double-crossing, deadbeat dad ass she does." Kobi glanced at me and shrugged. "Too much, baby?"

I shook my head. "Nah. Just right."

Dane rolled his eyes. "Are you two done?"

"Almost. Where was I on my mother's injuries?" I raised my fingers as I counted them off. "Taking her choice. Physical assault. Oh, and number three, using brute force to extract her powers from her."

"And what does that mean?"

"It means, I've been thinking. Castian said my mother's powers were different but equivalent to his. He has more power than you, *soooo* by extension, with my mother's powers added to my own, I should be more powerful than you, right?"

"Brains and beauty," Kobi said.

Reign and Samuel jogged into the mix.

"Got yer back, Zo," Samuel said, holding out a strange silver disc. "If yer able, drain his power and deposit it in this. Castian and I spelled a few of these as vessels, just in case."

Dane frowned. Without his power to dematerialize, his cave hideaway suddenly became more like a dead end than an evil lair. "Bullshit. I'm a fucking Original."

Reign smiled, his knuckles popping as he clenched his fists. "In five minutes, all you'll be is a bleeding asshole."

Dane's attack came fast and hard.

Samuel blocked the energy surge and held the silver vessel in the palm of his free hand. "Have at it. See what yer made of."

Lia

Lia appointed Tham to lead one group of undead warriors and Cameron the other. She failed to realize how many displaced souls the Scourge had left within the Realm of the Fair. Never had she imagined her elven brother would return with hundreds of reinforcements—but he had. The clearing was filled and vibrating with anticipation. Verily, this was their opportunity to exact revenge and find some measure of peace.

"Be of care, friends," she said, as they readied to disperse.

A large barbarian with a battle-ax chuckled. "What's the worst they can do, kill us? Too late for that."

A wave of male agreement rolled across the group.

"Then go with my thanks," she said, waving as they headed off. "The Scourge has long been the end of too many good people. It is past time for their end."

"You okay, Lacy? Kobi asked, unscrewing the metal top and handing me his flask. He and Aust had escorted me out of Dane's camp after we'd removed my father's powers. Samuel left to rejoin the fight, and Reign remained behind with Dane for a little one-on-one justice.

I took a quick sip and smiled as I swallowed. "Your flask is filled with fruit punch?"

He winked and lifted a finger to his black lips. "Kool-Aid, actually. Mika makes it for the cubs, and I'm addicted. Don't tell though. I have an image of being an edgy, dangerous guy to uphold."

He helped me over a fallen log and pointed to the pathway ahead. Faolan jogged along beside us, Paladin jumping and nipping at her ears.

"Back to my question," Kobi said. "How you doin'?"

I drank more and then handed it back. "I'm fine. A little drained but fine."

"You did the right thing, *neelan*," Aust said, squeezing my arm. "Those who wield their strength to harm others abuse the privilege of possessing powers."

"I know. It still makes me sad—"

The crack of a tree splitting had the three of us ducking for cover. Samuel groaned and slid down the trunk into the brush. He sat up, rolled onto his knees, and signaled to Nash that he was all right. The native apprentice continued the magical battle. And while Abaddon fought the two wizards on the magical front, Savage went at him hard with his fists.

"He's too powerful," Samuel sputtered. "He's absorbed the power of so many souls, he's unstoppable."

"Catch your breath," I said, arms raised as I jogged over to join Nash.

Savage took a massive hit and tumbled end over end. His mind exploded with a bombardment of violent emotion. Images and flashes, a life remembered in a split second. Twins. Born with the gift of persuasion. Inseparable until one betrayed the other, mutilated him, brutalized him, and sold him into slavery.

I stared at Abaddon. "You *are* a monster."

Savage struggled for breath on the ground. Beneath the tattoos, the scars, and the leather, I searched for the young man from the past. The man who glared back at me was nothing but the merciless warrior he'd become.

"You brutalized him for power?"

Abaddon laughed. "I needed it to discover the identity of the man who seduced our mother, who gave us this gift. I wanted to know if there were more abilities and power to be had."

Savage struggled up to one knee, regaining his strength. He stumbled back to the ground and cursed in my mind. *He's distracting you. Fight him.*

I wasn't distracted. The images of my father in his memories shocked me, true, but also brought things into perfect clarity. "So, Dane finally got the sons he'd always wanted."

"Son," Abaddon corrected. "Our boy Savage, didn't want anything to do with a father who left us to rot. So, I didn't think he deserved the gifts the man gave us."

Savage straightened. *He's no father of mine.*

"Or mine," I said, coming to terms with the words, even as they hung in the air. "The two of you deserve each other."

Reaching out with my mind, I found Paladin's energy. Hell Hounds consumed malevolent souls, and Abaddon possessed more malevolent souls inside him than anyone in all the realms.

He's all yours, pup. Eat your fill.

Paladin's head canted to the side. Black velvet ears cocked a moment before he barreled down the path. On a run, the Hell Hound's fur-covered body exploded in height and mass.

On my count, I said into the minds of the Talon warriors, *drop your attack on Abaddon in three, two, one.*

Nash, Samuel, Savage, and I all stopped our strike of force as Paladin took Abaddon to the forest floor. The size of a small horse, he was as intimidating and fierce as his mother had been when we faced her. And there had been three of us.

I gagged as the hound tore Abaddon to shreds. Chunks of soulless sorcerer landed in heavy, wet heaps among the trees. The foul stench of rot contaminated the air and clung to the back of my throat.

Savage stared at the carnage as if he could hardly believe what he was seeing. I suppose if I were him, I'd be in shock too. It's tough when you dedicated yourself to one purpose for a lifetime, and then it's suddenly gone.

In a strange twist of fate, I'd lost one brother and gained another in the same moment.

Lia

Lia stared out at the field of battle. In every direction, Scourge Raiders were crumbling to the ground in rotting heaps. Her army of the dead straightened, looking confused. "Why are they dropping over?"

"Abaddon is dead, Luv," Samuel said.

She smiled at her husband jogging out of the trees to join them. "Are you sure?"

He nodded. "Aye, Luv, I watched him die myself. He'll not bother ye again, I swear it."

"And the raiders?"

"Abaddon held the dark contract of their lives. Without him, there's nothing to keep them alive."

That reality would take time to process. "And Rheagan?"

"Not sure. The others are converging on the battle between her and Castian. We'll know soon enough where we stand on that front."

Her husband took her in his arms and smiled. "Kiss me like ye missed me, *mo chridhe.*"

Samuel looked tired and smelled of sweat and blood, but she had never been more content in her life.

Abaddon was dead.

Lexi

Lexi took the stairs two at a time up to Jade's suite and burst in without knocking. "Chiron told me Jade collapsed and was bleeding. What happened? Where is she?"

Rowan caught her as she raced across the sitting room and staggered back. "Slow down, Trouble."

She gripped him by the elbows and ass-planted him on the chair. "What's wrong, Doc?"

He looked terrible—like he'd just been hit head-on by a Mack truck. "Nothing. Just got zapped by your sister during delivery. I'll be fine."

"Delivery? It's too early."

"Too late now. We've got two healthy babies and one mother who healed herself back to normal. She's in the shower, getting cleaned up. All is well."

She looked at the two incubators glowing gold against the wall. All is well? She exhaled a heavy breath. Jade's pregnancy had been a nightmare since the beginning but they'd all made it through. "Aww, they both have Jade's red hair. Oh, and look at their cute little ears."

Galan came out of the bathroom. He looked as battle-worn as any of the warriors on the Haven grounds.

"What's up, Highborne? You look like someone nailed you in the gem-pouch. S'all good, right? Boy. Girl. Mom."

Galan nodded and swept the burgundy mating braid behind his pointed ear. "I just told Jade the truth about the hawk and Rheagan taking possession of her mother's body."

She sighed. "I guess with the pregnancy over, there was no avoiding it. How'd she take it?"

"Too well." Galan stepped over to the little boy, bundled up and starting to fuss. "She nodded and thanked me for letting her know, then asked to be left to finish cleaning up."

That didn't sound like Jade. "I'll go check on her."

Leaving the hubbies to take care of the young, she slipped into Jade's marble mausoleum of a personal spa. "Hey Blaze, you decent?"

Nothing came back except the echo of her own voice.

After checking the shower, the walk-in closets, and the entire bathroom, she eyed the open window.

Yep. *That's* more like her sister.

"And I know exactly where you've gone, girlfriend."

Kobi, Aust, and I found Castian battling Rheagan, and two dozen *Aina Ohtar* warriors in the clearing beyond the marketplace. Unlike human fights, a battle between immortals could go on for days, or even weeks. The entire two-hundred-foot area glowed silver against the darkness of night. An iridescent sheen radiated off a privacy dome erected to keep the two of them and their destruction in, and everyone else out. Smart man.

"Can you hotwire us an entrance?" Jade asked, Flashing in beside me. "I'd like to weigh in on this."

I eyed my cousin, fresh from the shower and looking tired. "Weren't you pregnant two hours ago?"

"Babies born. Powers unbound. Raring to go. There, you're all caught up."

"Shit, Blaze," Kobi said, eyeing her up and down. "You look damn good for just dropping two kidlets. Shouldn't you be home so that they can suck on your boob or something?"

I punched him in the gut. "Don't be an ass."

Jade waved his words away. "Back to getting us inside the dome. Can you?"

Lexi Flashed in beside us. "Hey, guys. What did I miss?"

"We were discussing Jade's breasts," Kobi answered.

Lexi rolled her eyes and checked out the battle in progress. "Twenty against one is rude. Zo, get us inside this giant bubble to even the odds. Rheagan and I have unfinished business."

Jade frowned. "That's my mom. You can't kill her."

"And she cannot be allowed to escape," Aust said. "Castian has contained her with deliberate purpose."

My mind spun with the random, rapid chatter of my Haven family. I thought about the issue at hand. "I'm sure I can open a small door, but Aust's right, we'll have to be quick. Kobi, you go in first in your demon mist. Block any attempt she makes for the opening. The rest of you, be ready. And keep Paladin out. I don't want him attacking Aunt Abbey."

Kobi nodded and dissolved into a swirl of black mist.

I touched the wall of the dome and let the energy tingle up my arm. My uncle's power was like my mother's but powerful in different ways. I matched his energy signature and created our opening. A heartbeat later, we were inside.

Castian cursed as we breached the dome. It echoed in my head at the same time it boomed in the air all around us.

"Close the door, Zo," Lexi said.

"I'm trying." I worked feverishly, trying to reseal the seam.

"Heads up," Jade said, pushing further into the dome. "She knows there's an out, and she's coming."

Kobi swooped away and assumed the form of his demon dragon. Catching Rheagan mid-air, he flew her up toward the concave peak.

Rheagan stiffened, arms raised. In a voice nothing like my aunt's, she started spellcasting, emitting a dark field of magic.

Work fast, Lacy. This is . . . unpleasant.

Chaos broke out around me, and I focused on the rift.

"Let me be of aid." Aust linked our fingers and squeezed my trembling hand. "Allow Shalana's powers to unite."

Aust's calming strength and the uniting of my mother's power was all I needed. The seam sealed before my eyes and the dome was once again whole. "Done. Put her down, Kobi."

But he didn't.

The dragon's path in the air became erratic as his head thrashed back and forth. "What's happening?" I said, heart pounding. "What's she doing to him?"

"Nothing pleasant," Lexi said. "How do we stop her?"

"I'll get Kobi away from her." I retrieved the metal disc Samuel had given me for Rheagan and raced across the clearing to my uncle.

"Here," I said, shoving the enchanted amulet into his hand. "While she's distracted, drain her powers and trap her in this."

Castian threw out his arm to stop me, but my feet were already ten feet off the ground. Wind swirled beneath me like a cyclone, and I pushed myself up and up farther still. Kobi's shrill wail tore at my insides. For a moment, I considered whether his life was worth saving Abbey's body.

Kobi was tough. He'd proven that more than once.

I didn't have any rescue plan in mind as I catapulted myself straight at the mid-air struggle. I collided unseen and gripped Rheagan around the waist. Yanking her away from my demon love, I directed us across the clearing so Castian could get a clear shot at his sister.

Tumbling through empty air, we plummeted before wind buffeted our descent. The hours of battling Castian had likely weakened her, but she was in no way weak.

Dark magic edged inside me like a toxic wave. "You must be Shalana's daughter," she said, grabbing a fistful of my hair and yanking my head back. "You have her powers. It seems your father underestimated you."

I grunted, resisting the intrusion of evil burning my skin. "And overestimated you."

Zo, Castian said into my mind. *You need to get away from her. I won't risk the spell draining your powers too.*

Easier said than done.

I pushed on her chin, forcing distance between us. My controlled descent was less controlled than I hoped. Rheagan's dark energy soured in my stomach, and though I could defend myself with physical force and magical abilities, I didn't want to hurt Abbey's body.

She's immortal, Castian said. *Get away from her.*

Rheagan uttered something unintelligible, and I was blown backward like I'd been electrocuted. The thud of my head to the wall of the dome sent black spots into my vision.

Aust was there in a heartbeat to help me up. "Are you well, *neelan?*"

"Well enough," I said, straightening and forcing my legs to hold me.

"Watch out." Aust grabbed me and rolled, shielding me from a bolt of flame as we dropped to the grassy battleground.

I blinked up at my cousin. She and Lexi were completely letting loose on Rheagan's warrior followers. "Jade's on fire."

"Literally and metaphorically," Aust said.

He helped me up a second time, and we jogged over to help Castian. My uncle looked ill and worn.

"This is taking too long," I said, raising my palms and calling on my mother's strength.

"As with Dane, so it shall be—" Aust staggered, hitting the ground with one knee.

Locked in with Castian's fight, I pushed harder and doubled my efforts. Draining Rheagan would stop Aust's suffering. "Hang in there. It's almost over."

Aust twisted on the ground, and a moment later, a massive ghost tiger stood in his place. The piercing, ice-blue eyes of the beast were Aust's without a doubt. I reached out with my newfound gift and felt his suffering.

He wasn't a Fae immortal. Rheagan's attack was painful and disorienting for him. She was twisting his thoughts, making Castian and I the enemy. He dropped his broad, striped head, and bared his canines.

The growl that tore from his throat sent chills up my spine.

"Easy, Highborne. You don't want to hurt us. Castian and I are your friends."

"Don't trust him," Castian said beside me. "He's not Aust right now, Zo. She's got control of him."

I dropped my hands and watched the beast prowl closer. "No. He's Aust. He's in there . . . aren't you?"

Castian grunted. Without my help, he was having a harder time shutting Rheagan down. It didn't matter. Aust was my primary concern. I eased down on my knees and reached into his mind. *You know me, Aust. You and I are connected.*

He growled again, his eyes hard and cold. A foot in front of me, he opened his mouth, panting to take in my scent.

Fight her. Even before Shalana's death, we were bonded. You, me, and Kobi. Somewhere in the back of my mind, I wondered where Kobi was.

Was he hurt? Was he battling Rheagan's henchmen?

My distraction lasted only a split-second. The moment I started to turn my head, the white tiger lunged. I screamed, raising my hands as a 500-pound jungle cat attacked.

Except, he didn't attack me.

With my heart hammering inside my chest, I raised my hands and rejoined my uncle. Aust had taken Rheagan by surprise and brought her to the ground.

"That's it, son," Castian said, a triumphant grin spreading across his face. "Hold her there . . . for just . . . two more . . . seconds." He dropped to his knees beside the tiger and his sister; his fingers gripped around the metal disc. "Your magical abilities are drained. All you are, and ever will be, is immortal. If I could take that too, I would. You have one chance to survive this, Rheagan. Get out of my wife's body and stay out of our lives for good."

"What if I like this body."

"I'll not have you in my wife's body. I'd rather she be laid to rest." Castian flicked his fingers, and the dome disappeared. He placed two fingers in his mouth and let off a shrill whistle. "The Hell Hound is coming, dear sister. And the pup will tear this body to shreds and devour your soul. You've lost."

I straightened, and Paladin was, indeed, barreling toward us. Growing in size and mass as he galloped closer, the pup's eyes locked on his malevolent prey.

"Get out, or you'll be dead in five, four, three—

The moment Rheagan vacated her vessel, Abbey's body went lax. In the same instant, Abbey and Castian vanished. I knelt on the ground and gathered a confused Paladin into my lap. Without the tainted soul to trigger his demon side, he was instantly a silky, black pup once again.

"Where are they?" Jade said, running over.

"Alone together somewhere. My guess is reuniting your mother with the hawk."

"But she's alive? And Rheagan's gone?"

I nodded. "I'd never say forever with an immortal, but for now, yes, she's powerless and gone."

Aust pushed against my shoulder, and I buried my fingers into the depth of his long, white coat. The moonlight overhead had long ago drained the color out of the clearing and left the world bleached. His coat glowed a beautiful shimmering silver.

"Noble the child of argenteous mane."

Jade's eyes widened as the last line of the prophecy fell into place. She smiled and kissed his wide nose. "Well done, Aust. It's no surprise that you saved the day. Those of us who know you, have never doubted that you are a true male of worth."

Aust shape shimmered and morphed back to the sleek and sexy man I'd grown to not only respect but love. "Gratitude, Jade. I love you as well, but this was very much a group effort."

It was. I glanced around the clearing for Kobi.

There were dozens of bodies on the ground, all dark and unrecognizable in the shadows and at a distance. "Where did he fall when I took Rheagan off him?"

Aust shrugged and took my hand. Together, we jogged around the clearing, checking bodies, searching.

"Kobi?" I called, my anxiety notching up with every dead warrior we found. "Kobi, where are you?"

"He's not here?" Lexi said.

"Where did he go?"

CHAPTER TWENTY-ONE

"*H*e wouldn't leave us in the middle of a battle. Something is wrong." I followed Aust as he used his Elven skills to track Kobi through the forest. His absolute ease in nature never ceased to amaze me.

"His scent is off," he said. He held my elbow as I climbed over a downed tree. "I fear Rheagan's dark energy infected him somehow."

"Then why leave?" I jogged to keep up, his pace increasing with each step. Faolan and Paladin got more excited the faster we moved, bounding along beside us. "If he's hurt, he knows we'll heal him."

"I hope he knows. He was deeply hurt in the library."

"I couldn't say I loved him when I wasn't sure."

"And I forced him to admit something the two of you should have handled in your own time."

I shook my head. "That wasn't your fault."

"The outcome weighs on me regardless."

A warm wind whistled past me as we emerged into a forest clearing. Nestled, hidden against a wall of overgrown shrubs and trees sat a weathered, wooden clubhouse. Moonlight highlighted the front wall of the little shack, and the chipped message scrawled in faded and dripping, lime-green paint. "Shitstorm Survivors: Come in peace or leave in pieces."

"Inside," Aust said, exhaling. "He suffers."

Swallowing, I stepped softly to the door. "Knock-knock. Want some company in there?"

"If I did, why haul my ass to butt-fuck-nowhere?"

Testy, but he had a point. "Why leave the battle at all? That's not like you."

His laughter came out in a harsh hiss. "You only *think* you know me. You don't. The man you know is an illusion."

I rolled my eyes at the disdain in his voice and pulled the rusted handle. The door creaked, and something shuffled in the shadows within. "What's going on with you? I'll heal you if you're hurt. If it's worse than that, Aust's here too."

He groaned and shifted again. "*Go.* Don't you get it? I don't want either of you here."

"Why?" I inched my way inside. Even with heightened night vision, I had to navigate with my arms outstretched. "Aust can smell your suffering. Let us help."

"I'm not a fucking fixer-upper. I'll take care of myself."

"That's not nearly as fun." I hoped I could break through whatever foul temper had taken him hostage. My foot bumped his leg, and I waited for my eyes to adjust. "I've heard sex after a battle is a great way to work off adrenaline."

"I'm not a charity case either. Just go."

"If you think ordering me away will work, you don't know *me* very well. Guess that's what we get for falling hard and fast. There are lots of things to learn about each other."

"Now you're patronizing me? We both know I was the idiot who caught a case of the feels. You shot me down."

"No, I didn't."

He shifted in the corner and hissed again. "Whatevs."

I clenched my fists and tried to remember that he was hurt. "Not *whatevs.* I wasn't ready to put a name on my feelings, but after the past few days, I've thought a lot about it. I *do* love you. Though, at the moment, I'm wondering why. You can be a real ass, you know that?"

"It belches up from the demon gene cesspool. Get over it."

I followed his leg up to his hip and eased onto the dirt floor beside him. "Stop being a dick. I said that I love you."

"Bullshit. That's sex talking."

"And that's insecurity talking. What the *hell* did Rheagan do to you? Where's my cocky demon with the massive ego?"

I expected him to say something like, 'Thank you for using cock and massive in the same sentence,' but it never came. I shifted closer until our hips touched and followed his arm up to his jaw. His head was lax and flopped to the side, hanging heavy from his shoulders.

Cupping his face in my hands, I lifted his head and felt rough, scaled skin. Contact with Rheagan's rancid magic was hard for me; I couldn't imagine what it was like for a demon.

"Kobi? Are you with me here?" He didn't rouse in any way. "*Aust?* I think we have a problem. Help me get him outside."

Aust rushed in and carried Kobi to the grass of the clearing. Clouds blocked the direct light of the moon, but even the dim glow from above was enough to reveal that Kobi was no longer able to hide his demon side.

"What has she done to him?" Aust asked, kneeling beside him. He stroked a finger along the plated skin of his jaw.

"It's his true self," I said, unbuttoning my pants. "If we see it, he's in more trouble than I thought."

Aust pulled Kobi into his arms and brought their mouths inches apart. "Take from me what is freely offered. Heal and be strong, warrior."

As Aust kissed Kobi, it struck me, once again, how right the three of us were. The misfit toys, as Lexi put it. Each of us searching for acceptance and family and love.

"I love you, Aust." The words came without thought or hesitation. "I know it's too soon after Bree for you, but you should know, it's not just Kobi I fell for. I love you *both*. And it's not that you each have half of my heart, it's this glowing warmth of the three of us swirled together and blended most amazingly."

Aust

Aust glanced up at Zophia, his thoughts and emotions tumbling in his head. He had known she cared for him. Their connection had grown, first in the caring for Shalana, and then in the sharing of her powerful energy. He never expected her love. And she gave it so freely. Without reservation. He began to form the words of his reply when Kobi regained consciousness.

"Fuck. Don't look at me." He pressed his palms against Aust's shoulders and turned his head. "I don't want this."

"Too bad," Zophia said. We're saving you, despite yourself. And you're ruining a beautiful moment, by the way. I was saying how much I love you both."

Kobi cursed and covered his face with his arm. "You're delusional."

"No. I'm not. Kobi, look at me."

A groan broke free from his chest. It sounded like a mixture of desperation and dark plea. The tension of indecision grew, but finally, his eyes opened and met her gaze.

Kobi's eyes had glowed scarlet before, had held the orange flames dancing in their depths, but never had Aust seen the vulnerability that his true demon face brought out in him.

"No matter what you think happens next," Zophia said, "I won't run away screaming."

"We'll see."

"No, *you'll* see," she insisted. "I don't judge you for what you were born. I accept you as I always have."

"I do as well." Aust felt the heat of a blush coloring his fair skin, but kept his gaze locked on Kobi. "We are an unexpected union of mirrored souls, and whether you possess the Goth beauty of a human, the magical state of your dragon, or the fierce visage of a demon, you remain the same male to me."

Kobi swiped rough fingers across his eyes and swallowed. "You're both crazy. I don't know how to deal with this."

"Verily, truth is not to be dealt with. It is fact. Despite your acerbic demeanor, you are loved."

Zophia knelt beside them and pulled her shirt over her head. Aust watched her chestnut hair fall back into place. It rained down the column of her neck and brushed the smooth skin of her bare shoulders. Wearing just her underthings, kneeling before them, and bathed in the light of the summer moon, she truly stole the breath from his lungs.

She took Kobi's hand and ran a gentle thumb over his demon skin. "Whether you believe us right now, or not, it's an implicit, unreserved, unconditional, absolute, wholehearted kind of love."

Aust eyed the iridescent rounds of her breasts, and his blush crept to the points of his ears. Those lace underthings stoked hunger deep within him. He forced his focus back to Kobi. "Let the humiliation and anger go and trust me to heal you. Now and e'ermore."

"Evermore?" she asked, a whisper of emotion catching on the word. "What are you saying?"

Dizzy with fear of speaking his mind, he bit his bottom lip and pulled in a deep breath. "Kobi commented once about me joining your pairing. If that invitation remains open, I wish to accept. I, uh . . . I wish to lay with you both and make it official—for only as long as the joining remains beneficial for each of us," he clarified.

"But Highbornes are bound for life."

"I do not expect to bind you two to Highborne laws."

The smile on Zophia's face had his heart rate quickening. "Well, that works for me."

Kobi smirked. "Works for me too."

Thank the gods. Aust fought the urge to explode forward and take what he needed. The pressure in his cock was a mixture of pleasure and pain, the two merging as they fired in his blood and ignited in his cells.

Gods, he wanted this.

It was no surprise that Kobi initiated things. "Zophia, you get our boy warmed up, and I'll enjoy the show. With any luck, I'll heal back to myself, simply by stroking off to the sight of the two of you."

"I can do that." Zophia stood and held out her hand.

Aust rose and stepped before her without hesitation.

She loosened the tie of his tunic and swept a soothing hand over the magical burn he suffered earlier. As her palm brushed his chest and the ribbing of his abdominals, his flesh tingled beneath her healing touch. When the damage was no more, she eased her hands over his shoulders and dropped his tunic.

Another graceful sweep of her hand brought a gossamer tent to the clearing, anchored within by a round bedding platform. The sudden appearance of opulent accommodations reminded him of the campsite Castian had erected each night in those first days of their *Ambar Lenn*.

"Your first time should be everything you've hoped for," Zophia said, trailing a suggestive finger down the ridges of his chest. "Any requests? Whatever your heart or body desires. Tonight's about you."

About him? Had anyone other than his parents and Mika ever focused solely on him? He lifted his hand, and after she gave him a nod, he tested the weight of her lacy breast in his palm. The throb in his cock grew even more demanding.

"Tonight, you two may guide me. You have experienced more than I have dreamed. No matter what passes between us, I shall be in ecstasy."

"Done deal," Kobi said, his voice a husky growl. "Lacy, untie the man's laces. Let's get this Three-way started."

Zophia glanced down at his groin and coaxed the ties of his pants loose. "I'm surprised these Elven leathers haven't split already. You must be very uncomfortable."

He was. He'd been aroused many times before but never to this extent. Knowing that they wanted him—knowing it was going to happen for them—he almost couldn't bear it. His cock twitched as his excitement raised another level.

"Breathe, Highborne," Kobi said, lounging back on one hand while he stroked himself root to tip with the other. "S'all good. We're going to take good care of you."

Aust exhaled, his blood throbbing in his temples.

"Look at me, Aust," Zophia said. "Is this nerves, or second thoughts?"

"Nerves," he said, his breath coming out more in pants than voice. "I swear, I want this. I am simply out of my depths."

She took his trembling hand and squeezed. "Then there's nothing to worry about. We'll take this one inch at a time."

"Yeah, we will," Kobi said, sexual innuendo dripping in his voice. "I bet you want Zo naked, don't you, Highborne? You want to trace her silky skin with your fingers and then your lips. Am I right?"

Aust swallowed. Unable to speak, instead, he nodded.

"Thought so. Okay, lesson one, slide a gentle hand across her collarbone and under her hair. Bring her against your chest and kiss her."

Aust did as he was told and found that following Kobi's instructions allowed everything else to fall away. The pressure of decision was gone, and in its absence, he was able to simply absorb the sensations. His body shuddered as their mouths met.

Zophia's lips were softer and less aggressive than Bree's. Despite the perfection of the moment, insecurity reared inside him. Bree had never been truly content with the male he was. He had tried long and hard to convince her, yet still, she failed to see him for who he was to his depths.

Zophia eased back. "Everything all right?"

He nodded and forced his pain back into its box. This moment was about them. Just the three of them.

"Now," Kobi continued. "wrap your arms around her and unhook that lacy bra. Let the girls out. Toss it to me . . . yeah, that's right."

He tossed the bra to Kobi and splayed his hands across her back. Gods. Her skin was soft as velvet, and as iridescent as the most precious pearl. One hand slid up to pull her closer; the other dropped to the edge of her panties.

"There you go," Kobi said, his voice less demon and more himself. "Now slide that hand under the lace and feel her ass. Zo has an incredible ass."

As his fingers slid into her underwear, Zophia brought her own down the back of his unlaced pants. His cock jerked hard, and she ground her belly against it. He groaned into their kiss and wondered if males ever passed out from being too aroused.

Breaking their sweeping connection of lips and tongues, she glanced up at him. Thankfully, seemed as breathless as he. "You have a great ass too. I've always thought so. In fact, all the women of Haven think so."

She shifted her hold and with both hands, pushed his leathers down his thighs until they dropped at his feet. The touch of the summer breeze across his heated flesh was erotic, and he worried he might well climax before they truly started.

"And after tonight," she said, a stunning grin spreading across her divine features, "this fine ass is mine."

"Ours," Kobi said, stepping against his back. Naked and once again his dark and beautiful human self, Kobi reached around them and linked them in an embrace. "One Highborne bonding coming up."

In a lifetime of watching encounters of all kinds from my station, I'd seen everything. The good, the bad, the joyous, and the heartbreaking. I'd never seen anything more sensually seductive or romantically rousing than Aust and Kobi getting familiar with each other, the strength of their bodies as they rubbed against each other, the glistening of their skin under the late June moon, the scent of sweat and sex.

The mingling of our three scents was an aphrodisiac which burned my heated core even hotter. I was so damp, I couldn't imagine how wet I'd be if one of them reached between my legs and ran their fingers across my—

"Are we neglecting you, Lacy?" Kobi asked, catching my wrist as I was about to touch myself. "Aust, our lady love needs some attention. You should have the honors. Zo, would you like kisses or touch?"

"Kisses." I laid back on the plush mattress of the platform bed and dropped my knees open wider to make room for him. "Watching you two has me wound. I won't take long."

"Take as long as you like, *neelan*." Aust settled between my legs and met my gaze from below. "You honor me with the use of your body. I shall cherish every touch."

"A girl could get used to that smooth and sultry talk."

"Then get used to it," he said, nuzzling the inside of my thigh. "It is a great honor for a Highborne to pleasure a woman. I intend to pleasure you thoroughly . . . and honor you often."

Yes, please. Aust dropped his head, and my back arched off the ground. I groaned, and my eyes rolled shut.

"So, fucking hot." Kobi crawled over me and suckled one nipple before moving over to the second. "Learn your way around, Aust. Zo's not shy, and she's not quiet. You can figure out what's working pretty easily."

"Bastard." I pinched his nipple ring, and he laughed.

His eyes flashed scarlet, and he trapped the tight bud of my nipple between his teeth. I cried out, afraid he might bite. "You win. Behave. Let me focus on what Aust's doing."

Aust's laughter tickled, his breath warm between my legs.

Every brush of their lips was a fantasy come true. The hard, strong man of battle. The brave, sweet man of nature.

And they were mine. Both mine.

"Do you feel how she's tensing, Aust? Finger her."

Aust shifted his weight to one shoulder and dragged two fingers through the damp mess they'd made at my core. Slicked and strong, he eased inside.

It took only the slightest pressure to make me seize up. A cry ripped from my chest as waves of pleasure crashed through me. Aust gripped my hips with a growl, lapping at me like he needed to consume every ounce he could.

"That's it," Kobi said, his voice a breathy whisper. "Ease back a bit and let her ride it out. Tease out her shudders. Fuck, I'm losing it just watching."

The slap of skin on skin preceded Kobi arching back and him coming with a shout. His hand gripped hard, his punishing pace shooting creamy jets out and over his hand. I watched his chest pump as he rode out the aftershocks and slowed his rhythm.

"Well, that's new," he said, breathing heavily. "Not like me to go off early, but holy fuck. Aust, you have to get inside her. You must be dying."

"Aching, yes," Aust said, tension noticeable in his voice. "But not dying."

I pulled his shoulders, and he crawled up my body. Reaching between us, I notched his erection where he needed to be. "Then let's take care of that. Are you still sure this is what you want—that we're *who* you want for a lifetime?"

His answer was a thrust and a groan as he mated me.

Aust pressed inside me and stilled, eyes closed, jaw tight. The look on his face burned straight into my heart—erotic yet vulnerable. As he began the sway of his hips, his rhythm was cautious, tentative.

I laid back and brushed his golden waves back from his face while I etched the moment into my memory—the image of him, sweat beading on his brow—the look in Kobi's eyes as he knelt behind him, watching the two of us—the feeling of security settling over me for the first time.

Highbornes mated for life. Despite Aust's offer for us not to feel obligated by the laws of his race, I wasn't about to back out on that. "For life," I whispered.

"For life," they both repeated.

CHAPTER TWENTY-TWO

*D*awn came all too soon. The gossamer draping of our mating platform swayed in the breeze as the gray of morning began to warm to gold. When I woke, Faolan sat next to the bed, her head on the sheets as she watched me sleep.

"Were you told to watch over me?"

Her tail thumped on the grass of the clearing.

"And where are our men this morning?"

The stunning wolf stood and turned toward the trees. Gathering Aust's suede tunic from the ground as I walked, I swung it over my shoulders and followed. Bending my head from shoulder to shoulder, I stretched out some of the kinks brought on by an active night. And though I was a little stiff and sore, I had never felt so gloriously content.

"Quite an evening," Castian said, appearing out of the bergamot scented mist unique to him.

I tied Aust's tunic it at my hip and pulled my hair free. There was no hiding the flush of my cheeks. Privacy was something no member of the Fae Pantheon took as a given. At any point in time, there was certainly someone watching what you were doing. "The battle, or what came after?"

Castian shrugged and swept his hand. A breakfast buffet table appeared by Jade's childhood clubhouse. I poured two large butter-caramel coffees—milk in mine, black for him. I handed his over and picked out a berry pastry. "How's Abbey?"

Now it was he who blushed. "Well and whole. It will take time for her to adjust to realm life, but she is with us once again, and that is all that matters."

"Agreed. Has she been to see Jade and the twins?"

He shook his head. "I'm taking her in a few hours, once she's had a chance to get her bearings. Residual effects of Rheagan's possession still linger. She wants to be wholly herself when she sees them."

He sipped his coffee, and I smiled. He had the same look of a man well-sated that I'd seen worn on two other faces this morning. "I'm happy for you, Uncle. I'm happy for all of us."

He nodded. "The both of them, eh?"

"I know it's likely not what you expected for me—"

"In truth, it is exactly as I expected. Abbey foresaw it almost two decades ago. The trick was getting Kobi free of Hell and on the path for him to be worthy of you. And keeping his demon enemies from finding him."

I blinked up at the sparkle in his emerald eyes and remembered the warding in the hawk tattoo on Kobi's shoulder. "I wondered why a demon was one of your Talon Enforcers. You knew all along?"

"I knew of the possibility. Fates versus free will, right? Any of the three of you could have decided to take a different path. I'm only glad it worked out. They each are loyal, strong males."

I chewed on my pastry and thought about something Kobi said a week or two ago. "Did you cockblock the men in my life—make it so this path stayed open to me?"

Castian sipped his coffee a little too long, and I had my answer. I thought about how unlucky I'd been in love.

"Well, I suppose I can't be angry with you. The ends justify the means, right?"

"That's what they say."

"And what of Dane and Rheagan?"

"With their powers drained, I doubt they'll cause much trouble. Your sisters are beside themselves though. I'm letting Zora and Zana stew in the worry that you and I have had enough and can take their powers if we so choose."

I laughed. "Looks good on them. What about Zinnia and Savage?"

"Zinnia will surface, I'm sure. It'll do her well to be lost and hated within the realm for a while. A little taste of what she put you through, I think. And Savage is well enough. With his brother taken care of, he'll take a leave of absence. I hope he finds some happiness in his own life. He deserves it."

I agreed. "I hope he comes back, though. I'd like to get to know him."

Castian tipped back his coffee and set the empty mug on the table. "He'll be back. Savage is a Talon Enforcer in every fiber of his being. Before too long, he'll be back."

"I'm sad Mom didn't get to see how it all ended."

Castian pulled me against his chest and kissed the top of my head. "She'd be thrilled you're finding your own way. She never once doubted that you would rise to be revered in the realms. I think it was solely her love for you that kept her tethered to this world at all, in the end."

"I'll miss her forever."

Castian squeezed me tighter. "I will too, Zozo."

By the time Kobi and Aust sauntered out of the trees, I'd pulled myself back together and was ready to face my men. Both of them had damp hair and a mischievous look that said they'd been off forming their own bond while I slept.

"If you were going skinny-dipping, you should have woken me up," I said, kissing each of them as they came to see the wedding feast Castian left us. "Or was I not invited?"

Aust tasted like berries and sunshine, a mouth-watering combination. "We thought we wore you out last night and wanted to allow you some rest from your insatiable males."

Kobi came up behind me, and I became the creamy middle of the misfit Oreo. He moved my hair away from my neck and, tugging Aust's tunic out of his way, trailed a kiss to my shoulder. "If you're going to bathe, might as well make it worth the effort. Aust, take her back to bed and strip her naked, will you? I've got an idea."

Aust's eyes were brighter than usual, and that was saying something. They were also lit with wild excitement, maybe even a touch of naughty. I knew, after multiple shared orgasms, how turned on he got when Kobi went all dominant lover on us. "*Neelan?* Are you game to see what is in store?"

I gave him my hand, and he led me back to the bedding platform. Standing toe to toe, he reached for my hip and tugged loose the tie of the tunic. "As much as I savor you wearing my shirt," he said, opening the two halves of suede to stare at my body. "Your naked body is too resplendent to cover."

I ran a hand over the seductive ridge rising against the laces of his pants and set him free. My gaze dropped as I shoved his leathers to the ground beside the discarded tunic. "You're easy on the eyes too. You don't mind if I look, do you?"

Aust held his arms out to his sides and gave me the honor of ogling him as he made a slow runway turn. Broad shoulders, lean hips, toned and tanned musculature, and the hairless, silky skin of a Highborne elf. When he came back around to face me, his smile was even naughtier. "Verily, looking is wonderful, but I prefer touching."

His arm came around my back as he guided us down onto the wide, round mattress. With a gentle tug, he had me centered and sprawled out for his pleasure like a seasoned lover.

"You're a quick study at the whole seduction thing."

His smile warmed my insides and tightened in my belly. "I have time to make up for but, fear not, Kobi has vowed to teach me everything he knows."

I laughed. "I bet he has."

As if to demonstrate his commitment, Aust's head dropped, and he sucked my nipple into his mouth. With a reverence I'd grown to expect from him, he toyed with the tightened bud, nipping, licking, and suckling until I started to squirm. "I do have two of those, you know?"

He released my breast with a *pop* and slid across my body to the other side. "I would never neglect either one of them."

"Good job, blondie," Kobi said, setting a heaping tray on the mattress above my head. "I hoped to find you two getting things started. Now, time for breakfast."

I was about to ask what he meant when he picked up two honey pastries and placed them perfectly over my breasts. "Am I breakfast or the table?"

"Both." Kobi picked up a dish of raspberry puree and a little silver spoon. With the attention of an artist at work, he drizzled the sticky red topping over each pastry and into my navel.

"And we males shall feast?" Aust swept my hair out of the splash zone and fanned it out on the sheet above my head.

"Once the table is set." Kobi set the puree down and picked up the chocolate chips and syrup.

"Those were supposed to go on the pancakes. Do I look like a pancake?"

Kobi handed Aust a stack of fluffy, silver-dollar pancakes, and winked. "You look like a delectable canvas. Gentlemale's choice, my man. Place these wherever you feel they would serve us best."

Aust's cock twitched as he took in my body laid out beneath him. "Verily, I am a great admirer of art and have more than a few ideas. Have you any whipping cream?"

"I like the way you think. Yeah, here you go."

Kobi handed Aust the bowl of cream, and he began laying the edible, golden discs in an overlapping circle around the raspberry puree in my navel.

"A flower," Kobi nodded. "And the whipped cream?"

Aust leaned in and plopped two dollops on my rib cage. With his fingers, he spread and shaped the creamy mounds until they met with his approval. "Clouds. Have we anything for a stem for my flower?"

Kobi roused himself from staring and walked over to the tray. "Um . . . bacon?"

Aust nodded and accepted a few strips.

Kobi poured warm honey onto a spoon and lowered it to the freshly shorn mound at the junction of my legs. The cool spoon moving over my skin, the heated look in his eyes, the smell of chocolate, honey, and raspberry in the air—it was all too erotic.

My knees fell wider, and I undulated against the contact.

"Aust, I think our hot little mate is getting impatient." Kobi wriggled his brows suggestively, shifted the tray onto the grass, and crawled up the bed.

Aust sat back on his knees. He stared at me with unchecked lust and licked his fingers. "Then I suppose it is time to eat."

"Fuck, I'm hungry." Kobi unwound a leather tie from his wrist and stepped behind Aust. He gathered the long, flaxen waves of hair in his fingers and tied them back. "All right, let's dig in."

I groaned as my two hungry husbands crawled over me. They licked and lapped and devoured their edible art, and it was a wonder I didn't orgasm simply from the nuzzling touches and warm swipes of tongues.

My breath hitched, but I clutched the sheets and managed to remain still. "Whenever you're ready, boys. I'm on fire here."

Kobi lifted his head and frowned. "You're never supposed to rush while eating. How rude."

Aust chuckled against the inside of my thigh, his breath warm. Thankfully, he took pity on me and lapped at Kobi's honey pool between my legs. My eyes rolled closed as he cleaned me with tender pulls of his mouth.

"Thank you, Aust," I panted, pushing to strengthen the contact. "Sweet ecstasy, you're a fast learner."

"*Amin mela lle, neelan*," Aust said, gazing up at me from between my legs. "And please, I want you two to call me by my soul name. I am *Rynn*."

I blinked back tears. A Highborne's soul name was a cherished secret, a declaration of commitment and trust. It was Aust's most precious possession and he shared it with us.

"I love you, *Rynn*," I said, reaching down to brush his cheek. He pressed against my palm and closed his eyes. "Thank you."

Kobi straightened and shifted down the bed. When he opened his mouth, I prayed that he wouldn't be a dick and ruin the moment. "*Amin mela lle, Rynn*. You honor us both, and I swear, we will never let you down."

Cue the tears. Our demon was an ass at times, but beneath that façade of mouthy selfishness, was a true, loyal gentleman. "How did I ever get so lucky."

Washed, dressed, and ready to face the world, the three of us headed to Jade's house. Despite wanting to keep our private lives private a little longer, until we each wrapped our head around our bonding, the events of yesterday demanded our participation in Haven life.

"And your uncle seemed cool," Kobi asked, for the third time, "you know, with the three of us? He's not going to cut my balls off or char-broil me with a bolt of lightning, is he?"

I squeezed his hand. "Aunt Abbey foretold the three of us almost twenty years ago. He knows she's never wrong, so he's had ages to get used to the idea. He's not going to strike you down—either of you."

Kobi laughed. "Why would he strike down the Highborne? The guy is the perfect husband, but I'm—"

I stopped abruptly, and Aust, Faolan, and Paladin collided outside the iron gate to Jade's grounds. I pressed my fingers over his lips and frowned. "I won't let you finish that sentence. You are as much a part of this marriage as Aust or me. You're not a fallback or a bit of kink when things get dull. You, my precious, self-loathing demon, are an equal player here. As necessary in the mix as a salt rim on a margarita or the bitters in an old-fashioned."

"Agreed." Aust wrapped a possessive arm around Kobi's lower back and kissed his cheek. "What we share is our own. Let those who know no better judge and form an opinion. We three know what it is between us. That is all that matters."

I nodded and waited for Kobi to acknowledge we were right.

He nodded but didn't look at all convinced. "It's hard not to hold my breath and wait for it to fall apart. I'm so damned scared I'm going to fuck this up."

"That's not going to happen," I said, smoothing a thumb over the frown in his pierced brow.

"We are committed to loving one another," Aust said. "That, and amazing sex will see us through anything."

We all laughed, and Kobi relaxed. "'Kay, group kiss, then we face the music."

Despite my urge to ensure we were alone, I joined the love in. I needed to follow my own advice. This was ours, and we needed to own it.

Straightening, Aust caught something on the wind and frowned. "I shall join you inside in a moment. There is someone I need to speak to first."

Kobi seemed to understand what was about to happen and gathered me to his side. "You sure you want to do this alone?"

Aust nodded, the frown on his beautiful face unwelcome.

"'Kay, we'll wait for you inside. We won't break the news until you're there to share it. Good luck, Highborne."

Aust

Aust's footing faltered briefly as he headed along the boundary wall surrounding Jade's compound and entered the trees. And for a Highborne, the lack of coordination was telling. From where Cowboy stood, leaning against a wide, old oak, he had a perfect line of sight to where, just moments ago, Kobi, Zophia, and he had shared a kiss, thinking themselves in private.

He stopped before the male who had been his closest friend and scuffed his suede boot against the soft earth. The wolf Were looked tired and sorrowful. And though it was obvious the male suffered for what happened, Aust found no pleasure in it. Instead, he drew a steadying breath and met his friend's guarded caramel gaze.

"Hey, buddy." Cowboy adjusted his black hat and cleared his throat. "I, uh, wanted to tell you how sorry I am you lost Shalana. I know what she meant to you."

Aust swallowed, his heart's mourning of his goddess, idol, and mentor a huge weight in his chest.

"Bruin's having the Weres dedicate our next run to her. We're all, well, everyone is at a loss. She was a beloved mother to us all."

"Thank you." He absently scrubbed Faolan's head where she pressed against his thigh. "Shalana loved the Weres as much as any of the animal species. She would be honored to be remembered in your ceremony."

Cowboy scratched his palm absently, the ink of his bonding mark now black. A Were's bonding mark only went black after the mating was accepted and consummated. Cowboy and Bree had accepted their future together.

Aust studiously studied the track of earth he was making with his toe and let that reality settle over him. Despite the newness of everything, it no longer hurt as acutely as it had just days ago.

Cowboy cleared his throat and shifted his stance. "I'm gonna make things right with you. Whatever it takes, I swear."

"I have nothing to offer you right now that is not rooted in pain or anger."

Cowboy nodded and squared off. "Then give me your worst and get it off your chest. I deserve that and more. Seriously, doesn't matter what it is—let it fly."

And so, he did. With nothing held back, Aust unloaded the heavy burden his heart carried. He let Cowboy see his pain. Unleashed his anger and the stabbing betrayal. And once he voiced his soul's truths, he punched Cowboy in the face. Twice.

Cowboy seemed relieved to be struck. He leaned against the wide trunk of the tree behind him and dabbed the corner of his shirt to his bloody nose. "Thank you," he said. "I hope that didn't just make me feel better."

Aust shrugged, a hint of a smile tugging at his mouth as he inspected his knuckles. "Well, not worse in any case."

The Were chuckled. "So, tell me . . . Zophia and Kobi? You three look like you've locked in and made things official."

Aust eyed the male closely, relieved there was no judgment in his gaze. "It was unexpected . . . but amazing."

He nodded. "Well, for what it's worth, I'm truly happy for you, my brother. Zophia is one-in-a-million, and Kobi is a great guy—once you get past the guyliner and pin-cushion thing."

Aust extended his hand. "I do wish the best for you and Bree, and hope one day, I might even be happy for you."

Cowboy clasped Aust's proffered hand and pulled him in for an embrace. "I hope so too."

After a firm hug and a few heavy pats on his shoulder, Aust stepped back. The awkwardness between them was new, but he hoped that once their lives grew in the directions they were headed, they might reclaim their camaraderie. "So, are you headed inside?"

Cowboy nodded. "Yeah. I'll walk with you."

CHAPTER TWENTY-THREE

*K*obi and I waited for Aust in the foyer of Jade's home. Everyone was there. Between the Talon Enforcers celebrating at the bar in the living room, to the visitors who'd come to meet the babies, our entire Haven family was accounted for.

"Stop staring at the door. He'll be fine. He's a big boy."

Kobi was right, but the thought of Cowboy bringing up his pain and humiliation again didn't sit well. "What if he gets thinking about Bree and regrets moving on with us? It's all so new. What if they fight or say something they can't take back?"

Kobi slid his fingers into the hair at the back of my neck and pulled me against his chest. "He's our boy. We love and support him. He knows it. There's nothing to regret."

"And, it was meant to be," someone said behind me. I turned at the sound of a melodic female voice I hadn't heard in almost twenty years.

"Aunt Abbey." I ran to where she stood with my uncle and hugged her. She smelled the same, her own sweet floral mixed with the lavender and bergamot of Castian on her skin. "I can't believe you're here. Are you okay? Rheagan didn't hurt you or anything, did she?"

Abbey stroked a gentle hand along my cheek and touched the

sheared ends of my hair. "I like this look on you. Far more spunk to it than that floor-length braid."

I drew a deep breath and soaked in the sight of her. "I can't believe you're finally here. I missed you, so much."

Another hug left us both wiping away tears.

The front door opened and Aust and Cowboy walked in together. There was no hiding the split lip and swelling on the side of the wolf's face, but they seemed to have sorted themselves out.

"Oh, Abbey, let me introduce you." I waved my two men over and smiled. "This is Kobi, and this is Aust."

Aust pressed his lips to my aunt's tanned knuckles and smiled. "It is a pleasure beyond measure to meet you. You are as lovely in life as the images painted by those who have long held you in their hearts."

Kobi laughed. "Well, that's a hard act to follow. Thanks, Highborne. It's nice to meet you, Abbey, and to have you home in time to share in Jade's big arrival."

"Have you seen the young?" Castian asked.

I shook my head. "No, we just arrived. That's on the list of stops though. I think we're headed to talk to Elora first."

Castian nodded, an all-too-knowing look clouding his eyes. "Come, the three of you, allow me to bless your union."

Kobi looked like he might choke. Aust looked humbled.

I nodded and took his hand. "Yes, please. Oh, and I've always admired Jade and Galan's binding braids."

"Subtle hint, Zo," Kobi said under his breath. "Not sure I can pull off a braid."

Castian took Aust's hand, and Kobi closed the circuit. When our hands were linked, an electric charge tingled from my scalp through my body and sent goose bumps prickling along my skin. The tingle soon grew to a white-hot fire spreading across my shoulders. "Let everyone know destiny fated this union. Your life together is embraced by the God of gods."

I gritted my teeth, and Kobi squeezed my hand. The scent of bergamot grew until it was rife in the air and a moment later the burn was gone. I glanced at my husbands and eyed the inked edges of a tattoo disappearing under their shirts to cover their shoulder. I wore one as well and couldn't wait to rip off our shirts and see what we looked like.

Castian raised his gaze, his expression serene. "I bless your union, with all my heart."

I reached for the braid hanging to the right of Aust's face first. The deep chestnut of my hair was woven with Kobi's ebony and Aust's flaxen gold. The contrast in color of the intricate braid was striking.

Hesitantly, Aust lifted his hand and touched the braid in my hair. His ice-blue eyes sparkled with wonder as the ribbon of our intertwined lives slid through his fingers.

"You are exquisite, *neelan*." Emotion laced his husky voice. It was there too, behind his eyes, unmistakable despite his attempt at composure. He turned to Kobi. "I am proud to wear a symbol of our joined lives. I am proud to be mated to you both."

When Kobi didn't have a comeback, I started to worry. When his chin started to quiver, I knew he was in real trouble. *Uncle, would you mind excusing us?* A moment later, the three of us were alone in a parlor off the main hall, and Kobi's defenses broke completely.

Aust had strong shoulders to cry on, and I couldn't have been more moved by the two of them. I wrapped my arms around them both and held on while our tough warrior fell to pieces. "We are forever, Kobi. You'll see. You don't have to hide yourself anymore. Not with us."

Aust pressed their foreheads together. "Never with us."

I raised my knuckles to the thick, inlaid panel of the door to Reign's private library.

"I am literally terrified." Aust turned to face us. "Mayhap we should wait. Knowing my mother, she has, no doubt, been very busy caring for the young. If she stepped away for a quiet moment, let us respect that."

I brushed his cheek and he pressed against my palm. "You haven't checked in since the battle ended. She's likely worried sick about you. Even if Reign and the others told her you were healthy, as your mother, she'd need to see it for herself. Besides, waiting won't change anything."

I knocked on the door in three quick raps.

"*What?*" came the graveled boom from within the room.

I dropped my head against the door, suddenly agreeing with Aust that this might be a mistake. "Reign, it's Zophia. Lexi mentioned that Elora might be in the library. We didn't mean to bother you. If this is a bad time, we'll find her later and can talk then."

The scrape of chair legs on hardwood preceded the heavy footfalls of Jade's adoptive father crossing the room. Chosen by Castian, I couldn't imagine a more fearsome protector for his only child. As the knob turned, I stepped back.

He opened the door only a few inches, his massive frame blocking all view of the room. His dark suit highlighted his olive skin and how his long brindle-colored hair cascaded down his lapel. I'd never seen it not tied back in a leather thong. Reign eyed Aust and something hardened in his gaze.

"I'm sorry," I said. "We're interrupting."

"Yes, you are," he said.

The door was about to slam shut when Aust's palm pressed flat against the panel. He stepped around me, inhaled, and his ice-blue eyes narrowed. "Reign, I would like to speak with my *naneth* for a moment."

I drew a deep breath and cursed our timing. The scent of a cooked meal hung heavy on the air of the library, but not as heavy as the scent of arousal.

"Not a good time," Reign snapped.

Aust, leave them, son, Cameron said. The displaced spirit came through the wall, looking annoyed. *Your mother finally reclaims some measure of happiness. Do not take it from her.*

Unaware of his father's wishes, Aust strengthened his position. "I insist. I must needs speak with her."

"Let him pass, Maximus," Elora said within the room.

223

Reign cursed. Aust pushed through the doorway and strode straight to the candlelit table in the corner where his mother sat, sipping a glass of wine.

Reign stepped into the hall with Kobi and me and after Faolan's tail cleared the threshold, closed the door with a quiet bump. Aust's ghostly father followed his son inside.

Reign leaned a shoulder against the doorframe and glared at us. "And what vitally important errand brings the three of you knocking on my door?"

Unsure if he truly wanted an answer or simply intended to fill the air with conversation, I hesitated . . . just long enough for him to take in the binding braids Kobi and I wore.

"Yeah," Kobi said, "so . . . uh, yesterday was a big day."

Reign stood stoically, arms folded across his banded chest, his broad back covering the width of the closed door.

In my mind, I argued with myself about Kobi and I leaving the three of them to discuss what was a family matter, or staying to accept our part in the situation. Kobi was no help. He stood there, awkwardly pretending we hadn't interrupted his commander actively seducing our new mother-in-law.

"I apologize," I said. "We had no idea you were entertaining and certainly didn't mean to—"

"—bring Elora's son into a private moment."

I winced. "Yes, that."

"It's been almost a year since Cameron's death."

"It's honestly none of my business—"

The door whipped open. Aust shoulder-checked Reign out of his way as he stormed into the hall, followed by his wolf and Paladin trotting behind.

Reign stretched his neck side to side and exhaled. "I'm not one to share the personal matters of others. I expect you to extend me the same courtesy."

"Of course. We'll leave you to your evening." I bowed my head and gave him a slight curtsy before starting my retreat.

"*No,*" Elora said from inside. "Send them in, Maximus."

Kobi gave me a wide-eyed look of horror, and I rolled my eyes. Elora was a kind and gentile woman. There was nothing to be afraid of. Was there?

Feeling the devastating loss of *my* mother, I decided maybe we could smooth over the unpleasantness with Aust's. Reign opened the door wide and ushered Kobi and me inside.

The woman standing in front of the fireplace was both regal and fierce at the same time. Long, blonde hair, gathered back and braided, exposed gently pointed ears. She wore a modest, yet flattering, dress that accentuated her hour-glass figure. The lifespan of an Elf was a millennium or two, but Elora looked more like Aust's older sister than his mother.

"Excuse the intrusion," I said, stepping in far enough that Reign could swing the door closed behind us. "I'm Zophia. I've been looking forward to meeting you."

"Have you?" Elora drummed her fingers on the mantle as she eyed me up and down. "It seems to me, that if you truly wished to introduce yourself, you had ample opportunity. You stayed in this house for a few days and visited more after that."

I cast a quick glance to Kobi, who looked stunned.

I'd always heard how amazingly loving and docile Elora was. What had I done to set her off? Then it hit me. I'd mated her son. "I'm sorry, I should have made it a point to meet you, especially when we started getting involved with Aust."

She reached to the wine flute at the little luncheon table and drank almost all of it down. "Aust is a grown male. In no way do I expect him to check with his mother before giving his heart to a female, but *bonding?* In what, two weeks' time? Do you two even understand what you have done? What this means to our community? Our family?"

"We do," Kobi said.

Elora raised a finger and cut him off. "I am speaking to my new daughter. I shall get to you in a moment, young man."

I fought the urge to defend him but knew it wouldn't do him or Aust any favors if I made an enemy out of the woman. "I understand your worry, but yes, we discussed the ramifications and laws more than once. With all due respect, the Highborne community spat in Aust's face for the past century. He lives in *this* realm now. He deserves to find his own way. That's the whole point of his *Ambar Lenn*. He's on Fate's Journey and found what he needs."

"And you two are what he needs? An exiled Fate and a promiscuous demon? Ridiculous as it sounds, in the century since I gave birth to him, raised him, and nurtured him, I never once thought, if only my son could grow up and mate a female who holds no purpose in her community and a male who thinks his cock is public property."

"Okay, stop," I said, a breeze swirling around me as my hair lifted from my shoulders. "Our bonding is a shock to you, granted, but we love him and have no intention of dishonoring his Highborne beliefs."

"It is too late for that. He has lain with *both* of you. *One* mate. *One* love for an eternity. That is what we believe."

I settled my nerves, hearing what she wasn't saying. I turned to Kobi and Reign and gestured to the door. "If you wouldn't mind, can the women have the room for a moment?"

Reign laughed. "Kicking me out of *my* library? I think not."

Elora raised her hand. "Let her have her say in private, Maximus. I shall be fine."

When the door closed, I strode over to stand before Aust's mother. "One love isn't how it worked out for you either, is it? Despite High-born views on bonding, sometimes, due to circumstances beyond your control, love doesn't follow the laws. You love who you love."

"This is about Aust, not me."

"I don't think it is, but all right, let's address Aust. You and Cameron spent the past century worrying over a boy who was mistreated and disrespected his whole life because of the gifts my mother gave him. Despite that, he grew up to be kind, loyal, and to possess a depth of love and compassion I've never had the pleasure of experiencing before. He saw the love you and Cameron shared and wanted that for himself."

Elora's ocean-blue eyes narrowed on me. "And what do you know of Cameron?"

Say nothing, Cameron pleaded, coming to stand just inches from us. *Please. Let her move on. She is safe now. I will leave her to a new life, I swear.*

"I know enough to know that when Aust saw you with Reign—when he smelled the attraction in the air—he was terribly hurt. And when you saw that he had bonded without your knowledge and without including you, you were hurt in return. I'm sorry about that. Both of you are adjusting to new lives. It's difficult and uncertain, but maybe I can help ease the tension between you."

Elora stepped to the table, refilled her glass, and gathered a clean glass from the butler's stand, offering me a red wine peace offering, I hoped. "Your concern is kindly received, however unnecessary. Aust spoke to me from his heart, and yes, for now, his heart aches. I hold nothing but the greatest love and respect for him. I understand how he misses his sire. His loyalty to his *eda* is yet another reason I adore him."

I made a conscious effort not to look at Cameron. Instead, I sipped at the delicate rim of my glass. "I can't imagine your loss, but I think it's healthy that you're finding love again. Aust will see that too. He has more love in his heart than any man I've ever met."

Elora swirled the burgundy liquid in her glass and watched the surface settle. "Cameron was my perfect mate. With him, it was easy, natural. He was the air that I breathed and the blood in my veins. When I lost him, I lost myself."

Cameron brushed her cheek with the back of his ghostly fingers. *You were my life as well,* neelan.

"But the difference between my loss and Aust's is that I am accustomed to people. I talked through my heartache, cried about it, drank with new friends, reminisced about the things I missed most. I came to terms with the fact that my life is not as it was. Aust, to my knowledge, has never spoken of it. He endured too much in that village of judgment and narrow-minded attitudes. It left him protective of his heart."

I swallowed and let the robust flavor of the vintage wash over me.

"My life as a Fate, with Dane and my sisters as my family, conditioned me in much the same way."

"When he lashed out at me, just now, I realized that now that he has you, there are things he shall never turn to me for, never confide in me. He is a grown male with a mate." She frowned. "*Two* mates. That struck my heart with as much of a blow as his anger about Maximus."

"Having Kobi and me in his life doesn't lessen his need for your love and approval. He was tied up in knots coming here. Your involvement with Reign took him off guard, but he desperately needs you to approve his choice to be with us—to understand that we complement each other and are happy."

Elora emptied her glass and balanced it on the fireplace mantle. "Then it seems we each disappoint the other today."

I shrugged. "Maybe, but there's always tomorrow."

Kobi had waited for me in the hall, and pushed off the wall the moment I exited the library. I don't think I would ever tire of watching the lithe strength of his body when he moved. Delicious. "Everything okay?"

I left the door open and smiled at Reign. "Thank you for the use of your private space. Again, I am sorry we interrupted your afternoon."

Reign could scowl with the force of a thousand curses. It was quite a skill. When he left us and closed the door, Kobi whisked me down the hall and up the main staircase.

I paused on the steps. "We can meet the babies later. Right now, we should check on Aust."

Kobi pointed up the stairs and placed a gentle hand at the small of my back. Tugging me back into motion, we continued toward Jade's suite. "While you were in with Elora, our boy went up to talk to his Elven family. He wanted to rip the bandage off and get everyone's disappointment with him over with all at once."

"Oh, no. He should have waited for us."

Kobi shrugged. "His call. Well, other than Jade. I guess you had a right to be there for that one."

I jogged to keep up with his long legs. "I honestly don't care. Other than Castian, Abbey, and my mom, everyone in my family considered me a disappointment my whole life. Why worry about it now?"

Kobi chuckled. "At least you had a family. I was thinking about it down there. I don't have anyone to tell. Who and what I left behind aren't even worth the breath to give them the news. No baggage here."

"Nothing wrong with traveling light."

We reached the top landing and headed down the hall to the open door of Jade and Galan's suite.

A loud *pop* sounded, and several people yelled. Something crashed, and the babies began to cry.

"Stay here, Lacy," he said, drawing his dagger and pressing me to the wall.

I waited, heart racing, as Kobi burst into the space.

A moment later, he popped his head out the door and waved me in. "False alarm, s'all good."

It took me a moment to take in the bustle of what was happening inside. Julian was filling champagne flutes. Bruin and Mika were hugging Kobi. Nyssa and Iadon were over by the window with Aust. Cowboy and Samuel were fussing over the baby in Lia's arms. Ella had a hold on Faolan's tail and was toddling around the room, singing.

"It's not a real party 'till something gets broken," Lexi said, bouncing the other baby. "Rogue cork took out a wall sconce. No worries. Hey, Aust told us the exciting news. Congrats."

Lexi hugged me with her free arm, and I got my first look at Jade and Galan's little boy. "Oh my goodness, how sweet. Can I hold him?"

"Yeah, sure, but you take him, you change him. He's wet."

Jade joined us, taking possession of her newborn. "Come into the nursery, and then you can have a turn with a fresh one."

Jade led us through the master bedroom, laid him on the nursery change pad, and undid all the necessary snaps and tabs. With sure hands, she exchanged wet for dry and was handing me a tiny bundle in a matter of moments.

"Wow, you're a natural."

Jade laughed. "Hardly, but Galan is Ella's mentor guardian, so we've spent time with her since she was born."

I gathered the baby's little fist between my fingers and brushed it against my lips. His skin was so soft and smelled sweet. "What's his name?"

"That's Rain, and his sister is Ember."

The baby blinked up at the sound of his mother's voice, his green eyes bright but unfocused. He had Jade's copper skin and deep, red hair and Galan's soft features and pointed ears. "Hello, Rain."

He is a wonder, is he not? Tham asked, standing next to me.

I nodded, wondering if Galan and Jade knew their elven brother was never far away.

Aust joined us and nestled into my side. He leaned close to brush Rain's cheek with his finger, and I kissed his cheek. I was pleased to see that his upset with his mother didn't seem to be ruining this moment.

Maybe this emotional strength stemmed from him knowing that no matter what people thought, he was secure and loved. Or maybe he knew they'd work it out. I had no doubt they would.

"Are he and his sister not the most stunning young elves you have ever seen, *neelan?*"

"He's the *only* young elf I've ever seen. Up close anyway. And I haven't met his sister yet."

"Maybe someday soon," Jade said, hugging Aust's arm and leaning in to join the group staring, "you two will hold your own babies. Ella and these two will want more cousins to play with while growing up."

"From your lips to the ears of the gods," Aust said, a blush coloring his cheeks. "It is too early yet, I think, to plan such things, though I look forward to having young of our own."

I exhaled, thankful he didn't have me slotted as a baby maker just yet.

"And how are we handling that?" Kobi said, bouncing in to join us. "My demon swimmers were dammed upstream for a good reason.

Elven babes are all that are in store. Are we gonna be able to rock a my-two-dads kinda thing?"

"Why not?" Jade said. "The more love, the better. Your kids will be lucky to have three amazing parents."

Despite my comment about not caring what people thought, I loved that there was no hesitation in Jade's answer.

Rain started to squirm and fuss, and Jade took him back into her arms. "Feeding time. If you'll excuse us."

"Don't be shy, Blaze," Kobi said. "Breastfeeding is natural. A wonder to be shared."

Jade snorted and pointed to the open door. "Why does every conversation with you lately come back to my breasts."

Kobi laughed as I shoved him through the bedroom. "I appreciate the beauty of the female form. It's a compliment."

Back in the living room of Jade's suite, the celebration of family and friends amazed me. I'd been to countless Fae parties over my centuries Behind the Veil, and never had I seen such genuine love and affection flowing between a gathered group.

"Can I get everyone's attention?" Bruin raised his bottle of beer, clinking the glass with the Were ring which recognized him as king. When the room quieted, he cleared his throat. "I want to say a few words and make a few toasts. Does everyone have a glass to raise?"

Cowboy handed Aust and Kobi each a bottle of beer.

Lexi put a pink and orange swirl drink in my hand and winked. "All set, big brother. Have at it."

Bruin nodded. "All right . . . first off, congratulations to Jade and Galan. The pregnancy was tough, but my sister proved, once again, that she's tougher. Welcome, Rain and Ember."

"Woohoo!" Lexi squealed, and everyone drank to toast the safe arrival of the young.

"And congratulations to Kobi, Aust, and Zophia. May the three of you be as happy together as anyone can be while living with the ego and attitude of an incubus demon."

Everyone laughed, and Kobi flashed his best friend a middle-fingered salute.

Bruin chuckled and shook his head. "No, I'm just fucking with you —Kobi's a keeper. I love you man, and I'll miss having you around morning 'till night."

"Yeah? Where am I going, exactly?"

Bruin tossed a security fob, and Kobi plucked it from the air. "The house in the ruin clearing is vacant and yours for the taking. A wedding present from Mika and I, to you three."

Mika hugged Aust and kissed his cheek. "Anyone around during the first weeks and months of our mating knows that new couples need space to figure things out and gain their stride. Now, you have a place of your own to do that."

Aust kissed her forehead and whispered something to her, while Kobi went over, grabbed Bruin by the jaw, and kissed him squarely on the mouth.

Bruin rolled his eyes and wiped the kiss away. "Yeah, well, good luck, you two. And remember, there are no returns. He's yours now."

"For better and for worse," I said.

"Likely more of the latter," Lexi said, leaning against Rowan's chest. "But he's handy if you lose your lighter."

Bruin drank deep and raised his bottle again. "And two last announcements."

The room settled down, and he pulled a velvet box out of his pocket. "With the excitement and drama of the past forty-eight hours, you might not all know that the Weres accepted me as king and that I named my Beta."

I met the gaze of Kobi and Aust, and they both shrugged. Nope. We'd been too busy with our own lives to keep up with what was happening. Ha. So much for the Keeper of Lives in Progress. I was out of the loop.

Bruin opened the velvet box and lifted a Were signet ring for everyone to see. "May I formally introduce Cowboy as the Were beta and aide to the king."

Everyone broke into a wild round of applause as Bruin placed the ring on Cowboy's finger. I was proud of Aust. He patted the man's shoulder and was genuinely happy for him.

"You said two more announcements, Bear," Julian said, taking pictures with his phone. "What's the last one?"

Bruin smiled and turned the ring box out for the room to see. "Samuel, Lia, and I have been working on a surprise. It was Lia's idea and her husband's unsurpassed talent which brought the idea to fruition, but these two rings belong to two very special people. Lia assures me that my sister and Tham are in the room. I'd like them to come forward."

The two ghostly lovebirds stopped chatting in the corner. They looked as confused and curious as the rest of the room.

Lia turned and waved them on. "Come on, you two." She picked up, first the male's silver band and then the daintier one fitted for a young woman's finger. "When I first asked Samuel if he thought it possible to bring you two back to the visual plain, he was skeptical."

"But ye never argue with a female who's got an idea lodged in her heed," Samuel said, raising his tumbler of whiskey toward his bride. "Especially, a Highborne female."

Galan, Aust, Iadon, and Tham all nodded, as if that was common logic.

"So, anyway," Lia continued, "my amazing and sexy mate researched, experimented, and consulted with a dozen other wizards, mages, and sorcerers to come up with these."

She slid the rings on Tham and Gemma's fingers and bit-by-bit, moment-by-moment, their ghostly translucence began to solidify. A hushed gasp of excitement fell over the gathering as the two became visible once again.

"Now," Samuel said, stepping forward, "if all is right in my figurin', we should be able to see, hear, and even touch them while they wear the rings."

Galan reached for Tham at the same moment Bruin pulled his

twin sister against his chest. The room broke into a great wave of joyous hugs and tears. Lexi, Jade, and the elves huddled around their fallen brother, while Lia, Mika, Bruin, and Cowboy hugged Gemma.

For the first time since my banishment from Behind the Veil, I truly missed my station in life. I squeezed Kobi's hand. "Are you okay to leave and help me with something?"

His glassy gaze, as he looked over at me, made me laugh. He swiped his eyes and inhaled. "Yeah, anything. Boy, you really contaminated me with the feels. This is bad for my rep."

I laughed harder. "Are you sure that's my fault? I think, beneath all that cold, dark, demon armor you surround yourself in, you've always had a big, squishy heart."

Kobi made a face. "What an awful thing to say to someone you supposedly love. How rude."

CHAPTER TWENTY-FOUR

Aust

*A*ust jogged along the path between Jade and Galan's manse and the home Bruin and Mika built in the ruin clearing. He loved the couple dearly, but did they truly intend to give him, Kobi, and Zophia a matrimonial home? It defied all expectation of friendship. He supposed that was where his mistake lay. It was not an act of friends—Mika and Bruin were family.

The summer breeze blew warm with the breath of blooms and evergreen spice. He stopped at the edge of the trees and took in the beauty of the house. The soft curves and angles mirrored the lines of nature. The expansive glass let the beauty of the surroundings spill inside. The serenity of it being located remotely enough to offer privacy, yet close enough that he could aid his family in mere moments should they need him.

He never imagined himself worthy of something so perfect. And then there were his mates.

Faolan's ebony ears pricked and turned to capture the soft sound of footsteps behind them. Aust waited, the quickening of blood pumping in his veins making him feel like a silly youth.

"Glad you're home, *Rynn.*"

Aust's eyes rolled closed as Kobi spoke his soul name and pressed in behind him. Strong arms wrapped around his ribs as the male nipped the point of his ear. "We've been waiting for you. Come see what we've gotten done."

Not ready to give up the contact, Aust flexed his spine and pressed against his lover's groin.

The resulting groan made him smile.

"Haven't had your fill, Highborne? Up for more torture, are you?"

If the torture he spoke of was the delicious penetration and slow, riding rhythm that their joinings brought them, the answer was a definite no to the first question and yes to the second. Aust turned in Kobi's embrace and relished how the demon's physical affection brought him to life. Every scent, every sight, every touch bombarded with more power and clarity than he had ever experienced before.

"I doubt my hunger shall ever truly be sated. The more the three of us share, the more I want of that connection."

Kobi's hand slid to the laces of Aust's suede pants and stroked the length of his arousal. With deft fingers, the incubus freed him from constraint. It was almost too much to bear, the male's unceasing desire, the kissing, the touching, the all-encompassing acceptance they both offered him.

"Insatiable hunger, eh? Challenge accepted. Now, let's get you inside, our girl is waiting. Then, we'll see about taking the edge off those needs of yours."

"I can hardly wait."

Kobi led him to the door, opened their way, and stopped.

"What is it?"

He turned, a wicked smile Aust recognized on the male's face. "There's a human tradition that a husband carries his bride over the threshold of their new home. I carried Zo earlier and think we should mark our first entry together in some way."

Aust chuckled. "Do you intend to cradle me like a female against your chest?"

"No. I was thinking something far more manly."

"I cannot wait to hear what you have in mind."

Kobi pressed a firm hand to Aust's chest and pushed him against the door frame. Aust's head fell back as Kobi finished unlacing his pants and took him by mouth. Breath hissed from his lungs, and he braced himself against the wooden frame.

"Life with you shall never be boring, I am certain." Aust gripped the doorframe above his head.

In answer, Kobi grew rougher and more demanding. The male's possession took him straight to the brink of orgasm. "You're mine, *Rynn*." Kobi gazed up from his knees. "Say it for me."

Aust's breath caught. "I am yours."

Kobi returned his attention and his hips seized. He gasped, his muscles shuddering as his release hit hard and fast. Kobi devoured every ounce of his pleasure. He was a demanding lover, but also endlessly attentive. When the tall, dark, and handsome male straightened to his full height once again, Aust was all but falling to the floor, unable to stand.

"That was quite an entrance," Zophia said, smiling from the entranceway of the living room.

Kobi chuckled, adjusted Aust's pants, and tied them up again. "Our boy deserved a grand entrance and commented on being randy. What kind of self-respecting incubus demon could let that slide."

Zophia laughed, kissed them both hello, and took Aust's hand. "Come on. I want to show you something."

Aust caught Hoola as she launched from a jungle gym climbing frame in the great room. The little gibbon hit his chest with a *thud* and nuzzled into his neck, quite content with her new accommodations.

"We are fortunate this place has a cathedral ceiling. This works well in here."

Zophia nodded at the green tubing that reached up at least fifteen feet in front of a glass wall. "We thought so too. Now, come in here and see what I'm excited about."

Zophia led the way to one of the large guest rooms down the hall. Near the window, a loom sat threaded and empty, then, along the far wall, rows and rows of tapestries hung in open-ended wood frames.

She swept her hand through the room and smiled. "Welcome to Zophia's new life on earth."

Kobi gestured to the hanging tapestries and winked. "I told her it looks like a carpet sale at a housing store, but I suppose, as the woman of the house, she has the right to overrule me."

Zophia smacked him in the stomach and rolled her eyes. "It's my loom station, or at least part of it. Seeing the babies this afternoon, and hearing all the exciting news, I wanted to record it. Kobi and I went Behind the Veil and took all the tapestries for our Haven family and friends. Then, we set them up here. Now, I can do what I love, and my meddlesome sisters can't affect their lives."

Aust strode over to the hanging frames of fabric and ran a gentle finger over the intricate weaving. "This is a wonderful idea. I wish I had helped you."

"We knew you'd say that and not to worry," Zophia said, taking his hand. They walked through the spacious new home, toward the enclosed garden off the library. "You're helping me with the second part of my plan."

Aust had seen portal mirrors several times since moving to Haven but wondered why there would be one affixed in the middle of an atrium garden.

"This opens up to my mother's property. I want to keep up her sanctuary and everything she loved. It's too much for me to do alone. Even with her powers now, you're far better at communicating with the animals. I thought you might like to help me keep her passion alive."

"It shall be my honor." Aust fought to swallow past the lump constricting his throat. "The celebration at Jade's brought about a decision for me as well—if the two of you are agreeable."

Kobi shrugged.

Zophia nodded. "We're game. Whatever you want."

Three days later, I stood on the lush, manicured grass of Jade's back lawn, dressed to impress, and in the company of several other stunning ladies. Jade, Lia, Gemma, Elora, Abbey, and I were decked out in the style and hemline of our choice, and the six of us awaited the arrival of our men.

The guests of the Highborne commitment ceremony milled around an intimate semi-circle of highboy tables, drinking their refreshments of choice, everyone ready to stand witness. Lexi and Bruin each held one of the twins, while Julian took their pictures and recorded everything with his latest, high-tech toy. All three of them were utterly captivated by their newborn niece and nephew.

I had hoped Savage would come. No one had heard from him since Abaddon's defeat. I wasn't sure if he'd taken our brother's death as a good thing or bad. Didn't matter. We'd both been wronged by our siblings. With that common ground and our lives and friends at Haven interwoven, someday, we'd find a way to be close.

Grandfather Hawk and Mika walked past me to set carnival-glass vases in the center of each table. Then, Iadon and Nyssa followed, placing two or three small bottles of fine white sand next to each.

My table had three.

"You look resplendent, Zophia," Elora said, joining me as I brushed a fly away from our table. "Thank you for doing this for him. Aust is beyond excited to have you both honor our traditions."

"Why wouldn't we?" I said, more curtly than I meant to. "When you love someone, you want nothing more than to make that person happy, right?"

"I deserved that," she said. Her genuinely warm smile made me regret my comment. A little. "And you were right. Aust is free to love as his heart demands. We live in *this* realm now. It is difficult to ignore ideals long taught, and accept happiness without the restrictions of guilt and judgment. I made amends with him and hoped you can forgive me as well."

I exhaled. "There's nothing to forgive. I'm irrationally protective of Aust. He's been hurt too often. I don't want him to suffer anyone's sleight ever again."

"Then we are one in that." She raised her wine and smiled. "May love conquer all in all our lives."

From your velvet lips to the ears of the gods, Cameron said, beside us. *Life is long and wonderous. It is meant to be shared.*

Though Elora couldn't hear or see her deceased husband, I thought it lovely that he came to give his blessing. It seemed, being protective of the ones you loved defied even death.

"Reign must be thrilled about your mating."

Elora nodded. "He is. Despite the harsh edges and autocratic command Maximus shows the world, he is a true romantic with endless heart. He accepts my eternal love for Cameron without pause and is confident enough to know he has his own place in my heart. He is my future . . . and a wondrous future he is."

Right you are, my love. Be well and blissfully happy, my beautiful wife. Blessed be. Cameron's form faded away, and I knew, deep in my soul, that since Aust and Elora had made peace—with each other and their futures—he'd finally passed to the After. He didn't need to protect them anymore.

That was someone else's honor now.

I blinked back tears, hoping if Elora noticed, she'd think me emotional. Music started, and I glanced toward the back deck of Jade's home.

The men emerged as a group, a virtual runway of hot and handsome. Castian led the pack, stunning in an ivory pantsuit. His trademark blue velvet cloak billowed in the breeze as he jogged down the tiered deck toward us.

Galan, Tham, and Aust wore traditional suede pants, crisp white tunics, and tailored embroidered jackets. They three strode out the sliding glass doors, their Elven grace in motion, a thing of breathtaking beauty.

Reign came next. The brawny warrior wore a fitted, ebony tuxedo with his brindle hair loose and long as it flowed behind him. Though his outfit was sleek and designer, it didn't lessen the intimidating edge the man always radiated.

"Looking good, old man," Lexi catcalled, letting off an ear-piercing whistle.

Then came Kobi. Tall and sleek, he wore black leather pants and jacket, and a white dress shirt with the top buttons undone.

As they drew closer, Kobi took Aust's hand, and the two of them became the only men I saw. Aust's smile lit up my whole world, while Kobi looked green and almost ill. I knew the reason, the moment they drew closer. Without his piercings, black eyeliner or lipstick, our husband had laid himself bare for our commitment ceremony.

"So," he said, his voice thin and breathy. "This is me. You still game to claim me?"

I raked my fingers into the silky strands of his hair—the chestnut of mine and the blond of Aust's a stylish highlight. I pulled him closer, and his body fit against mine perfectly. "I saw the whole you from the start, tough guy. You couldn't get away from us if you tried."

"I said as much inside," Aust said, giving Kobi a smug look.

Kobi lowered his forehead to rest on mine. "I wanted to be a hundred percent authentic today. No smartassed comments. No ego. No deflection. This is as real as it gets for me."

I kissed the clean shave of his cheek, and let his sacrifice sink in. "We'll take you however you come. You're not going to screw this up, I promise. We won't let you. Now, relax. Let's get hitched and excuse ourselves early. We still have quite a few rooms to christen."

"Sixteen," Aust added, "to be exact."

Kobi laughed. "But who's counting, eh blondie?"

Aust shrugged and directed us toward the tables.

When everyone stood at their table with their respective partners, Grandfather Hawk smiled at the group and began. "Highborne Elves mate for life—that is common knowledge. What may not be known by other members of the realms is that they take the oath of commitment just as seriously as their pledge of fidelity and love. With any mating comes struggles."

He smiled over at Mika and Bruin, and the congregation laughed. "And, with time shared, there will inevitably be obstacles and conflict.

The merging of the sand is a physical reminder that your lives are forever intertwined."

He lifted a shaky, weathered hand and gestured for each of us to pick up our bottles. "As you pour the sand, slowly into your vase, watch how the grains mix and grow together. They jostle and fall, giving way and settling, to make room for the next layer and the next after that."

Aust, Kobi, and I each tipped our little bottles and watched the sand mingle and rise.

"Now, if a mated Highborne pair ever wished to end their commitment, the disgruntled lovers must first sit down together and separate each grain of sand back to their original bottles."

Kobi snorted, eyeing the millions of identical grains. "Good luck with that."

Aust chuckled. "That is the point. The task is impossible."

"Elven logic at its best," Galan said.

"So," Tham said, smiling at Gemma, as he dumped the last of his bottle, "you are well and truly stuck with me, *neelan*."

Gemma laughed. "I'll deal. Besides, who else would take either of us? We're ghosts."

"At least everyone can see and hear you now," Samuel said, setting down his empty bottle next to Lia's.

"And thank the gods for that," Bruin said.

"No. Thank my *mate* for that," Lia corrected. "No offense to you, sire."

Castian chuckled and kissed Abbey's temple as she set the lid on their vase. "None taken. Free will over fate, for the win. From now on, carve your own futures."

"And Zo will record them," Jade said, waving to Lexi and Bruin to bring the babies to join them.

"Yeah, thanks for rescuing our tapestries," Lexi said, taking Ember to her mother. "We all breathe easier knowing you are safeguarding access to our lives."

"It's what I live for," I said, smiling at my Haven family. "As the

Keeper of Lives, you'd think I might have known where my own life would take me."

Kobi snorted and pointed at our vase of sand. "Bet you never saw this coming, did you, Lacy?"

As if they'd practiced the move, Kobi and Aust each kissed one of my cheeks and the group laughed.

"Honestly, no, but I couldn't be happier. One year ago, three High-borne elves began their *Ambar Lenn*, but it seems we were all part of Fate's Journey. *Amin mela lle*, everyone."

"*Amin mela lle*," everyone responded.

My two husbands closed in, and the world fell away.

Ironic, don't you think, Zozo, Castian said into my mind, *that Fate's Journey should end with the journey of a Fate.*

I smiled across the tables of commitment vases and lovers and friends to meet the emerald gaze of my uncle. Ironic, eh?

Or had he orchestrated these Happily Ever Afters all along?

AFTERWORD

THANK YOU FOR READING

I sincerely hope you enjoyed *Blind Spirit*, book four in the Scourge Survivor series. If you'd like to be kept in the loop on my release dates and receive my newsletter, subscribe here: newsletter

If you'd like to know more about my other series, drop by my website at: www.jlmadore.com

If you'd like to read an excerpt from book 6 in the Scourge Survivor Series, *Savage Love,* scroll to the next pages or find it on Amazon here: Fate's Journey

May the Fates be kind,
JL Madore

ABOUT THE AUTHOR

Author Notes
Written on 20/07/2018

As a novelist of many genres of romance—fantasy, paranormal, timeslip historical, and contemporary—I love to twist Alpha heroes and kick-ass heroines into chaotic, hilarious, and magical situations, and make them really work for a Happily Ever After.

My journey with writing began in 2008, when I moved with my husband and our children to a rainforest area in Panama. We went to start up a wildlife sanctuary and help animals displaced by the copper mining industry there, but the crash of the world economy soon after changed the course of our plans.

But, for one glorious year, we lived another life. Galan and Jade came to me there, and stayed with me, even after we moved back to Toronto. The only problem was, I didn't know a thing about writing a novel. So, I learned: I studied, took courses, wrote badly, learned more, wrote better. I even became the president of my local writing community and guided our 300 members on their paths of writing.

It's never been work to me. I love the hours. I love my characters. And I love, most of all, that readers like you find enough value in my stories to trust me with your time. Thank you. I hope my imagined adventures continue to live up to your expectations.

While I said this was the last in the series, and I've wrapped up the five affinity females and the three Elves on their Ambar Lenn, you never know. Savage and Julian, might still have something to say.

I'll keep you posted on that.

All the best to you and yours.
JL

ALSO BY JL MADORE

Find Me:

Social Media – Facebook, Twitter, Instagram

Web page – www.jlmadore.com

Email – jlmadorewrites@gmail.com

Reader Group – JL Series Updates

JL's Reverse Harem Titles

Guardians of the Fae Realms

Guardians of the Phoenix – Calli's Harem

Book 1 – Rise of the Phoenix

Book 2 – Wolf's Soul

Book 3 – Bear's Strength

Book 4 – Hawk's Heart

Book 5 – Jaguar's Passion

Darkness Calls – Keyla's harem

Book 6 – Dark Curse

Book 7 – Dark Soul

Book 8 – Dark Crown

Guardians of the Crown – Honor's Harem

Book 9 – Honor Restored

Book 10 – Honor Guards

Book 11 – Honor Bound

Book 12 – Honor Empowered

Rise of the Amberloq – Lark's Harem

Book 13 – Find the Fallen

Book 14 – Rise from Ruin

Book 15 – Trust and Triumph

Exemplar Hall – Jesse's Harem

Book 1 – Captured by the Magi

Book 2 – Jesse and the Magi Vault

Book 3 – The Makings of a Magi Knight

Book 4 – Clash with the Magi Council

Book 5 – The Unstoppable Storme

JL's More Traditional M/F, M/M, or Menage

The Watchers of the Gray Series (Paranormal)

Watchers of the Gray Boxset – Complete Series

Book 1 – Watcher Untethered – Zander

Book 2 – Watcher Redeemed – Kyrian

Book 3 – Watcher Reborn – Danel

Book 4 – Watcher Divided – Phoenix

Book 5 – Watcher United – Seth

Book 6 – Watcher Compelled – Bo

Book 7 – Watcher Unfeigned – Brennus

Book 8 – Watcher Exposed – Taharqa

The Scourge Survivor Series (Fantasy)

Scourge Survivor Series Boxset - Complete Series

Book 1 – Blaze Ignites

Book 2 – Ursa Unearthed

Book 3 – Torrent of Tears

Book 4 – Blind Spirit

Book 5 – Fate's Journey

Book 6 – Savage Love – epilogue novella